Feelings of anger flooded her all over again, but Prue suppressed them

She needed to remember things clearly.

The woman's arm had been straight, as though she was pushing on Gideon's chest. Pushing him down? Pushing him away? But what had he been doing? Had he simply tried to push her off him and his hand had connected with her breast?

Prue punched the pillow. She couldn't believe that. She was obviously desperate to make it seem as though he had a defense. So, why was she doing it?

Because Gideon's kindness now made her second-guess herself. She had to get some sleep. Tomorrow she had to play the role of loving wife. Curiously, that role had seemed easier to undertake when Gideon was her enemy.

Now that she wasn't so sure she hated him, acting as though she loved him would be dangerous.

Dear Reader,

Old love rekindled is one of my favorite plotlines because conflict is built in. No relationship is as interesting as one between two people who know each other's faults and foibles and are forced to reconnect. The old dynamite that once brought them together will certainly be present, and there'll be new discoveries to be made because of the years spent apart.

That's precisely the case with Gideon and Prudence Hale. You can be sure that the road to love between a politician and a designer will be anything but straight and narrow. Thank you for wanting to join them.

Sincerely,

Muriel Jensen
P.O. Box 1168
Astoria, Oregon 97103

The Man She Married

Muriel Jensen

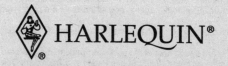

HARLEQUIN®

TORONTO • NEW YORK • LONDON
AMSTERDAM • PARIS • SYDNEY • HAMBURG
STOCKHOLM • ATHENS • TOKYO • MILAN • MADRID
PRAGUE • WARSAW • BUDAPEST • AUCKLAND

ISBN 0-373-71208-1

THE MAN SHE MARRIED

www.eHarlequin.com

Printed in U.S.A.

To Todd and Sarah Dielman, the world's best neighbors.

Books by Muriel Jensen

Don't miss any of our special offers. Write to us at the
following address for information on our newest releases.

Harlequin Reader Service
U.S.: 3010 Walden Ave., P.O. Box 1325, Buffalo, NY 14269
Canadian: P.O. Box 609, Fort Erie, Ont. L2A 5X3

CHAPTER ONE

PRUDENCE HALE THOUGHT later that she should have known it was all too good to last. Her first line of clothes had been a tremendous success at the fashion show to benefit the Maple Hill Library. She'd made a small fortune for them and for herself.

And as she stood in the parking lot of the Breakfast Barn Restaurant, along with a crowd of other nosy onlookers, watching her sister Paris and Randy Sanford—the town's favorite EMT—kiss and make up with embarrassing sincerity, she thought the morning could not be more perfect. After a difficult courtship, the two were reconciled at last.

Life was good and moving forward on most levels.

Then Prue heard a deep voice say, "Hello, Prue."

Air seemed to leave her lungs and her pulse stalled.

No, she thought. *Not when I'm finally on the right track. Not after this long, dark year when at last I'm living* my *life and not his. Please!*

She turned slowly to discover that all her prayers had been denied. There he was. Gideon.

She didn't know what shocked her most, the sight of his handsome face in the town that had been her comfort and haven since the Maine Incident, or the fact that he was in the company of Hank Whitcomb, one of Maple Hill's foremost employers.

What was he doing here? Her pulse had picked up again, but old emotion was a hard lump in her chest. She didn't want to talk about the breakup, she didn't want to think about her loss, she didn't want to hear it all hashed over again. She just wanted to sign divorce papers and get him out of her life.

Of course, she hadn't filed them yet. And, apparently, neither had he.

She had a hopeful thought. Maybe *that's* why he was here.

As everyone else streamed back into the restaurant, he came toward her.

She squared her shoulders and met his dark gaze as he closed the space between them.

She could admit that Gideon was exceptionally handsome. He had brown eyes, a straight nose and a mouth that used to laugh often but had lost that skill while he was in the state senate. He was tall and big with a personality to match.

Smaller than average herself, Prue had found his size intimidating at first, until she'd observed his kindness and compassion and his complete dedication to the people he served.

Curious, she thought, that the very things about him that had made her fall in love had become a sore spot between them when they'd continually kept him away from her.

She smiled just a little in an attempt to convince

him that, even when surprised, she was a woman of style and composure. That hadn't been true in the old days.

Well, it wasn't really true now, but she could pretend.

"Hello, Gideon," she said, hands in the pockets of a red wool jacket. She didn't want him to think she was willing to shake hands or otherwise touch. "What are you doing at the Barn?"

He indicated Paris, who stood nearby, hand in hand with Randy.

"I called a cab from the airport," he replied, "and Paris picked me up. I had no idea she operated a taxi service. I thought she was in law school."

Prue shook her head, the small smile still in place. "A lot has changed for her and for me in the last year."

He nodded once. "I see that. Anyway, we were happy to see each other, I asked her how things were going for her and she started to cry. So I suggested we go somewhere for coffee, she brought me here, and…well…" He swept a hand at the few stragglers in the parking lot making their way back inside. "Randy showed up, she ran off, he chased her, everyone came out to watch… Some town this is. Don't you guys have television?"

"Why don't you two sit in the cab if you need privacy," Paris suggested, handing Prue her keys and giving her a quick hug. "You should talk. It did a lot for us."

Randy clapped Gideon on the shoulder. "Good luck," he said, then drew Paris toward the restaurant.

Prue didn't want to talk, but Gideon was waiting expectantly. And she didn't want to be confined inside the cab with him. So she asked, "What were you doing with Hank Whitcomb?"

"He and his friends were at a table nearby when the Randy and Paris row started," he replied. "Paris took off on me, so Randy sort of put me in their care before he chased her out the door."

Okay, that explained how he'd gotten to the restaurant. "But what are you doing in Maple Hill?"

She saw his expression change. He was going to give her an answer she wasn't going to like. Not that he'd said or done anything she'd liked since she'd found him with another woman.

"A friend has invited me into a business partnership in Alaska," he said, his manner growing serious. "He's turning an old family home in the wilderness into a fishing lodge. It's pretty spectacular. An ancestor built the place when he made a killing in the gold rush. Anyway, I thought I'd try to talk to you one more time before I went away."

"What about the winery?" she stalled. "I thought you went back to running it when you left the senate."

"Blake has it running like a well-oiled machine." Blake was his younger brother who'd taken over the family winery when Gideon was elected. "Since my term ended, I opened a law office in White Plains, did a little work for the family, taught martial arts at the high school, but…I need something else.''

Alaska. That brought to mind ice and snow, days without sunshine, people bundled up in furs. But Gideon was someone who thought the sun was shining even when it wasn't. He never remembered a hat or an umbrella. It didn't seem like the right place for him.

Still. It was his life and she was no longer involved in it.

''Then you should go to Alaska,'' she said, trying to sound amiable rather than snide. It didn't quite come off. ''Because I don't want to hear whatever you have to say, Gideon. Oh, I know you could make it sound good. You have the politician's gift of gab. You talked me into believing I was going to love the state of New York, that I was going to have no trouble being a senator's wife. You talked me into waiting to have a baby.'' A small tremor broke that last word, and she had to clear her throat to go on, the pretense of amiability slipping away. Instead, all the old grudges were demanding attention. ''And as I was busying myself with charity work, living an almost nunlike existence while you claimed to be swamped with work, you were fooling around with Claudia Hackett.''

He hesitated a moment, drew a breath, and in a voice that sounded as though he had difficulty controlling it, he said, ''I came specifically to say one more time—I was not fooling around with Claudia Hackett.''

"I saw you with my own two eyes!''

"Your two eyes,'' he said quietly, "misinterpreted what they saw.''

"How do you misinterpret,'' she demanded, "a woman in nothing but panties?''

A man and a woman who'd just climbed out of a van turned as Prue raised her voice, clearly prepared to listen to them instead of going into the restaurant.

"Will you please sit in the cab with me,'' Gideon asked, "so that we don't make any more of a scene than we already have?''

"I don't want to talk about it,'' she insisted. "It's taken me a whole year to get over you and over the—'' She stopped and drew a steadying breath. "Over everything.''

He shifted his weight and folded his arms. "Well, I'm not leaving until you listen to what happened.''

"Then I hope you're happy in the parking lot,'' she said, moving past him, "because you're going to be here for a long time.''

He caught her arm and took the cab keys from her. "Look, Prue,'' he said, pulling her with him toward the cab. "You listen to my explanation. That's all I ask. Believe me. Don't believe me. I really don't care. Give me ten minutes, and then I'm out of here.''

"What's the point, Gideon?'' she asked, pulling against him. "We are so out of love, there's no going back.''

"I'm not trying to *get* you back." He sounded convincing. Well, that was a comfort. Sort of. "Why would I want to live with you if you won't trust me? It's just become a matter of personal necessity that I tell you what happened, even if you don't believe it."

She huffed a noisy breath and stopped struggling. If it meant he'd go away and she could forget, it was worth anything. "All right. Ten minutes. And I'm sitting behind the wheel."

"Fine." He unlocked the driver's-side door of the old station wagon, reached in to hit the button that unlocked the passenger door, then returned the keys to her. He walked around the cab and climbed in.

She tossed the clipboard that held Paris's daily log onto the dash, and her cell phone with it. She pushed the sun visor out of her way, leaned an elbow on the window and rested her left hand comfortably on the steering wheel.

He studied her posture. "You look comfortable," he observed.

She straightened, dropping her hand to her lap. "Force of habit. I used to drive a shift for Paris off and on."

He raised an eyebrow in surprise. "Really. Does she know you sometimes drive on the sidewalk and can fell a parking meter without looking back?"

She glowered at him. "That was an accident and you know it."

"I would hope so."

"My heels were too high." They'd been driving

home from a party and quarreling. She'd insisted on driving.

"A lead foot in high heels is not a good thing."

She turned slightly to give him her most arctic stare. "I thought you wanted to talk about you and Claudia."

That stare had never intimidated him in the old days, and it didn't now. "Still the same old Prue. Ignore your own transgressions but remind everyone else of theirs."

She reached for her door handle, but he caught her arm. "All right, all right. Let's not waste ten minutes arguing."

"We wasted a whole marriage arguing," she countered. "When you were around enough to argue."

GIDEON WONDERED why he'd come. It wasn't that he wanted her back; he'd been honest when he told her he didn't. He'd thought the absolute adoration he'd had for her in the beginning had completely disintegrated, but it hadn't. One look at her made him forget the bad times, remember the fun.

She was not very tall, but nicely rounded where it counted, and still absolutely beautiful. She had long, golden-blond hair that was piled atop her head today, but if he concentrated, he could remember it running across his face in the throes of lovemaking, silky and cool.

Her blue eyes could be lively with laughter or

stormy with petulance, her mouth soft and full in the raspberry shade of lipstick she'd always preferred.

She was also still capable of raising his blood pressure.

But he planned to move his life in a new direction, and it was important that she hear him out. He was probably wasting his breath—he'd be damned if he'd just be quiet and disappear as she wanted him to.

"A lobbyist for industry," he began without preamble, "was offering bribes to push through his particular agenda, and the attorney general's office invited me into this scheme to flush out Senator Crawford from Vermont who was suspected of having accepted a boat and a place in the Caymans."

She rolled her eyes. "I believe good old Crawford was crooked, but you're telling me Claudia was a lobbyist?"

"No," he replied patiently. "I'm telling you that I was aware that Crawford had a mistress who was a stripper. Several members of the ethics committee ate together when we worked weekends, and I'd seen him meet her afterward."

She thought she had him when she asked, "And you saw him with this mysterious woman and *knew* she was a stripper. How was that?"

"One of the others who frequented the club where she worked told me. And Crawford was such a posturing braggart, I was sure he had to have told her what he was doing."

"So she got down to her panties and poured her heart out to you, is that what you're telling me?"

He closed his eyes, hoping to summon patience. "No," he said. "I'm telling you that she told me she'd tell us everything she knew if we could guarantee her safety. The attorney general suggested we take her someplace quiet and remote to record her story."

"Ah." She nodded as though in understanding. Then she asked, "And where were these members of the ethics committee when she was in her panties?"

She'd never believe this, but it was the truth, and all he could do was reel out what had happened.

"They hit a moose," he said, maintaining his patience in the face of her open disbelief, "and never made it to the house. Took them two days to get back to Albany."

"How thoughtful of them. And in sympathy for the moose, she decided to go *au naturel* for you."

"She was a young woman accustomed to using her body as a commodity to get what she wanted," he explained as Prue let her head fall back to the headrest with a groan. "I told her that, in exchange for her help, we'd see that she could go to New York University, something she told me she's always wanted to do. She thought she had to pay me for that."

"So if I call New York University," she challenged, "they can assure me she's enrolled."

"No," he had to admit. "She did a semester and fell in love with a pharmacy student who moved back home to take over his father's pharmacy. She's now at a college somewhere in Indiana." Her disbelieving expression made him add with mild sarcasm, "I don't know which one, but you're welcome to call them all if you like."

"Oh, Gideon." Prue shook her head as though trying to clear her mind of what he'd told her. "How stupid do you think I am?"

"You left me without letting me explain," he said, finally losing patience. "How smart is that?" She'd left their Maine house and raced back to Albany, and when he'd gotten home, she wasn't there. A friend of hers called to tell him she was in the hospital with a nervous collapse and didn't want to see him.

"I'd say pretty smart," she retorted, pushing the door open, "if you expect me to fall for *that* line of fiction. If any of that was true, why wouldn't you have told me what you were doing? Why haven't I read about it in the paper?"

"I didn't tell you," he said, stepping out of the cab as she did and facing her across the roof, "because Mrs. Crawford was part of that women's fund-raising group you worked with. I thought it would be awkward for you if you had to watch what you said around her or did anything to make her suspicious."

"Thoughtful of you," she said stiffly.

"And no one's told the press," he went on, ignoring her comment, "because it's still an ongoing investigation."

"You have an answer for everything."

"Because it's the truth." He'd been sure his effort to explain would end this way, but there was just the smallest tug at his chest as he met her eyes. They were filled with anger, then he thought he caught a glimpse of the same regret he felt. Then it was gone. "Okay, I had to try," he said evenly, satisfied that he'd done his best.

"Goodbye, Gideon," she said. "I'll file for divorce so you can get on with your new life in Alaska, and I can get on with my life." Then she disappeared into the restaurant.

Gideon stood for a few minutes, examining his options. The suitcase he'd brought with him was still in the trunk of the cab. He'd stay the night in Maple Hill and go back to Boston tomorrow. Then it was off to Glacier Bay and the Kenton Cove Lodge.

Paris and Randy came out of the restaurant, Paris's expression troubled, Randy's sympathetic.

"She wouldn't listen?" Paris asked.

"She listened," Gideon replied. "She just refuses to believe me."

Randy nodded and offered his hand. "We have a lot in common," he said as they shook hands. "We're both in love with difficult women."

Gideon smiled grimly. "I can relate to the difficult part, but it's all become too complicated to resolve. I'm just going to move on. Paris, you said there were a couple of inns in town?"

Their conversation was interrupted by a loud group of men pushing their way out of the restaurant, talking and laughing. It was Hank Whitcomb and his friends, at whose table Randy had left Gideon when he'd run after Paris.

Hank broke away from the crowd, waving them off, then came to join Paris, Randy and Gideon. He hugged Paris and clapped Randy on the back. "All right, you two. Glad to see you've patched it up. Makes me winner of the pool."

Paris raised an eyebrow. "The pool?"

"They had bets on when we'd finally get together," Randy explained, lifting both hands to deny responsibility when Paris looked dismayed. "I had nothing to do with it. Except in falling in love with you."

Paris leaned into Randy and wrapped an arm around his waist, a beatific smile on her face. "Well, that's all right, then. Hank, you've met my brother-in-law?"

Hank nodded. "We empathized about women while you and Randy were having it out." He winced at Gideon. "I presume since Prue's now inside with her mother and Jeffrey that you're in the same situation Randy was in half an hour ago."

Gideon grinned mirthlessly. "No happy ending for us, though. I understand your wife has an inn?"

"No, no," Paris insisted. "If you're staying the night, you can stay with us, or with Mom."

Gideon shook his head. "Thanks, I appreciate the offer, but the two of you need private time, and frankly, so do I. I have some calls to make, some business to conduct that'd be best done without distractions.''

"Jackie covered the desk at the inn this morning and I promised to take her a cinnamon roll.'' Hank held up the to-go box in his hand. ''Why don't you just ride to the inn with me?''

Paris looked worried. ''So…you're just going to take off for Alaska tomorrow?'' she asked Gideon.

He wrapped her in his arms. ''There's little point in me staying. What about if the three of us meet here for breakfast in the morning before I go?''

''That'd be good.'' She heaved a sigh. ''She's changed, you know. I'm sure if you two had some more time together, you might be surprised by how much more…real she's become.''

He nodded grimly. ''She's always been very real to me. The trouble is, what we had no longer exists for her. So there isn't even a thread of the old life to hold on to and find our way back.''

''Maybe the way isn't back, but forward,'' Randy suggested. ''Approach it as two people *without* a past. Start over.''

''That sounds good,'' Hank offered, then added with a grin, ''And I fully appreciate that this is none of my business, but I've inherited an unfortunate buttinsky nature from my mother.'' Then he sobered and went on. ''But as someone in love with a woman with whom I'd had a past, I know you can't pretend it isn't there. It's *always* there. It affected you, it changed you, and it has to be resolved or there is no future.''

He frowned at Gideon. "The bad news, Gideon, is that if it's important to you, you have to hit it head-on. There's no way around it."

Gideon spread both arms. "I understand that. That's why I'm here. I didn't really think we could repair the relationship, I just wanted to make sure she understood what had happened. But she's not willing to listen and I'm tired of trying."

Randy shook his hand. "Maybe she'll miss you while you're in Alaska."

Gideon gave that suggestion the small, wry laugh it deserved. "I don't think so. See you two here in the morning. Is eight too early?"

"Eight's good."

Gideon followed Hank to a dark green van, Whitcomb's Wonders painted in white script on the side.

"The men who work for you are called Whitcomb's Wonders?" Gideon asked, climbing into the van. "That's quite a claim."

"It is. And I can back it up. Like I told you over breakfast, clients love that they can call one number for almost any kind of service relating to a home or business."

"Do you have a good shrink on staff? I feel as though I could use one right about now."

Hank laughed. "No shrink, but my mother loves to dispense advice. I'll spare you that." He pulled out of the parking lot and onto the highway. "I think I understand your frustration. My wife and I were high-school sweethearts. We were separated by a major breach in communication and finally got back together when I moved home a couple of years ago.''

"How did you heal that breach?''

"We fought a lot," Hank said. "But at least we were talking.''

That, Gideon thought, was the difference right there. Prue had a lot to say but wasn't interested in listening.

Well. That was fine. He was sure he'd like Alaska. Land of the Midnight Sun, of sled dogs and tales of the gold rush. Another adventure.

He just wished he felt more enthusiastic about it. He had to do something completely different, and a partnership with an old college friend in a fishing lodge in the wilderness had seemed like a good place to relax, enjoy the outdoors and try to get a little spirit back into his life.

He hated what had happened between him and Prue, but pleading with her to listen to the truth was as close as he intended to get to groveling.

Hank pulled up to the Yankee Inn, a three-story colonial with green shutters and a vine-covered pergola at the side.

Inside, as Hank leaned over the counter to embrace his wife and deliver the cinnamon roll, Gideon looked around. He saw worn wood floors, a cozy atmosphere provided by a fieldstone fireplace and a settee that was probably as old as the building.

Hank introduced Jackie, a pretty woman with strawberry blond hair and welcoming gray eyes. Hank wished him good luck, while Jackie checked Gideon in and then led him upstairs to his room. It was remarkably quiet. He could see some roofs, the tops of trees and birds in flight. He went to the window and looked down on the bucolic setting stretched out before him. Drying grass, the beautiful Berkshires and the occasional home dotting the road that led to town. He felt something reach out to him and take hold.

"One of my ancestors hid an injured redcoat in this room," Jackie said, smoothing the quilt on the bed. "And nursed him back to health."

He put his bag down and opened the window. Cool fragrant air filled the room. It smelled of wood smoke, and he could hear the musical burble of a stream. He turned back to his hostess to grin. "That was probably a dangerous and unpopular thing for her to do."

Jackie nodded. "She was sixteen. Danger doesn't always stop you at that age. Fortunately, he changed sides for her and survived the war. They raised eight children on this place."

"Courage deserves a happy ending."

"Yes, it does. And sometimes it takes time to get there."

She smiled pleasantly as she opened the door, a silent message in her manner that she understood his situation and sympathized with it. Of course. She'd dealt with and survived that major "communications breach" with Hank. And everyone in Maple Hill seemed to know and even care about everyone else's business.

"Drinks in the lounge five-thirty to seven this evening," she said. "And continental breakfast from seven to ten in the morning. Is there anything I can get you?"

He looked around the cozy, comfortable room and shook his head. "No, thank you."

"Just press nine on the phone for the desk. Enjoy the day."

She stepped out into the hallway and closed the door.

He didn't think there was any way that was going to happen, but he could get himself organized for the trip to Alaska. He confirmed his reservations from Boston, verified his flight on the small plane scheduled to take him from Juneau to Gustavus, then tried to call Dean Kenton, his partner in the fishing lodge, but got no answer.

He took a shower, closed the window in the room as the day wore on to early afternoon, then lay down on the bed, enjoying the unusual luxury of having the time and place for a nap.

The bedding smelled fresh and vaguely herbal as he settled his head into the middle of a plump pillow and closed his eyes. His back and shoulders relaxed against the mattress.

Peace, he thought, enjoying the moment. He was finally going to have peace. Loving Prue had been exciting, tempestuous and undeniably delicious when she was being sane and adult. But she'd displayed those qualities less often in the last year of their marriage, and he wouldn't miss the tears and shouting on her part, the exasperation and anger on his. Refusing to see him when he'd followed her home had been unreasonable, even for her.

Yes. Moving away was a good thing. Nothing like a clean break from the past, even though he couldn't completely separate himself from it, as Hank had said. It was a part of him, had changed him. But he would take what he'd learned and move on.

Somewhere there had to be a woman who was willing to give a man the benefit of the doubt.

He was just drifting off, when his cell phone rang.

"Hello?" he asked, sitting up, happy to put thoughts of Prue out of his mind.

"Gideon? It's Dean."

"Hi. I tried to call you earlier."

"Did you? Oh. Sorry." Dean's usually cheerful voice was grim and hesitant. "There's been a lot going on here."

Gideon could hear a commotion in the background, people shouting. Then he heard a wail—like a siren. He sat up a little straighter. "What happened? Are you all right?"

"I'm fine," Dean replied. "But there's been a fire at the lodge."

"A fire," Gideon repeated, a sense of foreboding bumping along his spine.

"Yeah," Dean confirmed. "The kitchen and the whole guest wing burned to the ground."

CHAPTER TWO

"I CAN'T BELIEVE I named you *Prudence*," Camille O'Hara said.

Prue stared at her mother, a woman in her late forties who was a model and an actress. She'd had her two daughters very young and was still gorgeous. She wore her expertly colored platinum hair in trendy spikes and had an artistic flair for line and color in her clothes. The fact that she was small and slender contributed to her youthful appearance. Prue knew that she got her creative talent from her.

Unfortunately, she'd inherited other things as well. Camille was charming and vivacious with a tendency toward theatrics—a quality probably well suited to her career. But those same qualities made Prue seem like the princess Gideon had often called her.

"Camille, don't be so hard on her." Jeffrey St. John, an actor, musician and old friend of her mother's who was recently rediscovered, had been visiting for a week and showed no signs of going home to Florida. He'd been a calming influence in the household. "She's had a shock, and strong feelings are involved. What would be right for you isn't necessarily right for her."

"How can a strong, dynamic man who loves her not be right for her?" Camille demanded.

"He said he didn't want me back," Prue reminded her. Now that the initial shock of seeing Gideon in Maple Hill had passed, Prue was dealing with a sort of posttraumatic depression. The need to be cool and disdainful in the face of his pathetic explanation had disintegrated and now all she felt was loss for the magic they'd known. "Neither one of us wants to be married again. And that ridiculous explanation of what happened was enough to make the most trusting woman laugh."

"Sometimes," her mother suggested more quietly after Jeffrey's reprimand, "truth is stranger than fiction. Remember when you and Paris were little and the dog stole the cookie dough and I thought you'd done it?"

It was a terrible time to confess to a twenty-year-old crime, but it did make Prue's point. "We did do it, Mom. That's what I mean. If you lie well enough, you can get away with murder—or infidelity."

"You *did* eat the cookie dough?" Camille asked in genuine surprise. She seemed to have missed the point.

"My point, Mom," Prue said patiently, "is that I once loved him very much. He cheated on me while I spent night after lonely night alone believing he was working, giving up my life so he could fulfill his noble calling. Now I don't give a rip about him. He's moving to Alaska to be a partner in a fishing lodge, and I'm going to see a lawyer and file for divorce so I can look for a new partnership. Someday. Right now I have too much to do.''

"Okay," Camille said. Prue was prepared for more argument. Her mother never gave up on anything. "But I think you're making a big mistake. It isn't easy for women like us to find the right man. They feel overwhelmed by us, even intimidated. We attract them all right, but holding them is harder because sometimes…we're just too much.''

"The right kind of man," Prue repeated her words with a roll of her eyes, "wouldn't be found in a compromising position with a stripper.''

"I understand he had his clothes on," Jeffrey said.

Both women turned to him in surprise.

"Well, Paris and Randy sat with us this morning while the two of you were in the cab, and she and your mother talked about it.'' He shrugged. "I just think if a man's as eager as all that to make love to a woman, he's going to get naked, too.''

Feeling besieged, Prue needed to get away. She snatched her jacket and purse off the arm of the sofa and drew a steadying breath. "I'm going to the studio,'' she said politely, though her emotions were hot and turbulent. Anger and pain and bitter disappointment gave her a heartburn that had nothing to do with digestion. "I have a lot of orders to fill and I have to make a plan, try to hire some help.''

Jeffrey stood. "Prue, I'm sorry if I…''

She came back to give him a quick hug. "You

didn't do anything, Jeffrey. I just need to get to work and think about other things.'' She went to her mother, who sat curled up in an overstuffed chair, and hugged her, too. ''I know you have my best interests at heart, Mom. Don't worry if I'm late. I have a lot to do.''

Camille patted her cheek. ''I'm so happy for you that the fashion show went well. Soon the whole world's going to know you're a brilliant designer.''

That was a nice thought.

Jeffrey tossed her his car keys. She tossed them back. ''Thanks, but it's a beautiful day and I'm going to walk.'' She'd sold her Porsche when she'd moved back home to help contribute to the household. The fact that her sister owned a cab company had helped her get around, but after Paris and Randy were reconciled this morning, she imagined Paris would have better things to do than drive her to her studio.

She blew a kiss into the room and walked out the door, breathing in the sharp, clear air. She set a steady pace and headed off toward town, thinking that the two-mile jaunt would probably take her half an hour or better.

It was just after noon when she reached town. Colonial homes and small businesses stood in the sun-dappled early afternoon, Halloween decorations on the windows, a black cat–shaped windsock puffed out in front of the hardware store.

Traffic picked up as she reached the square, groups of women and men from City Hall or businesses downtown hurrying to lunch appointments. The trees on the common caught the sunlight that also glossed the curved lines on the statue of Caleb and Elizabeth Drake, a couple who'd fought off redcoats. Prettily painted two-hundred-year-old buildings framed the square.

She tried hard to concentrate on her surroundings rather than think about Gideon and his sudden appearance this morning. Though everyone else seemed to think his visit was noble to try to clarify what had happened and an indicator that he still cared, she thought of it as just another attempt to convince her of a fiction she just couldn't swallow.

She didn't think she was being difficult. She simply needed to hold on to her self-respect. What woman in her right mind would have believed him?

She'd just reached the far side of the square, when a horn honked behind her. She turned to see Paris's cab pull up to the curb. The station wagon had magnetic signs on the front doors that read Berkshire Cab in tall yellow letters. Her sister reached across the front seat to open the passenger door.

"Where you going?" she asked.

"To the studio." Prue ducked down to reply. "Why aren't you and Randy making out somewhere? What's wrong with you?"

"One of the other EMTs' mother died and Randy was called in to cover for him." Paris shrugged. "So, I thought I may as well drive. Get in." She pulled a bottle of 7-Up and a package of saltines off the passenger seat.

Prue complied, fastened her seat belt, then took the bottle and crackers from her. "How's the nausea?"

"Comes and goes," Paris replied, watching her rearview mirror as she pulled out again. Taking her place in the busy traffic, she grinned at the windshield. "I'm feeling too obnoxiously happy to notice, really. Can you believe it? I'm in love! And I'm going to be a mother."

Prue patted her sister's arm, sincerely pleased for her, while her own heart reacted with a silent whimper. "A lot's changed since you woke up at five this morning, sick as a dog and determined to leave Maple Hill and Randy to go back to law school."

Paris nodded, still smiling. "I know. I can't believe that only hours ago I was so sure that all the wonderful aspects of my life were over, except for the baby. And here I am."

"Obnoxiously happy."

"Yes. And you know why?"

"Why?"

They'd passed downtown now and the Breakfast Barn sign was visible in the distance on the left side of the highway.

"Because I was forced to listen to. reason. Randy came after me and made me listen to him." She spoke amiably, then added with pointed emphasis, "Just like Gideon tried to do with you this morning."

If Prue wasn't wearing her favorite red wool jacket,

she'd have leaped from the moving car and taken her chances. But this fabric had been the devil to work on and she wasn't going to endanger it to escape her sister's advice.

"Do you want to hear what he told me this morning?" she asked Paris.

Paris sent her a quick and frankly interested glance. "Do you want to tell me?"

Prue recounted Gideon's story complete with the members of the ethics committee hitting a moose and the stripper harboring a lifelong desire for higher education.

Paris considered a moment, waving at the driver of a police car that drove past. "I don't think that's so unbelievable. Parts of the story are a little outrageous, but then Mom always says that truth is—"

"Stranger than fiction," Prue finished for her. "I know. Well, I don't believe it. There's been nothing about the incident in the paper."

"He said it was an ongoing investigation."

"That's what he said."

"Prudie…" Paris gasped, obviously frustrated with her. That came as no surprise. They'd learned to deal with each other since they'd each returned home a year ago, but they would always be two very different women.

Paris was levelheaded and practical, and if it hadn't been for a shocking discovery about their mother's history that redirected her entire life, Paris would probably be about to take the bar exam right now.

Prue had always thought Paris took after Jasper O'Hara, their father, who'd been an accountant and the voice of reason in their lively family. But it turned out that Paris was the result of a traumatic event in her mother's life, and whatever she'd inherited from Jasper had been by osmosis rather than genetics.

Prue, on the other hand, was artistic and mercurial like their mother, and tended to operate on emotion rather than reason, which oddly seemed more reliable to her. Reason was so black and white and allowed little scope for creativity. Emotion, however, could take one in a million different directions and always seemed to open doors rather than close one in.

"You know," Paris started again. "You're so creative about everything until it comes to love. It doesn't exist just to serve you, you know. Gideon's whole purpose in life wasn't to see that you were adored and that nothing in your life went wrong. It's entirely possible that things happened just the way he said they did, but you won't trust him because you'd have to open up your concept of what love is. Maybe he needed *you* at the same time *you* were so desperate for reassurance."

Prue tried to understand that and couldn't.

"What are you talking about?" she asked crossly. "Love is about supporting and respecting one another. You might remember that I've been doing this longer than you have. I did it for four years while he claimed to be working too hard to do it for me, only to find out that he was fooling around."

"He said he wasn't."

"I saw him!"

"You saw him fully dressed with a nearly naked woman in his lap. I think it's entirely possible his explanation could be true."

"Yeah, well, your future doesn't hinge on the possibility that it could also be a lie."

"Okay," Paris sighed. "I don't want to fight with you, especially now that I'm carrying a baby and you're about to become the next Donna Karan."

Prue drew a calming breath. They'd have never agreed to disagree in the old days; they'd have fought an issue until they weren't speaking. Both of them had learned a lot and gained some maturity over the past year.

"Okay," Prue said. "And I appreciate all you did to make the fashion show a success. The library made a lot of money, and so did I."

Paris grinned wryly. "I think my fainting on the runway earned you some pity business, but we can't take issue with that. So, how are you going to fill all those orders?"

"I've been thinking about that. Now that I have a little cash to play with, I'm going to hire help. And Rosie DeMarco from Happily Ever After might be willing to help me if her sister's around to watch the shop."

"Sounds like you have it all worked out."

"Planned out, anyway. Whether everything goes according to plan is another matter."

They'd reached the old Chandler Mill Building on the river where Prue had her studio in an upstairs space. Paris pulled into the parking lot. "Call me when you're done for the day," she said, "and we'll go for Chinese. Randy'll be at the fire station tonight and I can visit but I can't hang around too long."

Prue nodded. "That'll be fun. When you're not home, I feel like a fifth wheel with Jeffrey at Mom's. I mean, I love him dearly and I think it'd be wonderful if he and Mom got together, I just don't want to be in their way."

"I'm sure you're not. You know Mom. She'd tell you if you were. She'd put it charmingly, but she'd tell you."

They laughed together, not at their mother, but at their shared knowledge of her passive-aggressive honesty.

Paris gave her a quick hug as she reached for the car door. "I'll butt out of your business, I promise. I just want you to be happy."

Prue hugged her back. "Prudent Designs makes me very happy," she assured her. "And usually, having you for a sister does, too. Unless you try to convince me that candy is poison like you did when we were children, or…"

"You know, the Heart and Health Association proved me right on that one."

"Or—" Prue talked over her "—you interfere in my love life."

Paris gave her a look. "Do you even *have* a love life?"

Prue angled her chin. "I might someday, and I wouldn't want you to interfere."

"I understand," Paris said gravely.

"Incidentally…" Prue couldn't help the wide smile. "Remember when I was five and you were seven and we stole the chocolate-chip cookie dough while Mom was talking to Dad on the phone?"

Paris nodded. "We told her Mopsy got it. We were so bad at fibbing. Your creative nature apparently didn't kick in until later."

"She believed us," Prue told her. "I just found out this morning. When I told her we lied, she was shocked."

Paris grinned with the old mischief of their childhood. "You're kidding! That story was so transparent!"

Prue made a face. "Now I feel guilty. I suppose she loved us, so she trusted us."

Prue thanked Paris for the ride and promised to call her when she was finished for the day. Then she got out of the car and let herself into the building as Paris drove away.

Trust. There was that word Prue didn't want to hear again. At least not today, because it brought to mind the image of Gideon's face telling her he didn't want her back because he couldn't live with anyone who didn't trust him.

Well, she was embarking on her own future, and she didn't want to have to trust anyone but herself.

GIDEON SAT on an antique settee in front of the fire in the parlor of the Yankee Inn. He'd had a long telephone conversation with Dean, who told him there was little point in his coming to Kenton Cove until the lodge was rebuilt and, now that cold weather was setting in there, work wouldn't start until spring.

Disappointed but trying to put a positive face on the situation, Gideon had canceled his flights and was perusing the *Maple Hill Mirror,* trying to decide what to do with himself for the next seven or eight months.

The inn's door burst open suddenly and he found himself surrounded by a group of wet-haired children smelling of chlorine and carrying damp towels. There were three girls and a boy, and not an adult in sight. Jackie had disappeared into an office at the back and hadn't returned.

"Hi." A pretty little blond girl about ten or eleven sat beside him. "You're the senator, aren't you?"

Gideon smiled politely, wondering where she'd gotten that information. "Well, I was. I'm not a senator anymore," he said, folding down a corner of the paper. "You're that kid that's been to the swimming pool."

She giggled. "How'd you know that?" Then remembering her wet hair and her obvious towel, she giggled again. "Oh, yeah. We have swimming lessons after school."

Another little blonde, several years younger than the one next to him, stood with a scolding expression. "You're not supposed to get naked with somebody unless you're married to them."

"Rachel!" A dark-haired child with large brown eyes whose age appeared to be somewhere between the other two came to sit on his other side. She looked mortified. "I'm sorry," she said to Gideon. "My sister's too little to understand about gossip and how you're not supposed to believe it or pass it on."

Oh, good. Even children knew he was the object of gossip and what it was all about. He folded the paper and put it on the low table in front of him.

"I'm not too little!" Rachel denied. "Mom said that Grandma said—"

"Grandma gossips!" the older sister interrupted her. "And Mom doesn't want us to do that." She turned to Gideon. "Our mom owns the inn."

"Ah. You're Mrs. Whitcomb's children."

"Her name's Jackie," Rachel informed him. "Our dad's Hank. He's our second one. The first one died." She pointed her wet towel at the brunette. "That's Erica, and that's Ashley. She's our friend." She pointed to the young boy beside her. "This is Brian."

"He's my brother," Ashley said.

"Only, he's not really." Rachel seemed to have a compulsion for detail. "His mom's in jail, so Mariah and Cam adopted him. Everybody died in Ashley's family."

Erica rolled her eyes and groaned in dismay.

"That's private stuff!" she said to Rachel. "You don't just blab it to everybody!"

Rachel frowned in hurt surprise. "We know *him*." She pointed to Gideon. "Well, we know *about* him. He's Prue's husband, and Prue's friends with Ashley's mom and dad. And Dad said he liked him."

Gideon met Brian's eyes, wondering how he was taking the girls' candor. He was pleased to see that it didn't seem to be bothering him. Brian was obviously well adjusted to his new situation. Gideon had met Cam that morning over the eventful breakfast at the Barn. He'd seemed like a good guy. They all had.

He held his hand out to the boy. "Hi, Brian. I'm Gideon."

Brian shook his hand and smiled. "You know judo," he announced with enthusiasm. "Uncle Hank said! Can you throw me?"

"Sure." Gideon stood, and without giving the boy a moment, he tossed him spectacularly over his right hip, protecting the boy's landing with a firm grip on him. Then he pulled him up.

"Wow!" Brian was flushed with excitement.

The girls were all on their feet. "Do me!" Rachel demanded. Gideon complied. Squeals of hilarity reigned as he swung the other two girls to the floor.

Hank pushed his way into the lobby just in time to catch Brian pleading to be thrown a second time.

"Daddy!" Rachel ran to him, caught his hand and pulled him toward the laughing group of children, talking all the time. "He can do judo!" she exclaimed. "And he made Brian fly through the air, then he did it to me, then he did everybody!"

"And he's gonna do me again!" Brian shouted. "Go ahead, Gideon."

Gideon looked at Hank in question. He nodded his approval. Brian went over with a giggling cry.

"Whoa." Hank came closer, smiling. "You're going to have to teach me to do that." He frowned teasingly at the kids. "And when I take the trouble to pick you up, it would be nice if you didn't race off and leave me behind the minute the car stops."

"Sorry, Dad," Erica said, then without drawing a breath asked Gideon, "Can you throw Daddy?"

Gideon shook his head. "Space is too small. And I'm sure your dad's had a busy day and the last thing he wants to do right now is go flying through the air."

Hank studied him with new interest. "Do you think you could?" he asked.

"Could what?" He couldn't mean what Gideon thought he was asking. "Take you down?"

"Yeah. If you had the room."

"Sure."

Hank raised an eyebrow in challenge. "We're about the same size."

Gideon nodded. "It's not about size."

"Okay. Follow me."

The children jumped along beside them like little pistons, squealing as Hank led the way to a big empty room in the back.

"Jackie uses this room for banquets," he explained, "but it's empty at the moment because housekeeping just shampooed the carpet. This do?"

"Very well." Gideon pulled off his shoes and advised Hank to do the same. They pushed the eager children toward the wall.

"You stay back there," Hank told them firmly. "You don't want to get hit when Gideon comes flying at you." He grinned at Gideon. The children cheered.

It took just a few seconds. Gideon grabbed Hank, and when Hank tipped his weight, thinking Gideon intended to push in that direction, Gideon reversed and dropped him by hooking his foot with his own.

Hank went down with a thud and a shout and lay there for a moment, the breath knocked out of him. Gideon offered him his hand.

Hank took it, surprise in his eyes. He grinned again and flexed his shoulders. "Okay, I wasn't expecting that."

Gideon brushed off the shoulder of Hank's chambray shirt. "Assailants don't usually count to three," he said.

"True." Hank conceded. "Okay, let's go again."

"Come on, Daddy!" Erica shouted.

Brian called, "Go, Gideon!"

Hank, busy assuming a prepared stance, stopped to frown with teasing ferocity at the boy. "Whose side are you on, Brian?"

Brian smiled winningly. "Well, Gideon doesn't have anybody to cheer for him."

That was certainly true on more than one level.

Prepared, Hank was a stronger opponent, but knowledge won out over strength. Gideon grabbed him and, using the man's own strength, tossed him over his hip. Hank landed hard.

The children gasped.

Gideon would have worried about embarrassing Hank in front of the children if Hank had seemed worried about it, but he didn't. Hank propped himself up on his elbows and asked, "Can you do two men at a time?"

Gideon nodded, then looked around. "But you're the only man here. You're seeing double. That'll be gone in a minute."

"Funny man." Hank sat up. "Erica, can I have your cell phone?"

The girl dug in her backpack and handed it to him. He dialed. "Good," he said after a moment. "You're still there. Can you come down to the banquet room for a few minutes? Doesn't matter what for, you'll have a good time."

He winked at the children, who laughed. He tossed the phone back at Erica and got to his feet, flexing his left arm and groaning.

"What're you doing for dinner?" he asked. "Jackie told me your trip to Alaska fell through, at least for the moment, and you've booked an extra day."

Gideon nodded. "I thought a drive through the Berkshires would be good for my disposition."

"I'm sure that's true," Hank said. "Jackie makes a mean enchilada casserole. Want to join us?"

Gideon was a little surprised by the offer. It wasn't as though he knew him that well, and it was a curious suggestion in light of the fact that he'd just taken him down twice.

"Ah…that'd be nice," he said. "Thank you."

A man in paint-smeared coveralls walked into the room. Brian ran to him.

"Uncle Evan!" he said. "Gideon's going to throw you around!"

Gideon remembered the man from the breakfast table at the Barn.

"Gideon, you remember Evan Braga? Evan, Gideon Hale."

"Right." Gideon shook hands and said with a note of apology, "I just want to make it clear up-front that this is Hank's idea and not mine."

Evan looked doubtful. "Okay."

"He's a martial arts expert," Hank told Evan. "He's going to throw us."

"Throw us," Evan repeated blankly.

"Yeah."

"Is this in my job description?"

"No, but job description is what this is all about."

"Ohhh," Evan said as though that clarified things. Gideon was confused.

But not about what he knew. Hank and Evan backed away from him, each at an angle, then came toward him. Hank was easily dispensed with, but

Evan had had some training. Gideon struggled with him for a moment, then finally overbalanced him, hooked his left leg and used the weight of his own body to drive Evan's shoulders to the floor. Gideon leaped up again, ready for a counterattack.

Hank and Evan, both supine, looked at one another.

"What do you think?" Hank asked him.

Evan, breathless from their brief but fierce struggle, nodded. "Yes. But if you tell anybody he took both of us, I'll hurt you!" He frowned at the children. "And that goes for you guys, too."

The children giggled, obviously not taking him seriously.

Gideon offered his hand to Evan and hauled him to his feet. Then both reached for Hank.

"Am I still invited for dinner?" Gideon teased.

"Absolutely," Hank replied. "I want to talk to you about a job."

CHAPTER THREE

"THE FISHING LODGE caught fire, or something, yesterday," Camille said, handing Prue a bag of oranges. She put two bags of lettuce into the vegetable crisper in the fridge, then closed the door and looked into Prue's dismayed face. "I met him at the market. He was supposed to leave for Boston this morning, then fly out to Alaska, but his partner asked him to wait until the lodge is rebuilt. Hank offered him a job, so he's staying here until the lodge is ready."

Prue was stopped in her tracks by that news. No. That couldn't be. She had fifty-one special orders for her designs. She couldn't operate under that kind of pressure with the possibility hanging over her of running into Gideon at the market or the Barn.

"Tell me you're kidding," Prue pleaded.

Camille pushed a ten-pound bag of potatoes into her arms. "Can't do that. It's the truth. Put that stuff away before you get a hernia."

Prue carried the oranges and potatoes to the far corner of the room where an old-fashioned cooler-cupboard opened to the outside and kept produce cool. She placed the food on the slatted shelf, then closed the door and came back to her mother.

"But why would he want to stay *here?* I'm here. We're getting a divorce."

"Divorced couples often live in the same city."

"This isn't a city, this is a small town! We'll keep bumping into each other."

Camille smiled as she walked past her with a dozen eggs destined for the refrigerator. "Then you'll have to behave with grace and dignity when that happens, won't you?"

Prue sank dispiritedly onto a stool pulled up to the work island in the bright cream-colored kitchen. "I don't think I'm capable of that," she grumbled.

Camille, on her way back to the grocery bags, stopped to stare at her. "What?"

"Come on, Mom," she said, playing with the bag of green onions sitting on the countertop, waiting to be washed. "You know how it is. Paris has the smarts, and I have the…the reputation for reacting. She keeps her cool, and I just try to look pretty while I'm preparing to blow up or laugh nervously."

Her mother changed directions and came to sit on the stool beside her. "What are you talking about? You've always been the…the…"

"Princess…" Prue provided for her. "Yes, I know. The one who likes things her way, who forces the issue until it comes out her way. To some people, it looks like charming determination, but to those who know me well, it just means I don't know what to do when things don't turn out the way I planned. Because Paris is the brains and I'm like you."

Camille blinked, obviously uncertain whether or not to be insulted. "Thank you, Prudence," she said drily.

Prue touched her arm. "Mom, you know what I mean. Paris is a woman of today, all intelligence and quick wit. Who else could come home with nothing and make a taxi service a going concern?"

"You've opened what appears to be a very successful design studio," Camille pointed out.

Prue shrugged. "I can see designs in my head and I can sew. But my talents are the kind that would have gotten me through if this was nineteenth-century France. But this is twenty-first-century America where women run countries and corporations, fly in space, preside over colleges and hospitals. I'm out of date."

Camille blinked again. "Then, if you're just like I am…"

"No." Prue anticipated her conclusion and denied it. "You're not out of date. You're an actress and a model. You're supposed to look beautiful and be fabulous and charm everyone." She met her mother's eyes. "And we know how brave you've been. I've proved nothing, except that I can sew."

Camille put a hand to Prue's cheek. "Prudie, when did this insecurity begin? I don't remember you ever questioning yourself this way."

"I've had a lot to think about since I've come home." She took her mother's hand and held it. "I've watched Paris take hard news and still get on with it.

I've learned about all you went through that we never suspected. And you both found men to love who loved you in return.''

Camille squeezed her hand and said significantly, "So did you.''

"But I apparently wasn't enough.''

"Depends on what you choose to believe.''

Prue covered her eyes with one hand. "Let's not have that argument again.'' She dropped her hand to the table and said with a touch of regret, "My plan was to finish my orders, then maybe take my designs to New York where I can really compete. But if Gideon's staying here, maybe I'll go to New York now.''

"Well, that's foolish,'' Camille said. "You have fifty-one orders. Doesn't that involve fittings—probably more than one—for each garment?''

Prue had to concede that it did. She knew she couldn't leave, it just felt good to pretend that she could.

"Yes, it does. It's going to take me months.''

"You told me last night that Rosie DeMarco said she could help you in her spare time.''

Prue nodded. "It's going to take months even with help.''

"Then, you'll just have to decide that when you run into Gideon, you'll be civil and not make a scene.''

"I think you *should* make a scene.'' Paris walked into the kitchen holding a large bowl covered with plastic wrap. "I think the next time you see him, you should run into his arms, tell him you want to listen to his explanation one more time with an open mind, and try your marriage again.''

Prue rolled her eyes at her sister. "You're delusional. What's in the bowl?"

"Chilly's chili," Paris replied, handing the bowl to Camille. "I had lunch with Randy at the station and—you know his partner on the ambulance, Chilly Childress—sent me home with leftovers. You have to try this stuff. It's hellfire ambrosia." She took Camille's stool as her mother put the bowl in the refrigerator. "Did you know," she asked Prue, "that Gideon's rented that old A-frame on the far side of the lake? He's staying for a while. Something happened with the partnership deal. Addy told me. I guess Hank found him the house."

"A fire happened," Prue informed her. "Mom met Gideon at the market this morning."

"So, what do you think?" Paris asked, looking pleased. "I think it's fate. I think the cosmos is conspiring to force the two of you together so you have to work it out."

Prue caught her mother's eye across the work island as she prepared a pot of coffee. "And to think I said Paris was the smart one."

Paris broke into a wide smile. "She did?" she asked Camille. "Prue said I was smart?" She turned to her sister in suspicion. "You want something. What is it? A kidney?"

Prue swatted her arm and slipped off the stool. "I have to get to the studio. You just keep dreaming."

"Actually," Paris said, catching her arm. "*I* need something."

Prue stopped. "Yes?" she asked warily.

"You know the wedding dress I modeled?"

"The one you fainted in and got all dusty? Yes, I do."

"Can I get married in it?" Paris asked with a gleeful expression.

Camille squealed and started crying as she wrapped Paris in her arms. Prue forced herself into their circle until it was a three-way hug.

"Of course you can," she said. "Congratulations!"

Paris drew slightly away, her green eyes bright with happiness. "Randy and I talked about it when I was at the station for lunch. He wants to get married as soon as possible. We're thinking within the next couple of weeks."

Camille frowned. "But that's barely time to plan showers and invitations and—"

Paris interrupted with a shake of her head. "We don't want all that. We'll call everyone. The guys at the firehouse want to fix the food, and I've got a dress."

"But..." Camille didn't seem able to focus her complaints.

Paris hugged her again. "It's what we want, Mom. No fuss, just everyone we love around us. Okay?"

Even her mother found that hard to dispute. "Okay."

"I want you to give me away, Mom."

"Really? Is that…proper?"

"Yes. It's done all the time. And Prue, of course, will be my maid of honor. Chilly's going to stand up for Randy. What's the matter?"

Camille had a worried expression. "You're not moving away, are you?"

"No. Randy wants to stay and so do I. In fact, we're going to start house-hunting pretty soon."

Camille put a hand to her heart in relief. "Thank goodness. I thought the hurry meant he was going back to medical school or you really did want to go back to Boston. I know I lived without you and Prue for quite a while, but I've really enjoyed having you back."

Prue saw in Paris the excitement, the promise she herself had known when she'd burst into the house one rainy afternoon four-and-a-half years ago to announce her engagement to Gideon. She remembered the deep-down satisfaction she'd felt that life was progressing according to plan, that she'd found a handsome, smart and well-respected man.

She hadn't known then that her princess life was about to be dethroned. That it wasn't all as perfect as it appeared.

Paris's cell phone rang. "Berkshire Cab," she answered. "Oh, hi, Letitia." She listened a moment, then slipped off the stool. "Sure I can. I'll be right there. Ten minutes."

She turned off the phone, tucked it into the pocket of the baseball jacket Randy had lent her at a picnic about a month ago, and that had hardly been off her back since. "I'm picking up the Lightfoot sisters," she said, hugging Camille one more time. The Lightfoot sisters were a spinster pair who ran the Maple Hill Manor School outside of town. It had been in their family for generations. "Want a ride to the studio, Prue?"

"Yes, please." Prue ran for her purse and jacket and met Paris at the door. "Bye, Mom!"

"Bye, girls. Drive carefully. When Randy gets off, we'll all have to celebrate!" She shouted the last part as Paris closed the door.

Prue climbed into the passenger seat as Paris slipped in behind the wheel.

"I'm really happy for you," Prue said, buckling her seat belt. "I'll make you something special. I don't know what yet, but I'll think of something."

Paris backed out of the driveway, turned onto Lake Road and headed for the highway. "You won't have time to think about anything but all those orders you have to fill. Letting me use the wedding dress is enough, Prue. I suppose I should talk to Rosie about buying that headpiece I modeled with it. It was perfect."

"It was. Any thoughts on what color you want me to wear?"

"I don't know." Paris made a face as she thought. "Something fallish, I suppose. Like gold or pumpkin."

"I have a soft orange brocade I've been saving for something special. You think that'd be too weird for a wedding?"

"Not at all. You're not capable of weird when it comes to wearing the right thing. I swear, you'd look good in golf pants."

Prue laughed. "You're the one who wowed them at the fashion show."

"Of course. I was wearing your clothes."

"And you did such a good job of it, even the Lightfoot sisters ordered two of the cloaks. One midnight, one emerald. They told me they intend to wear them when they go to the opera in Boston."

Paris smiled. "That's great. The sisters are so cute." She pulled into the parking lot of the Chandler Mill Building and stopped near the door. "Will you have time to make yourself a dress for the wedding?" Paris asked as Prue stepped out of the cab. "I mean, with all those orders to fill?"

"Oh, sure," Prue replied. "I'll do something simple but special. How do you feel today?"

Paris waggled her right hand. "Early morning's the worst, then I'm usually okay. Have a good afternoon." She grinned mischievously. "Any messages for Gideon?"

"No." Prue was afraid to ask why, but she wanted to know. "Why?"

"I'm picking him up later so he can buy a car."
She smiled innocently at Prue. "You should come
along. You keep talking about buying a car, too."

Prue grabbed the leather wallet that always sat on
the console beside Paris, and reached into it for the
candy bar her chocoholic sister usually stashed there.
And there it was. Hershey with almonds. Basic but
delicious.

"Hey!" Paris complained.

"If you can be mean to me—" Prue pocketed the
bar, zipped up the wallet again and returned it to its
spot "—I can be mean to you. Just leave me alone
about Gideon."

"Prudie! Give me back my chocolate! I need se-
rotonin for two!"

Prue thanked her sister for the ride, stuck her
tongue out at her and let herself into the building.
Once inside, she stood for a moment with her back
to the closed door, absorbing the sense of safety and
security the building provided her. No one here ever
asked her about Gideon. No one here ever made her
think about the loss she'd kept from him. She wondered with a little wince why the grief was suddenly
so fresh. Because Gideon was back, probably.

She'd have to consider moving into her studio.

GIDEON LIKED the house Hank had found for him.
Hank had done work in it several months ago when
the owner was moving and preparing to rent it out
rather than sell it on the chance he returned one day.

"It's probably a little big for one person," Hank had said, "but then again it's nice to have space."

The A-frame had a large living room with the vaulted ceiling typical of the architecture, a long kitchen and dining area off to the right, and a bedroom and a bath behind the living room.

The loft bedroom was huge with a finely carved railing that looked down on the living room.

Hank had led him out onto the deck that ran the length of the structure and pointed across the lake. "See that dock on the other side?"

Gideon had squinted, but the sun was bright and the lake was a considerable distance across. He could barely make it out.

"That's Cam and Mariah's place. Used to be mine, but Jackie had the old family place in town and that's worked out more conveniently for us with the kids."

"I love this house," Gideon said. "And I appreciate your finding it for me considering how little you know about me. And considering the story circulating of the incident that led to my separation from Prue."

Hank nodded. "I've heard it. But I've been misjudged a time or two myself, and I think it's a good thing to make your decisions about people on what you witness firsthand. And so far all I really know is that you make good breakfast-table conversation, you were decorated for bravery in the Gulf War and you're a judo master. Hard to think badly of you on that information."

Gideon had appreciated that vote of confidence. It

was going to make staying here more doable than it might have been. And Hank asked him to set up the new security program that would become a part of Whitcomb's Wonders' services. Gideon was certain Hank wouldn't have asked that of someone he had any doubts about.

This morning Gideon had gone to the furniture store and bought a sofa, a dining table and chairs, a bed and a television. A small apartment-size washer and dryer had been left in the downstairs bathroom. He figured that would see him through his stay in Maple Hill.

A cursory look around the living room reminded him of Prue's flair for decorating.

It was weird, he thought as he went to the kitchen to make a pot of coffee. Now that he'd seen Prue again, he missed her. When she'd first taken off on him after refusing to see him and discuss what had happened, he'd been so angry at her unreasonable attitude that he hadn't cared if he ever saw her again.

Then, after almost a year without her, he'd begun to accept that it was over. Anger had evaporated and all that was left was a desperate need to set the record straight.

When Dean had offered him the partnership in the fishing lodge, he'd known he had to make one last effort to talk to her on his way out of her life. He'd wanted nothing more than to hear her say that she believed him.

The frustration had returned when he'd gotten here

and found that her attitude hadn't changed an iota. But he thought he'd seen pain in her eyes. She wouldn't change her mind because she was still hurt.

And the obvious conclusion was that she still cared about him.

He certainly still cared about her. As much as he could have cheerfully murdered her yesterday for trouncing all his explanations about what had happened in Maine, he had to admit that seeing her had affected him in a major way. All the old feeling was back. Everything he'd felt for her, and thought had been destroyed, had apparently only been suppressed.

He wanted her back. He'd told her he didn't, but if she wouldn't listen to the truth from him, it seemed pointless to be honest about his feelings.

The loud ring of his newly installed telephone jarred him out of his thoughts. He put the filled coffee basket into the machine and poured water into the well as he picked up the receiver.

"Hello?"

"Gideon?" The voice was low and female with a touch of Marlene Dietrich's dramatic alto. He recognized it immediately.

"Aunt George!" he exclaimed. Georgette Irene Hale Milton Didier Finch-Morgan was his favorite aunt, his father's older sister who'd worked for *Vogue,* been widowed three times and was now CEO of her third husband's considerable holdings. She lived in London. "How are you?"

"I'm *enmerdée* at the moment," she said, the

French word translating to a situation that involved considerable manure. "But I'm coming to see you."

"But…I'm not home," he said stupidly.

"Well, I know you're not home, Gideon. I called you there first and got this number from your mother. She told me about a plan you had to go into partnership in Alaska. I understand it just fell through."

"Actually, it's only been delayed," he corrected. "But why did you track me down? I hope it's because you decided I'm your favorite nephew and you're leaving me everything."

"Ha!" she scoffed. "You are my favorite nephew, but I'm having too much fun to leave anybody anything just yet. I've tracked you down because I want to talk to Prudence."

"Ah…Aunt George. You know Prue and I are separated."

"I do. But I also know that she's in Maple Hill, wherever that is, and so are you." .

"I just came to try to straighten things out with her before I went to Alaska. But she still doesn't want anything to do with me."

"But you're still staying there?"

"I've been offered a challenging job. And it's a beautiful place to be until I go to Alaska. Why do you want to talk to Prue?"

"Because I heard about her line of clothes. Your mother faxed me the photos that appeared in the *Boston Globe*."

"The *Globe?*" he repeated in surprise.

"Apparently their fashion reporter was there for Leaf-Peeper weekend and decided to stay for the fashion show. She was very impressed. So, I remembered that I never gave you kids a wedding present."

Gideon laughed. "That was probably wise, or it'd be in storage in New York with a lot of our other things."

"Well, I insist on making it up to you. Or rather, to her. I always did like that girl. In the communications division of one of my companies, there's a very prestigious little fashion magazine that would love to have photos and a story about a young American launching a sophisticated new line."

He knew Prue would be thrilled at that opportunity. And in spite of all her animosity toward him, he wanted her to have it.

"I can be there in three days with a photographer," Georgette said. "And I'll do the story myself. I often contribute to the magazine because of my fashion experience. Can we stay with you?"

Gideon hesitated, only because he knew his aunt's presence would put paid to all his hopes of peace and quiet.

"Ah…sure. But Prue doesn't want anything to do with me. If you want to deal with her…" And suddenly, like a shaft of sunlight through a storm cloud, he saw a way to turn this to his advantage.

Georgette waited a moment, then demanded, "What?"

"I…ah…" He stalled for time as his brain churned with an idea.

"Gideon?"

"Can you do some dramatic work for me, Auntie?" he asked as he mulled over the idea again, looking for flaws. There were many, but he was an optimist.

"You know me, dahling," she said in a theatrical tone. "I live for center stage."

"I'm thinking," he said, unreeling the plan, "that if you tell her that I told you we were reconciled and that she's living here with me, she'll come over demanding to know what I'm up to and I can explain that I didn't want her to miss this opportunity to make a big splash in the press. She'll think I'm noble. Maybe."

"That sounds plausible."

"So, she'll have to stay with me for the time that you're here so that it really does appear that we're reconciled."

"But would my opinion of your marital status be that important to her?"

"I think it'll be all entangled in her wish to have this opportunity. And in my noble and self-sacrificing insistence that she get it."

"Ah. Insidious. I like it. Give me her number."

As fate would have it, he'd run into Camille when he'd been in the supermarket buying coffee, and she'd given it to him—both her cell and the studio. He gave both numbers to his aunt.

"All right, Gideon," she said briskly. "I'm going to bring the fashion world a bright new star and possibly save a marriage in the bargain. Is there an aunt anywhere more wonderful than I?"

"I doubt it," he replied. "Go to it, Auntie."

She hung up, obviously pumped to come through for him.

All he had to do was wait.

And he might invest in a little body armor, just in case.

CHAPTER FOUR

PRUE SORTED THROUGH her orders, listed them according to garment and size to place her fabric order, then listed names and phone numbers in preparation for setting up a fitting schedule. She sipped at a cup of coffee, stared at her long list and fought a sense of panic. She'd have to work flat-out—with help—in order to get everything done so that her first customers could wear their fall and winter fashions before spring came!

She fell back against her chair, momentarily daunted by the task, and looked around at the studio she'd finally acquired after years of dreaming about it. It was far more functional than glamorous—a lot like her life. The room had a collection of tables, one for cutting fabric, one that held two sewing machines, one for simply working out patterns. There was a rolling rack of finished and half-finished projects, two overstuffed chairs for collapsing into, shelves with bolts of fabric, drawers with trim, buttons, notions.

On the wall above her desk, a bulletin board was covered with fabric swatches, design ideas, fast-food coupons and the occasional business card.

It occurred to her that she finally had this place

because Gideon had sent her half the proceeds of the sale of their condo.

But she didn't want to think about him right now, and was happy to be distracted by the ringing telephone.

She picked it up, hoping it wasn't a client already wondering when her order would be filled.

"Hello," she said with false cheer.

"Hi, darling! I never sent your wedding present and I'm coming to make it up to you!"

Prue was surprised by the vaguely familiar female voice and the odd, completely out-of-sync remark.

"Ah…" she began hesitantly.

"It's Aunt Georgette, darling!" the theatrical voice clarified. "Remember me? We only met once, but I'm generally considered to be pretty unforgettable."

Prue had to laugh, remembering the tall, attractive woman in head-to-toe Gucci she'd met in New York at the engagement party Gideon's parents had given them.

"What a lovely surprise." Prue remembered finding her funny and sincere. But she couldn't imagine why the woman was calling her. Last she'd heard, Georgette lived in Europe with a new husband, who'd since passed away.

"I'll tell you why I'm calling," Georgette said, launching into a story about receiving a fax of the *Globe* story about Prue's fashion show, and how she wanted to prepare an advertising campaign for her through the firm she'd inherited from her husband.

"I'm so sorry I missed your wedding, but I'd like to make up for it now. What do you say?"

Prue was flattered, astonished, and very aware of just what such exposure could do for the future of Prudent Designs.

"Well, I'd love that, of course," she said, then felt honesty required that she tell her just what had happened since the wedding she'd missed. "But I think you should know, Aunt Georgette, that Gideon and I—"

"Were getting a divorce," Georgette interrupted. "Gideon told me. But since you've patched things up, you're still deserving of a wedding present."

Prue repeated dumbly, "Patched things up?"

"Gideon explained about the misunderstanding, but I'm so happy you had the good sense to hear him out and trust that he'd never do such a thing to you."

Prue was trying hard to grasp what Georgette was telling her, but her brain just wouldn't make sense of it.

"When I decided to offer this little gift, I called Maggie." Maggie Hale was Gideon's mother. "She told me Gideon had followed you to Maple Hill. He must really love you to leave New York for a tiny town on the edge of the Berkshires to put your marriage back together."

Prue opened her mouth but could think of nothing coherent to say with it. A male voice in the background shouted Georgette's name.

"Got to go," she said quickly. "I have a few

things to clear up before I leave. Oh, incidentally, when I first got this idea, I thought we'd have to hire a male model to be in the shots with you, but now that you and Gideon are reconciled, I can't imagine a more photogenic couple. What do you think?''

"I...I..."

"Good. And it'd simplify things for me if I could just bunk with the two of you while I'm there. I'll book a hotel, motel, whatever you've got there for the photographer."

"Ah..."

"I'll be there in three days."

Prue's mind tumbled over and over itself trying to make sense of what was happening. Then necessity made her grasp the important issue. A very influential woman in fashion was going to create an advertising program for Prudent Designs. At the moment, that was all she needed to know.

"We'll see you then."

"Good. I'll call Gideon with details of my arrival."

The moment she hung up the phone, Prue realized what she'd done.

She'd gotten herself an ad campaign! And into a tangled mess.

She called Berkshire Cab. "Paris, you've got to take me to Gideon's!"

Paris's voice exuded hope. "Really?"

"Yes," she said. "I'm going to kill him. You know where this A-frame is?"

Paris sighed. "Yes, I do. He bought a new truck

this afternoon. I dropped him at the car lot, then tooled by later to see what he'd decided on. It's beautiful!''

"Can you pick me up?"

"Do I have to search you for weapons?"

"Paris…"

"I'll be right there."

THE A-FRAME WAS on the wilder, less populated side of the lake. It had a full front porch and big double-glass doors. On either side of the doors was a large pot of flowering cabbage, and the boxes under large square windows were filled with yellow mums.

Parked near the porch steps was a red pickup. Prue remembered that Paris had told her he'd bought a truck, but it hadn't registered at the time. As long as she'd known him, he'd driven a sports car.

Then the doors opened and he appeared with a Berkshire Cab coffee mug in his hand. Paris had had the blue-and-white mugs printed when she'd first started the company, offering them to anyone who took a trip of twenty miles or more. It was easy, Prue thought, to see whose side she was on.

He wore jeans and a gray Whitcomb's Wonders sweatshirt with red lettering. The jeans were as out of character for him as the truck, though he looked wonderful in them—long-legged, lean-hipped and dangerously informal. She didn't like the fact that her pulse accelerated ever so slightly.

Prue paid Paris for the ride.

Paris tried to push the money away. "What are you doing?" she asked with a frown. "I never charge you…"

"Well, that's going to stop," Prue insisted. "He told his aunt we were back together!"

"What aunt?"

"Georgette. The one who lives in London."

Paris nodded slowly, as though trying to figure out how one thing related to the other. "Why does that mean you have to pay me for the ride?"

Prue knew it had nothing to do with that. It was because the cup and the sweatshirt were examples of how he'd been accepted by everyone, and it made her want to do something mean.

"It isn't the mug, is it?" Paris asked suddenly. "Because it was just a friendly gesture—not a slight against you, just something for him. And if you're offended, you should know that there's a small set of Fiestaware Mom sent over for him when I picked him up at the dealer's. So you can hate all of us."

"I don't hate you," Prue said, chin raised in affronted dignity as she unlocked her door. "I just think it's interesting that you're all helping him, when he's making my life so difficult."

"I don't understand about his aunt."

"She's coming to visit," Prue explained, "and she says he told her we've patched things up. So she's expecting us to be together when she arrives."

"Well, why didn't you just correct her?"

Prue opened her mouth to explain about the advertising campaign, but she didn't know where to start. It was all so convoluted.

"Never mind," she said, climbing out of the car. "Thank you for the ride." Her tone didn't sound very grateful.

"Sure," Paris replied stiffly, then put the cab into gear and turned around to head out onto Lake Road.

"You two still fight all the time?" Gideon asked as Prue approached the steps.

"Yes," she replied. Then realizing that wasn't entirely true, Prue amended, "No, not as much. Sometimes." Remembering that wasn't what she wanted to talk about, she met his dark gaze as she climbed the steps. "Georgette called."

GIDEON SMILED in a friendly way, keeping any sexual suggestion out of the gesture and adding a look of understanding. "Ah," he said, pulling the door open. "Come on inside. I'll pour you a cup of coffee."

She used to like his coffee, he remembered. She'd usually made breakfast when they were married, but he'd made the coffee. She'd claimed to be unable to strike the perfect point between strong and too strong the way he did.

He'd always loved her "Mmm!" of approval when she took her first sip.

It had been a simple but comfortable routine, the memory of which could bring him to the edge of despair when he made coffee in New York in his quiet and lonely kitchen.

But despite his warm memories, he felt fairly sure she didn't have any so he half expected her to refuse his offer of coffee and choose to have this discussion on the porch. He was pleasantly surprised when she preceded him inside.

He pointed her to the new leather sofa and went to the rustic bar that separated the kitchen from the living room. He poured coffee into a bright yellow cup, her favorite color, and carried it out to her.

"You told Georgette we've patched things up," she said, sitting on a corner of the sofa, looking like a duchess displeased with one of her serfs. She reached up to accept the cup. "Thank you."

"She seemed to have that impression when she called me," he lied easily. This could work if he was convincing. "I think she probably got it from Mom, who was sure when I told her I was coming here before going to Alaska that you'd either want to come with me or plead with me to stay here."

"Why didn't you set her straight?" she asked coolly. Then she took a sip of his coffee. There was no "Mmm!" this time, but she did close her eyes for an instant, her appreciation there but silent.

"Because she started raving about Prudent Designs," he replied, looking her in the eye because that part was true. "Then she started reeling out this whole ad campaign idea launched from the article using the two of us as models, and before I could explain to her that she was mistaken, she was giving me names of publications where the ads would appear, numbers of consumers who'd be reached, big names who'd be clamoring for your clothes." He shrugged with what he hoped appeared to be sincere nobility. "So I let her think what she wanted to think. I figured if you thought it was all just too distasteful, you'd correct her yourself." He took a sip of his coffee and asked innocently, "Did you?"

He knew very well she hadn't. If she had, she'd have simply called him and chewed him out. Only a strategy meeting would require her physical presence.

She sighed and glanced away, obviously feeling guilty about maintaining the deception. "No, I didn't," she admitted. "Selfishly, I thought the opportunity too good to pass up." She angled her chin in that infuriatingly disdainful way he'd grown so used to in the last few months of their marriage. "Now, I suppose, you're going to tell me you've done this just to set me up so you can refuse to go along with this after all?"

She made him wish they'd bring back thumbscrews and the rack. "Now, that's a nice thing to say to someone who's gone out of his way to help you. After all you've put me through this past year, how much fun do you think this is going to be for me?"

She studied him, apparently searching for a chink in his believability. He guessed that because he was sincerely dedicated to the project—even though for entirely different reasons than she thought—she couldn't find one. She finally sighed and said grudgingly, "I'm sorry."

He accepted that with a shrug and sat in the opposite corner of the sofa with his own cup. "No matter what's gone between us, I couldn't blow this for you. But I think it'd be a good idea," he said reasonably, "to try to put away all the old stuff between us, at least until Aunt Georgette's gone again. I'm sure if we put some effort into it, we can be civil to one another in the interest of your career."

She took a sip of her coffee and studied him with uncertainty. "I'm sure we can," she finally conceded. "I guess I just don't understand why you're willing to do it."

"I thought I explained that," he replied. "Even though our marriage is over, I'd never be vengeful enough to step on your dreams. If Georgette can help you to realize them, I'll do what I can to help."

He thought he sounded sincere, but she still appeared unconvinced. Because he *was* sincere, he snapped at her. "Okay. I'll do it because if you make a bundle, you won't need alimony. Is that easier for you to believe?"

He expected her to find relief in that fib so she could go on believing he was the rat she thought him to be. But she didn't seem to. There was a brooding quality about her, and she looked just a little lost— an unusual state of affairs for the usually confident and capable Prudence O'Hara Hale.

She tossed her hair, a sign that meant she wanted to change the subject. "She said she'd be here in three days." She looked around the room as though noticing her surroundings for the first time. Then she patted the sofa. "This must have cost you a fortune."

He shrugged. "I liked it. And I think it'll fit into a fishing-lodge atmosphere when I go to Alaska."

She nodded and got to her feet, walking around the large, mostly empty room. "You were lucky to find such a great place to rent month to month," she observed.

"I know. It's good to have friends in the right places. Hank knew about the house and put in a good word for me with the owner."

She turned away from a perusal of the bare walls to focus suddenly on his shirt. And with a gesture that completely surprised him, she pinched a small amount of fabric at his chest and said drily, "And he provided you with a change of shirt, I see."

He nodded, leading the way around the bar to the kitchen. "It's all part of the employment package."

She looked around, nodding, then walked to the door that led onto a back porch. A fairly large pet door had been cut into the bottom.

"Must have had a Saint Bernard," she guessed, turning around and walking out again, following a small corridor to the bedroom.

He indicated the empty room with its wide window looking out onto the woods behind the house. "I think Aunt George could be comfortable in here."

"*Employment* package?" she asked, his previous reply apparently just catching up with her.

"Yes," he said, leaning a shoulder in the doorway. "Hank was looking for a way to provide security services as part of his offerings. While I was having breakfast with him and some of the other guys the morning Paris abandoned me in the booth at the Barn, we happened to talk about my experiences in Iraq. Then I was playing with his kids in the lobby of the Yankee Inn and…"

She looked confused and he felt called upon to explain that he'd just gotten the call from his business partner telling him to delay his trip, when the kids walked in from their swimming lessons. "They knew who I was," he said with a grin. "And Rachel, I think it is, told me you shouldn't get naked with people you aren't married to."

Prue shifted her weight. "Yes, I've always thought so, too."

"Yeah. So have I." Before she could offer doubts about that, he raised a hand to stop her. "I know. Never mind. Anyway, the kids also knew I was a judo master, so they asked if I could throw them. Hank showed up while we were doing it, and we got into a little hand-to-hand."

"You threw children?" she asked in disbelief.

He rolled his eyes. "Yeah, right. I wanted to see how high they'd bounce. Of course I didn't *throw* them. I just made some flamboyant moves and floated them to a landing. I used to do it to you all the time, remember?"

On several occasions the playful combat had led to lovemaking. Judging by a sudden stiffening of her stance, she remembered the same thing.

"You did judo in the inn?"

"In a banquet room, I think. They'd just shampooed carpets and the room was empty."

She winced and shook her head. "Go on."

"Well, once I took him down a couple of times, he called for a friend of his working in the building and asked me to fight both of them at the same time."

"You won, of course."

"Of course."

"So…he hired you as security director or something?"

She was fishing. He could tell by the way she avoided his eyes, then made herself look into them. She wanted to know if he was staying. And she wasn't sure if she'd like that idea or not. "No," he answered, trying to make it sound as though he had no intention of staying. "I'm writing a security model for them. You know—what they need in employees, what they can provide and how they should do it. It'll pay for the delay in going to Alaska."

Now she did look relieved. He tried not to notice.

"Your aunt will need a bed," she said as a complete non sequitur. "And a dresser and a chair. It'll look more as though we're settled here if our 'guest room' is well furnished."

He wanted to cheer that she was into making this work. But he simply responded, "Makes sense."

"I'll have my things moved over from my mother's for this room," she said, walking into it, checking the wardrobe closet at the far end, pausing to look out the window. "Then you won't have to buy anything."

"You're sure your mother won't mind?"

"It's our old set from the Albany condo," she said. She caught his eye for an instant and he could see she was momentarily trapped in memories of that place. It had been wonderful, a sort of French Country oasis in their tumultuous lives. Then she shook her head to dismiss the recollection, and he was forced to do the same as they headed back to the living room.

"Our bedroom's upstairs," he said, knowing the quickest way to relieve her of painful memories was to annoy her.

She made a scornful sound as though she had no words strong enough to respond to his suggestion that they *had* a bedroom.

Before they started up the stairs, he pointed to the only door on the right side at the back of the house. "Bathroom. Shower, makeup lights, exercycle. Hot tub on the back porch."

She went to look, then returned with a cool nod. "Very elegant."

He led the way upstairs.

The entire loft was a bedroom. Had he had more

furniture, part of it could have been sectioned off into a sitting area, but this way it was just one vast space. A large bathroom with a sunken tub and two separate sinks, mirrors and medicine cabinets occupied the far end of the room. Next to it was a walk-in wardrobe with enough room to hold clothing for a family of seven.

"Wow!" she breathed in surprise.

He went to stand beside her as she studied the largely empty closet. He'd hung up the two changes of clothes he'd brought and his overcoat. He remembered that in their small French Country paradise, she'd grumbled often about the tiny closets.

"Your aunt will wonder why you don't have more clothes," she said.

It was on the tip of his tongue to say that he doubted his aunt would be going through his closet, then he remembered his aunt. She considered nothing off-limits to her lively curiosity.

"I closed the condo the day before I flew here," he explained. "I left my clothes at my parents'. I'll call Mom and ask her to ship them here."

Prue frowned over that as she walked into the closet as though unable to believe its size. "Then she'll really be convinced we've reconciled. You'll have to explain."

"No," he disputed. "She's so honest, she'll feel compelled to tell Aunt George. Then where will we be?"

She considered that, then turned to him, her wide eyes worried. "We shouldn't do this." She sounded as though she was trying to convince herself. "It'll put your mother in the middle of a lie and that isn't fair."

"We've already done it," he said, trying to maintain a calm tone while praying fervently that she didn't change her mind. "The wheels are in motion. It's too late to turn back."

That wasn't entirely true, but she seemed to believe it. She walked out of the closet, then turned to him. "We're taking advantage of your aunt."

That wasn't true, either, but she didn't know that. And it was important she didn't find out.

"We're letting her do a nice thing for us, for you, that she really wants to do. When you achieve star status, you can give her all the credit. She'd love that. Take a breath." She had a nervous habit of holding her breath when experiencing a crisis of confidence. It was his opinion she was hoping to pass out and avoid the whole thing.

Prue drew a deep breath, then let it out slowly and seemed to calm down.

"It's going to be fine," he said bracingly. "It's a little bit of a lie, but not big and awful." Then he grinned. "And if you feel that badly about it, you can just make the whole thing true."

"Ha! Ha!" she scoffed. Then she swatted his arm.

It was the first time she'd touched him in a year and he had to admit he enjoyed it.

She walked to the middle of the room and folded her arms with sudden determination. "Well, if we're going to do this," she said, "we're going to have to do it wholeheartedly or it isn't going to work."

Now she was talking. "I agree."

"We're going to need a few things."

"What kind of things?"

"Photos, knickknacks, warm touches to make it look as though we really do live here."

He had to concentrate to keep the pleasure out of his voice. "I have a box of photos with my clothes that are going to Alaska with me. I'll ask Mom to send them along. No knickknacks, though."

She was looking around as she thought. "I've got some things I can bring over with my clothes. And we'll need a few more pieces of furniture."

"Sure. I opened an account at Fenton's Furniture."

She shook her head. "No, we'll go to the Bargain Basement."

"Where?"

"The Bargain Basement. It's a secondhand store." When he would have disputed that he'd be happy to buy whatever she wanted new, she shook her head, reading his mind. "If we want it to seem as though we live here, things should look like they've been handled, used. She knows we just moved in, but our things should be old and familiar."

"You sound as though you've done this before," he teased. "Tell me the truth. You've pretended to be married to someone else, haven't you?"

"No," she replied with a direct look. "My heart was in it. You were the one pretending. Come on. I want to see what we need in the kitchen." She headed for the stairs like Napoleon planning a campaign.

He followed, ignoring her swipe at him. After all, she'd admitted that her heart had been in their marriage. It was going to be his job to lure it back again.

CHAPTER FIVE

GIDEON DROVE Prue to her mother's home in the new truck.

She was surprised when he simply looped the lake and found the right house without her directing him there.

"How did you know where I live?" she asked.

"I knew you lived on Lake Road, too. I met Hank and the guys here to jog this morning. They pointed it out to me."

She couldn't believe he'd been accepted so completely so quickly. According to the Wonder Women, the wives and girlfriends of Hank's employees, the morning jog was an important ritual.

Then something alarming occurred to her. "What are we going to do about the Wonders?"

He turned into the bungalow's driveway. "What do you mean?"

She unbuckled her belt and turned toward him anxiously. "They know we're getting a divorce, that we haven't patched things up at all." She put a hand to her forehead, wondering if this plan was going to fall apart before it ever really came to life. "God, every time I say that—'patched it up'—I think of a giant canvas patch on a tent that's collapsing.''

He laughed. ''Yeah, that's what it'd take all right to fix us up. Prudie, relax. It's going to be all right. I'll just explain to them and I'm sure they'll back us up.''

''You're going to explain,'' she asked doubtfully, ''that we're lying to your aunt to get me an article in a fashion magazine and an advertising campaign?''

He caught the hand she gestured with and squeezed it. ''Relax. I'm sure I can put matters in a good light.'' In the old days, he'd catch her hand to get her attention, slow her down. She was a little startled that he remembered that. And that she did.

She froze for an instant, her hand caught in his, and felt all the old electricity. Then she yanked her hand away and pushed her door open. ''Pick me up at nine,'' she said, assuming the businesslike manner she'd used all afternoon. ''And we'll be at the Bargain Basement when it opens.''

''I'll pick you up at eight,'' he corrected, ''and we'll have breakfast first.''

''That's not a good idea,'' she argued firmly. Making plans with him was one thing, sharing the intimacy of a meal was something else.

''It is,'' he insisted, ''if you want the rest of the town to see us together and become convinced that we're reconciled. Just in case Aunt George falls into casual conversation with someone. She likes to do that. Get the flavor of the town she's visiting.''

That made an irritating sort of sense. "All right," she agreed. "Eight o'clock." She hurried into the house before he could say anything more.

She was happy to see that her mother and Jeffrey were out, though her mother's car was in the driveway. They'd developed the habit of taking a walk around the lake in the evening. That was good—she could pack a box of photographs and other keepsakes in private.

She found a large box in the garage, took a stack of newspaper from the recycle box and went to work. She started with the family photos she kept on her dresser—one of her and Paris as children wearing mouse ears at Disneyland, one of the two of them with their father at the beach, Paris's high-school graduation, the three of them with her mother backstage at her opening as Lady Macbeth in summer stock. It always brought a smile to her lips to look at those.

She tucked them safely away in the box, then dug into the bottom of the closet for the photos that were harder to look at but that Georgette would expect to see while she was visiting.

She tossed her white brocade–covered wedding album onto the bed, along with other mementos of her wedding to Gideon—her garter, the ribbons from her bouquet, the cloisonné earrings with a lapis center that Paris had given her for the traditional "something blue." She loved them but never wore them, unwilling to deal with the memories they evoked.

Then she found the photos of Gideon's family—his tall, distinguished father and short, plump mother—George and Maggie. They were lovely people and had always been wonderful to her. She loved them like a second family, but looking at their smiling faces reminded her of all she'd thought she had and discovered she didn't.

She added the pictures to the box, took the alarm clock from her bedside table, a small jewelry box from the dresser and a poster of Audrey Hepburn wearing Givenchy that hung on the inside of her closet door.

There. She dragged the box to the door, then heard her mother and Jeffrey in the kitchen, talking and laughing. There was the sound of puttering and crockery. The preparation of a snack probably, to balance the healthy exercise.

Prue smiled to herself. Her mother had always been so disciplined about watching her famous figure, but now that Jeffrey had walked back into her life, she was far less preoccupied with herself than she used to be. Her work demanded it, of course, but she talked less about the next performance or modeling job now than she did about where she wanted to take Jeffrey next.

Her mother was in love.

Prue took a deep breath and squared her shoulders. She had to tell her mother about the plan because, though Camille and Georgette had also met only once—at the engagement party—they were two of a kind and had liked each other. Georgette might want to see her when she arrived.

Her mother would have to know the situation.

Prue put a smile on her face and walked into the kitchen, where her mother was filling a teapot and Jeffrey was cutting a wedge of cheesecake into two slices. The tea shop's lethal cheesecake was clear proof that her mother was besotted.

"Did you have a nice walk?" Prue asked.

"Hi, Prue," Jeffrey said. "Shall I cut this in three?"

"No, thank you," she replied. "I just…wanted to tell you something. Then I'm off to bed."

Her mother put the lid on the teapot and carried it to the work center where two china cups and saucers waited. She sat on one of the stools and smiled at Prue. "Paris said she took you to see Gideon. She wasn't tattling," she put in hastily. "Jeff and I were going to dinner and wanted to know if you cared to come along. You didn't answer the phone at the studio, so I asked if she knew where you were."

Prue accepted all that with a nod. "Gideon's aunt Georgette called me. Remember her?"

Camille's smile widened. "Of course I do. Lovely lady."

"Well, she's coming to Maple Hill."

"What? When?"

Prue explained about the story in the *Globe*, about Georgette's delayed wedding gift and her misunderstanding about Prue and Gideon's situation.

Camille blinked. "She thinks you're still married?"

Prue nodded. "Yes. I guess Gideon's mom is convinced he's here to work out our problems and passed that on to Georgette. So when Georgette called Gideon, he let her believe it so I could have the opportunity she's offering."

"Ah…well…that was good of him. So…" Her mother didn't seem to know what question to ask next. "How are you going to…you know…handle it?"

"I'm moving in there until she's gone," she said, looking her mother in the eye as she spoke and daring her to make more of it than it was.

Her mother seemed just as determined to behave as though it didn't matter. "If there's anything we can do…"

"If I can find someone with a truck," Prue began, turning her attention to Jeffrey, "and a few able bodies, can you move my bedroom set, my clothes and a few boxes to the house Gideon's renting on the far side of the lake?"

"Of course," Jeffrey replied. "I'll be happy to."

Camille frowned. "What's Georgette going to think if you're sleeping in your own bed?"

Prue struggled to maintain a bland look. "It's for Georgette's bedroom downstairs. I'll be sleeping upstairs in the loft bedroom."

Camille's calm expression wavered just a little.

"I know," Prue said with a wry smile. "That

might be a problem for any other man and woman, but Gideon and I are so angry and disappointed with each other that it'll be easy for us to share a room and never touch.''

"Good.'' The word was softly spoken, the smile that accompanied it completely unconvincing.

"And I remember that the two of you really hit it off,'' Prue added, going to the cupboard to get her own cup and saucer and pouring just a half cup of tea into it. "She might want to see you when she's here. If so, please remember that at least until she leaves, Gideon and I are reconciled. Okay?''

"Okay,'' Camille concurred. "When are you moving in?''

"Tomorrow.'' Prue sipped her tea. "I have to help him make the house look as though a couple really shares it. He bought just minimal furniture when he rented the place, so I'm going to hit the Bargain Basement and find some things to perk it up.''

"If there's anything I can lend you…''

"Can I take the yellow Fiestaware teapot? I noticed you've already lent him the dishes.'' She added that last comment innocently, not really condemning her mother for sharing her things with the man who'd done her daughter wrong, but hoping to tweak her sense of guilt just a little.

It didn't seem to work. Or perhaps it did…. Hard to tell when her mother turned right to the cupboard and took down the yellow teapot. She placed it on a corner of the counter.

"Take it with you in the morning. I'll put some tea bags in it."

"Thanks, Mom." Prue gave her mother, then Jeffrey, a quick hug and went to her room.

She showered, pulled on an old pair of flannel pajamas, then climbed into bed, thinking it odd that she'd soon be sharing a bedroom with her ex-husband. Actually, she could still sleep in this bed in the room Georgette would occupy until Georgette actually got there.

Then she'd sleep in that upstairs loft with Gideon. There was room for a love seat, she remembered. If she could find one that opened out, or maybe a futon, cohabiting in the room wouldn't be a problem. Although the way she felt about him now, she could sleep beside him in the same bed and never want to touch him. Except maybe to punch him in the nose.

She smiled, and on that thought, closed her eyes and went to sleep.

PRUE RAN out of the house the moment Gideon pulled into the driveway at five minutes to eight. She looked delicious in jeans, a short, yellow embroidered jacket over a white turtleneck, with her hair pulled back into a ponytail. He guessed she was the *Vogue* version of a woman dressed to go furniture shopping.

She got as far as the passenger door he held open, when she groaned and said, "I forgot my list!" and went back into the house.

Meanwhile, Camille and Jeffrey came out to say hello.

"Everything you told her about what happened in Maine is true, so help you God?" Camille demanded, glancing over her shoulder to watch for Prue's reappearance.

Gideon raised his right hand in keeping with her choice of words. "I swear."

She grinned broadly. "Then good luck with this little drama for your aunt's visit."

He hugged his mother-in-law. "Thanks, Camille."

Gideon had met Jeffrey in the grocery store the other day and offered his hand. "How are you, Jeffrey?"

"I'm good," he replied with a smile. "I promised to help move some of Prue's things over as soon as she finds a few able-bodied men with a truck. Let me know when it's convenient."

"I've taken care of the truck and the men," Gideon said as Prue ran out again, a folded square of paper in her hand. "Evan Braga's going to stop by after work with his van, if that's okay, and I'll meet him here with my truck. Between us, we should be able to carry a bedroom set and boxes."

"I'm going to make some calls," Prue said, coming around to the passenger-side door Gideon held open again, "and get us some more muscle."

"Hank, Cam and Hank's brother-in-law, Bart, are coming, too," he said. "I think it's overkill for one bedroom set, but I promised them beer and pizza and nobody wanted to miss out.''

She looked both impressed and disappointed that that had been taken care of. "Well," she said finally, "that's one thing off my list." She sat down in the passenger seat, unfolded the sheet of paper and crossed the top item off.

"Well, if you don't need me for the moving—" Jeffrey grinned "—I hope you need me for the beer and pizza."

"Yes, we do," Gideon replied, closing Prue's door and walking around to the driver's side. He waved at Camille, who winked at him, and climbed in behind the wheel.

"You'll have to run for office in Maple Hill," Prue said, a light tone of criticism in her voice. "You've certainly made enough friends already to have a strong political base."

"Nah," he said, amused by that suggestion of pique. "I'm just going to help you collect on this gift of Aunt George's, then I'm going to finish this security model for Hank, and take off for Alaska. The lodge won't be rebuilt until spring, but it'll give me time to learn my way around. This is a great place, but it's…hard to be here."

"Are you sure about Alaska?" she asked. "I mean, what do people do up there?"

"They fish from May to September," he answered. "I'll find things to do." He turned onto Lake Road, which would lead them to the highway and eventually the Breakfast Barn. He cast her a glance. "You're not worried about me, are you?"

"Of course not," she denied. "It just doesn't seem like the place for you, somehow. I mean…you were always so full of energy and ideas. It's dark there most of the time and if you're out in the wilderness, won't you be confined by the weather? I would think you'd find it boring."

He laughed lightly. "After the demands of political life," he replied, "and the trauma of the bribery case and our separation, boring would be welcome. But in the meantime…" He paused at the highway, waiting for an opening in the traffic. He found it and accelerated. "Some drama will be fun. It'll be like a Julia Roberts/Hugh Grant romance movie."

She turned to him in disbelief. "I thought it sounded more like an intrigue flick or a thriller."

"Why? Are you scared?" he asked.

She started to shake her head, then admitted with surprising candor. "Yes, I am. I'm afraid it'll all blow up in our faces and we'll hurt your aunt."

"It's not going to happen," he assured her confidently. She didn't have to know it was because her aunt was in collusion with him.

"I'm going to murder you if you're wrong," she promised with a sincerity that made him glad to know the plan was foolproof.

Rita Robidoux was on duty at the Breakfast Barn when Gideon and Prue walked in. Gideon had met her his first morning in town.

A short, plump woman in her late fifties with hair an unnatural shade of red, Rita waved to them, picked up two menus and the coffeepot, and intercepted them at a booth in the corner.

Gideon sat on the same side of the booth as Prue, and when she would have protested, he said under his breath, "Convince Rita we're reconciling, and it'll be all over the county by dinner."

Rita handed each of them a menu, turned over the two fresh cups sitting on paper coasters and poured coffee into them.

"You take cream, as I recall," she said to Gideon. "Gilbert, was it?"

"Gideon," he corrected. "And yes on the cream."

She walked away.

"Have you considered," Prue asked as he opened his menu, "how we're going to explain when Georgette leaves again why you're going to Alaska and I'm staying here?"

"Lovers are always trying again and failing," he replied.

"Yes, but I'm tired of failing." Prue opened her menu with an angry snap and frowned at him over the corner of it.

He let her see his surprise. "I thought your opinion was that I was the one who'd failed."

"It was," she conceded. "But it still felt as though I'd failed, too. I didn't know why you'd want someone else if I made you happy."

"I didn't want anybody else," he repeated, truly

tired of the argument. "And if I *had,* that would have been my failing and not yours."

Her eyes narrowed warily over the top of her menu. "But…you said I acted like a princess."

"You did," he agreed, closing his menu and putting it aside. "You do. But I knew that when I married you. And when you're not being a princess, you're hardworking and caring and generally remarkable."

She didn't seem to believe that. "Now you're trying to make points," she accused.

"Why would I do that," he asked, "when this whole thing is for *your* benefit to begin with?"

Rita was back with a small, white pitcher of cream that she set between them. "Kind of lovey," she observed with a smile, "for a couple contemplating divorce." Rita was known for her outspoken interest in everyone's private life. She was indulged because she could be counted on for information on anyone or anything at any time. She and Addy Whitcomb were considered the Aaron Brown and Anderson Cooper of Maple Hill. Possibly even of the entire commonwealth of Massachusetts. "How do you explain that?"

Gideon deferred to Prue, wanting her to reply in the hope that speaking the words would plant a seed in her brain that would grow.

"We're…reconciled," she said with a reluctance Rita probably translated to shyness appropriate to the situation.

Rita grinned broadly. "Well, that'll be good news to a lot of people. Everyone thinks you're beautiful and a brilliant designer, and we all took to Handsome, here, right away."

"Great," Prue said, suddenly focusing on the menu. Gideon was sure only he heard the irony in the single word.

She ate half a grapefruit and whole-wheat toast while he had a Denver omelette and tomato juice. They ate in relative silence except for the occasional request to pass the jam or the pepper, and she left her fourth triangle of toast as she'd done since he'd known her.

He reached for it as *he'd* always done, and she passed him the jam—as *she'd* always done. She looked up at him as she realized they'd just repeated a routine familiar to their life together. She seemed about to share a smile over it, then apparently thought better of the idea and sipped her coffee.

"It's all right that we have memories in common," he said, pushing his empty plate aside, then stacking hers on top of it. "We can't ignore our entire past together. Some of it was pretty good. It might help our performance to remember that."

He was surprised when she met his gaze and nodded. "I know it wasn't all bad," she said with a sigh. "But I think stirring all that up is going to make our performance harder rather than easier."

"Why is that?"

"Because whenever I remember the good times,"

she said, her eyes pooling with tears, "I'm grief-stricken and start to cry. Your aunt will wonder why a woman who claims to have a delightful marriage is sobbing all the time."

He folded his forearms on the table and leaned toward her, hurt by her obvious pain, particularly when he knew it was unnecessary. But encouraged by it as well. "That's self-inflicted grief," he said quietly. "You didn't lose me—or us—just your perspective on what happened."

A tear spilled over and he performed another familiar ritual from their time together. He reached into his pocket and offered her his handkerchief.

She took it from him and told him in a tight, high voice to "Move, please!" When he did, she slipped out of the booth and left the restaurant.

Rita frowned at him as she accepted his money and counted out his change. "Don't be discouraged," she said, her eyes going to the door through which Prue had walked. "It takes time to work out all the slights and emotional injuries."

"Thanks," he said, handing her a couple of bills for her tip and heading for the door, thinking that to do that, Prue would need—well—forever.

CHAPTER SIX

THE BARGAIN BASEMENT was literally in the basement of a building on the square that housed several shops. It had been opened just last year by a husband-and-wife team adept at finding unique items in estate sales, garage sales or manufacturers' closeouts.

They'd painted the basement walls white and strung lights all around to give a sort of flea-market, street-vendor atmosphere to the place. It was filled with interesting old furniture, architectural salvage, curios and old photographs that should never have left the families to whom they'd belonged. It always made Prue sad to look at them, and wonder what tragedy had befallen the family that their photographs ended up for sale. Even though her life had fallen apart, she'd saved all of hers.

"What are we looking for?" Gideon asked, following her down a narrow aisle between upholstered sofas.

A tall, slender gray-haired woman shouted a greeting from the doorway of a small office in the far corner. She was Jean Trenton, who owned the store along with her husband. "Hi, Prue! Still shopping for the studio?"

Prue had bought her tables here. She waved back. "No. We're shopping for a few things for…this gentleman's house."

Her smile was visible all the way across the basement. "Gideon, isn't it? I heard you reconciled."

Prue turned to a smiling Gideon in disbelief. "Do you believe it? How could news have possibly gotten here this fast?"

"Starla McAffrey told me," Jean said, anticipating her question. Starla worked at the Breakfast Barn. "Rita told her."

"But we only told Rita less than an hour ago."

Jean nodded. "Starla came over on her coffee break. She's having Clete Morrison and his children over for dinner and she needed a tablecloth." She pointed to the Mediterranean armoire filled with table linens.

Prue smiled. "Well. We're just going to look around, okay?"

"Of course."

She gave Gideon one more disbelieving look, then slung her purse over her shoulder, opened her list and perused it. "A few comfortable chairs for the living room," she read, pen in hand to check things off. "A library table…"

"What's that?" he asked, leaning over her shoulder to see the list. She caught a whiff of his subtle aftershave and had a sudden, unbidden memory of lying naked with him in the middle of their bed.

"Ah…" She shook her head to clear it. "It's tall

and skinny and goes behind the sofa. I love the leather, but it would be nice to soften it with plants, brass…something warm.''

''Okay. What else?''

''Um…a pot to go near the fireplace, a love seat or a futon for the bedroom, a hamper for the bathroom and a few things for the walls.''

''Is the pot near the fireplace for a wood box?''

''Yes.''

''Okay. I'll look for that.''

She caught his arm as he would have walked away, realizing suddenly that though he'd gotten them into this, she was taking over the redecorating of *his* home.

''Don't worry about getting stuck with all of this when you leave,'' she said. ''Maybe we can get the owner of the house to rent the place furnished, in which case he can pay you for the stuff, or I'll buy it from you and sell it off.''

He shook his head. ''I wasn't worried about getting stuck with the furniture. And you don't have to buy it from me. I'll just consider you my sales agent and you can send me the money as you sell it.''

''I am sort of…taking over.''

He smiled. ''I'm used to that.''

That was true, but she'd always wondered if he really understood why. ''When we moved into the Albany condo,'' she said, ''I tried to consult you on things, but you were always so busy, you either forgot to give me an answer or told me to do what I wanted to do. So I did.''

"I know that. I was always grateful that you were capable enough to handle it on your own."

She blinked. "You were?"

He seemed surprised that she was surprised. "Yes."

"You never said that."

He shrugged. "I was busy. And now that I'm no longer pushed at every turn, I realize that's no excuse for anything. But at the time, it seemed valid."

She was touched by the apology and the understanding behind it. Her world seemed to tilt, putting her off balance. She stared at him for a long moment.

He stared back, then when she was sure he was going to touch her, he took a step back. "I'll look for a wood box," he finally said, finding a route between the sofas toward the wall against which all kinds of odds and ends were lined up.

She struggled to regain her equilibrium and began to work her way methodically down the list. By noon, she had a collection of things grouped near the counter by the door where Jean would eventually check her out. She caught Gideon's arm and dragged him across the basement to approve her purchases.

She'd found an oak library table with a few aesthetic nicks that was just what she'd envisioned.

"With a basket of flowers and a candlestick or something," she said, drawing those things in the air with her fingertips, "it'll be perfect."

He nodded his approval. "And I like that." He

pointed to a white, farm-style hall tree with five hooks across the top and a bench for storage and sitting.

"I was thinking we could put it on that bare wall near the kitchen."

He nodded again.

She sat down on a red-and-green-plaid love seat and drew him down beside her. "This opens into a single bed," she announced. "Perfect for that edge of the bedroom. Along with the trunk and the lamp." She pointed to a more interesting than valuable flat-top trunk with corroding leather strapping still attached, and the red lamp with its beige linen shade sitting atop it. "It'll make a nice reading corner."

He gave her a knowing look. "And a safe retreat for you."

"Yes," she admitted candidly. Her conviction that they could occupy the bedroom with little chance of temptation was already wavering. She'd been so angry at him for so long, she'd forgotten he could also be the charming man sitting beside her.

He bumped her shoulder with his. "I remember a time when the safest place for you was in my arms."

She did, too, and the memory of that was both painful and pleasant. "Yes, but a lot's happened since then."

He nodded and pushed himself to his feet. "Okay, let's leave it at that so we don't ruin this mellow mood." He reached to the pile of things for a very large light blue pot on a wheeled base. "How's this for a wood box? We'll have to put a flat disc of wood in the bottom so we don't break it when we put the wood in.''

''I love the color,'' she said, both relieved and disappointed to have backed away from the issue of their relationship. ''And it picks up the color of this wingback chair.'' She pointed to a big chair upholstered in polished cotton.

Gideon turned to her with a moody smile. ''See? We haven't completely lost our ability to see things in the same way.''

''True,'' she said as she went to stand behind two twig chairs. Of course, that ability would work only if they could spend the rest of their lives picking out furniture. ''And these I thought would look great in the living room and could go out on the porch in the summer.''

The moment she saw his expression, she realized what was wrong with that remark. They wouldn't be there in the summer. He'd be in Alaska and she might very well be in New York.

With a toss of her head she tried to pretend she hadn't meant that *they'd* be there in the summer. ''The chairs…might be a selling point for the next renter since they can go out or in.'' Yes, that was lame, but it was the best she could do.

Mercifully, Jean arrived and Gideon handed her his credit card. Dwight, Jean's husband, appeared to help Gideon carry the furniture up the basement stairs to the street and load the truck. Prue picked up a few more odds and ends while Gideon and Dwight made the first delivery home.

When Gideon and Dwight returned for the second load, Prue told Gideon she was going to run to the flower shop across the street to pick up a few plants.

"Okay," he said. "I'll pick you up there. Then we should think about lunch. I'm starving."

When he returned for her, she put several plants in the back of the truck, along with a large oblong basket and an armload of silk and dried flowers.

"For the library table," she explained, pushing the plants into a corner of the truck bed so they wouldn't fall over. "Where'd you put everything?"

"Just in the middle of the living room. We need anything else?"

"Some towels for the bathroom and a few things to throw in the medicine cabinet so it looks as though we actually use it."

She frowned. "Then we have to get serious about groceries. Do you have any idea what your aunt eats?"

He shook his head. "If we're going to be taking photos around town, we can just eat out."

"Yes, but there's still breakfast and dinner."

"Then just get what you like, and as your guest, I'm sure she'll be fine with it." He grinned at her across the truck bed. "Promise me you won't dust lightbulbs like you did when your mom came to visit us in Albany."

She smiled reluctantly. She did get obsessive when

company was coming, feeling as though every detail had to be perfect, and that her value as a woman and a wife would be judged by her dustless, clutterless, errorless home. She remembered standing atop a ladder dusting the lightbulbs in a light fixture. Gideon had lifted her off the ladder and carried her to bed, insisting that she'd been cleaning like a maniac all day and it was time to get some rest.

As she recalled, she hadn't gotten any.

GIDEON COULD SEE by the faraway look in Prue's eyes that she was remembering the same thing that filled his memory. Their lovemaking had caught fire, and it had been 2:00 or 3:00 a.m. before they'd finally gotten to sleep.

Shortly after that, she'd begun to complain about everything, blame him for everything. Her sometimes charming princess behavior coupled with his own pressures and the inability to turn to her for comfort became a toxic mix for their marriage.

But he didn't want her to remember that now that she seemed wistfully happy with memories of their lovemaking.

"Lunch?" he asked hopefully.

She pointed down the street on the right side of the common to a sign depicting a tall cup of mocha mounded with whipped cream sketched in neon, and beside it a neon teapot. Below were the words the Perk Avenue Tea Shop.

"Just half a block away," she said. "The best desserts in town."

He winced. "A tea shop? I was hoping for something called Morty's Truck Stop. I have visions of a giant sandwich, potato salad, pickles and…"

She caught his hand and pulled him along with her in the direction of the tea shop. She probably wasn't even aware of the gesture, but he followed docilely, afraid to break the spell of walking hand in hand with her after a year of bristling hostility.

"They're famous for their thick sandwiches and deli salads," she said. "Lunch is on me because you've been so uncomplaining. You used to hate to go shopping."

He pretended a superior look. "I like to think I've matured in the intervening time. But if the sandwiches aren't all you claim, you're going to have to pay."

She spoiled his fun by refusing to ask how.

The sandwich *was* everything she'd claimed. It was a no-nonsense stack of roast beef with horseradish cream, tomatoes and red onion on sourdough. He was first a little disappointed in the deli salad that accompanied it—a sort of slaw. Until he tasted it and moaned his approval.

"They make it with honey–celery seed dressing," she said. "Isn't it marvelous?"

He nodded, his mouth full.

She worked on a Caesar salad with chicken and was ready for dessert when she'd finished, while he was too full.

"You have to share a cup of strawberries and mascarpone with me," she said. She sounded serious.

"I *have* to?" he questioned.

She confirmed that with a nod. "If you don't share it with me, I'll just order my own and eat the whole thing."

Sometimes her arguments defied reason. "If you want the dessert, why would that be bad?"

"Too many calories," she replied simply.

"Then why not just skip it?"

"Because I really want it," she replied, leaning toward him as though he were simple. "But you have to have some because half of it is only half as many calories."

That did make very basic sense. But he was having fun needling her. She was seldom this vulnerable to temptation. "I don't even know what mascarpone is."

"It's a light cheese they use to make a wonderful cream." She was already on her feet. "I'm ordering it. Are you in?"

"I'm in," he assured her.

He tortured himself by watching the sway of her hips as she went to the counter and placed the order for the dessert. Then a group of women walked into the shop, recognized her as she turned to head back to their table and intercepted her in the middle of a cluster of tables.

There were hugs, high laughter, fingers pointed in his direction. They were a particularly attractive group of women—four of them—and as he recognized Jackie, he presumed they were the famous Wonder Women married to Hank's friends in Whitcomb's Wonders.

Prue brought them to their table and he seemed to score points when he stood to welcome them.

Jackie gave him a hug. "Men never stand for women anymore," she said, bringing her friends forward to introduce them. "Haley, my sister-in-law, Mariah, Cam's wife—" two small dark-haired women "—and Beazie, who's married to Evan. You remember Evan? You threw him on the floor at the inn."

Beazie, a redhead, laughed at that. "Thank you for giving me something to tease him about."

"We need your help with something," Prue began quietly, gesturing them closer.

"We know about the make-believe reconciliation," Jackie said, just above a whisper. "The guys told us. You can count on us to back you up."

"Actually, the story's already getting around that you'd patched things up," Haley said. She owned the local newspaper. "Addy's friend Myrt writes a gossip column for me, and she included it when she filed her column."

At Prue's gasp of astonishment, Mariah said with a grin, "I think Rita told Addy and you know Haley's mom. She wears a satellite dish for a hat."

Everyone laughed, and the women welcomed Gideon, then wandered toward the counter in a group to place their order.

"I think Addy's faster than e-mail," Prue said with a shake of her head as she resumed her chair. Gideon sat down as well just as their dessert arrived. It was layers of strawberries and the cheesy cream in a large goblet topped with whipped cream and a chocolate-dipped strawberry.

"That's what we want," he said practically. "Everyone to be convinced it's true." He picked up his spoon.

"If I can have the chocolate-dipped strawberry," Prue bargained, "you can have the first bite."

"Deal." Since she'd already reached for it, it seemed a moot point. He dipped his spoon into the mixture and took a bite. It was surprisingly light and delicious.

"This Al Capone stuff is pretty good," he said, dipping his spoon in again.

"*Mas*carpone," she corrected, giggling. She pushed his spoon aside with hers and dug in.

SHE HAD THE LIVING ROOM upside down by early evening, when Hank and his friends arrived with her bedroom set.

Gideon looked mournfully at the dining-room table in the middle of the sea of things she'd moved around to reorganize. "I was going to have pizza delivered," he said.

"Why don't you just take them out for pizza," she suggested, "and I'll have this all put together by the time you get back."

He looked doubtfully at the heavy stuff. "You can't move these things around."

"I'll just decide where they go and wait for you to help me move them. Meanwhile, I'll organize Georgette's bedroom and put some things on the walls."

"Want me to bring you back some pizza?"

"No, thanks. I'm still full."

"Okay. We won't be very late."

She smiled good-naturedly. "You can be as late as you want to be. You're a free agent."

"I'm not worried about getting a rolling pin on the head for getting home after midnight," he said. "I'm more concerned about you trying to move this stuff alone."

"We'll do it tomorrow." She was a little injured that he wasn't concerned about being late. Then she realized that was completely ridiculous. This was all a game, and *she* was the one forgetting that. "We have two days to get everything in order."

"Prue!" somebody shouted from the bedroom. "The bed by the window or on the opposite wall?"

She excused herself to lend a hand and Gideon hurried to the door to help Jeffrey with her dresser mirror.

When everything was in place, Gideon caught her hand and led her back out to the living room. Everyone followed.

"Tell us where you want the furniture in here," he said.

"Will you please all go for pizza and let me—"

"No," he replied succinctly. "Tell us where you want it. The job can be done in fifteen minutes, then we can all go for pizza."

"I don't want pizza," she insisted.

"Then you can have salad and bread sticks. That used to be one of your favorite meals." He went to the sofa to take one end of it and Hank went to take the other end.

"Come on, Prue," Hank coaxed with a grin. "We're hungry here."

Unwilling to starve them further, she had no choice but to do as he asked. She pointed the sofa to one side of the fireplace. When Bart hefted the blue wing chair single-handedly, she stood where she wanted it, facing the sofa on the other side of the fire.

Gideon carried the library table to where he knew she wanted it, while she directed Cam and Evan to put the twig furniture in a conversation area near the wall. She carried a small round table to put between them, and Cam pointed to a lamp.

"How about that on the table?" he asked.

"Just what I had in mind," she replied. "But I think it'll need an extension cord."

Hank headed for the door. "Got one in the truck. Be right back."

Gideon and Cam flanked the hall bench and carried it to the bare wall by the kitchen.

"Won't the table and chairs go here?" Cam asked Prue, hands on his hips as he looked around to see where else the table could go.

Prue decided he was probably right. She smiled apologetically. "Okay. Can you take the bench to the wall by the front door?"

Cam pretended disgust. "She must have learned furniture placement from Mariah. It's never in the right spot unless you've moved it four or five times."

"That was only once," she corrected with a gracious smile. "And if you'll recall, I wanted to send you all for pizza. You're the one who insisted on putting the living room in place."

"I don't think straight when I'm hungry," he teased in return.

Hank was back with an extension cord and connected the lamp they'd placed on top of the trunk. He turned the light on against the darkening afternoon and Prue had a sudden, curiously startling sense of warmth and home.

"Looks good." Gideon handed her the basket she'd bought and the silk flowers. "You do something with those, and we'll take the love seat upstairs. This is going to take four of us. Hank, do you have rope in the truck?"

"Yeah." Hank frowned. "Why? Is there going to be a lynching?"

Gideon rolled his eyes. "It's a sofa bed. If we don't tie it up, it'll open on us."

"Okay, not as much fun as vigilante work, but I'll get it."

Gideon, Hank, Cam and Evan carried the love seat up. Their distracted laughter and complaints about the narrow staircase as they bumped against the wall and banister made Prue nervous.

"Gentlemen, this is not the time to be clowning around," she scolded. "Your wives will kill me if anyone gets hurt."

"Ooh," Bart said quietly. "That sounded severe. Straighten up, guys, or we might not get our pizza."

Prue turned to Jeffrey for sympathy. He followed her with a box of photographs. "You have to be nice to free labor," he advised. "It's in the Constitution."

"I wasn't criticizing," she denied. "I just want to send them home in the same condition they were in when they arrived."

"They want to go home full of beer and pizza," Gideon said as he topped the stairs with the front end of the love seat. He and Cam set it down and drew it backward. Evan and Hank hurried up the last few steps to catch up. "Where to?"

She hurried around them to stand where she wanted the piece, then moved quickly aside to let them place it there.

Jeffrey put the box down beside it.

"Thank you so much!" she said sincerely. The small sofa already brightened the bare corner of the room, but she decided she'd have to go back to the Bargain Basement for another table and lamp. The trunk and lamp she'd chosen for this spot looked so good downstairs. "You're wonderful to do this for me…for us," she amended quickly.

Hank dismissed her thanks with a shake of his

head. "We like to get everyone in an indebted position. You never know when we're going to need a babysitter, or an extra cake or salad for some function or other."

"Well, I am indebted," she assured him. "You guys go and have your pizza." She turned to Gideon with a smile. "Treat them royally. Double bread sticks and dessert."

"You're coming with us," he insisted.

She headed for the stairs, drawing him out of earshot of the others. "I have no problem with staying home. Really."

"You need a break," he argued. "Besides, how would it look, when word's getting around that we've reconciled, if people see me on a night out with the guys."

She made a wry face. "They'll think you're just like any other guy."

"Yeah, well, that won't do our story any good. Besides, Hank says his kids are at his mom's, so Jackie's joining us."

The other men approached to follow them down the stairs. "Our kids are on a weekend trip with Mariah's sister," Cam added, "so Mariah's coming, too. I wonder if Randy's off."

Jeff nodded. "He is. Paris told me they were looking forward to a night at home. But maybe they'd like pizza first." He smiled at Prue. "I'm sure your mother would love to come."

"All right, it's a party!" Bart said. "Haley's at the

office, but I bet I can steal her away to have dinner with us. Evan, what's Beazie doing?''

"She's home with the baby," he replied. "And I'm sure it's too late to find a sitter. Why don't you just have a good time, and I'll—"

"No," everyone replied simultaneously.

"Tell her to bring the baby," Hank said. "We're all used to having children around."

"But he's teething. I don't want to spoil your evening with a cranky baby."

"Come on," Cam said. "It'll give us a chance to show off our baby-calming skills."

Prue hooked an arm in Evan's and started down the stairs. "Seems neither one of us is going to be able to escape. Use the kitchen phone and call Beazie."

Evan grinned at her. "If the baby's whiny and you regret inviting me, it'll all be Gideon's fault."

"Most things are," she said with a bland smile over her shoulder at Gideon, following them down the stairs.

CHAPTER SEVEN

AN ELEGANT PARTY at Tavern on the Green could not have been more fun. Everyone squeezed around a large table at the back of Papa's, where five varieties of pizza went around and around the table.

They began the evening with couples seated together, but the cross conversations and a football game on the television mounted on the wall necessitated a change. The men moved to one end of the table, their eyes still glued to the television, and the women gathered at the other end to try to talk over the noise.

Paris had taken the sleeping baby from Beazie and looked down on the beautiful, pink-cheeked face in wonder. "How is he sleeping with all this racket?" she asked Beazie, seated across from her. Prue swallowed a painful breath. She kept smiling in an effort to maintain her composure.

Beazie shook her head as though the mystery was beyond her. "You got me. He seems to be able to sleep through anything as long as I'm awake. But if I'm trying to sleep, everything else wakes him up."

Jackie, with four children at home, laughed as she picked a slice of Canadian bacon off her pizza and popped it into her mouth. "It's just the beginning of a plot," she said after she'd swallowed, "to keep you off balance. And it continues in ever more sophisticated ways as they grow up. I got a call from the Maple Hill Store yesterday." She smiled as everyone leaned closer to hear her story over the men cheering. "Hank and I have a tab there, and the girls have heard us use it enough times that when they were walking back to school after lunch the other day, Rachel picked up snack treats for their classmates and told Harvey to "put it on the tab.""

Mariah laughed. "Clever little devil."

Jackie cast her a dry side glance. "Yes. Apparently she'd volunteered me to make treats, then when she realized she'd forgotten to ask me until the last minute and knew I'd be upset, she complained to Erica, who got the idea about charging treats."

"That shows great resourcefulness," Camille said with a laugh. "And a willingness to help one another. You have more good things going on there than bad."

Haley poured pop into her glass from the large pitcher in the middle of the table. "And early experience with the proper use of credit is good for any woman."

Jackie looked horrified. "She bought junk food for her friends!"

Haley blinked at her vehemence and indicated the empty pizza pans. "Didn't Gideon and Prue just do that for us?"

All the women laughed as Jackie swatted her sister-in-law's arm.

Haley turned to Prue. "Bart says you two have the A-frame looking great already."

"It's a wonderful house," Prue agreed, taking the pitcher from her and topping up her own glass. Then she reached across the table to fill her mother's and sister's. "And I found some great things at the Bargain Basement. I just have to put some finishing touches around—pictures, flowers."

"When's Gideon's aunt arriving?" Beazie asked.

"Day after tomorrow."

"And she thinks the two of you are still together?" Haley asked.

Prue nodded and grinned at everyone. "And if you help us carry on the charade," she said, "there'll be Chinese food for you when she leaves."

Mariah waggled her eyebrows. "Wow. How long do you think we can make this work for us? If we convince her you're sexually insatiable, will you take us to the tea shop for chocolate torte?"

At the same moment that the women squealed with laughter, the men fell silent. They obviously heard the "sexually insatiable" comment. Seven pairs of male eyes stared at the women.

"Who's sexually insatiable?" Bart asked from the other end of the table.

"No one," Jackie replied deflatingly. "It's just a fantasy."

Hank laughed. "It certainly is. And not fair taunting us with the suggestion that it exists."

The men at the next table got to their feet and cheered a play, redirecting the Wonders' attention to the television.

"Boy, are they touchy," Paris observed, rocking the still-sleeping baby.

Jackie leaned her chin wearily on her hand. "I work long hours, and with four children we have to schedule the time to be romantic. Romance shouldn't require so much effort."

Mariah nodded. "I know what you mean. We don't have little ones like you do, but that's almost worse. It's hard to find a quiet moment when they can't just walk in on us."

Beazie indicated her baby. "I'm so sleep-deprived, I wouldn't know a lascivious suggestion if it fell on my head. I'm sure it's the same for Haley. And you have to put out a newspaper every week. I'd fold if I had to do that."

"Henrietta's a few months older than baby Evan," Haley said. "She's starting to sleep through the night and, of course, my mom's a big help. It's those late-night deadlines that make me want to sleep for a week—without a man."

The sharing went on—the offering of advice, the tricks that worked and didn't, the comparing of experiences. Prue admired their openness and their lack of judgment. She'd been on fund-raising committees with Mariah and Jackie, but hadn't really experienced their friendship in a personal way. She felt warmed by it.

She looked across the table at her sister and found that Randy and her mother had changed places so that Randy sat beside Paris and, with an arm around her, stroked the baby's head. They talked quietly, anticipating, she imagined, the time when the baby in her arms was their own. Prue turned away.

Beside them, Jeffrey and Camille were checking their watches, taking a last sip of their coffee, their eyes smiling into one another's as he helped her on with her jacket. They were so happy together, she thought, they were like the characters in a novel whose love had gone unrequited over most of a lifetime until fate finally brought them together once more.

Prue experienced a strange sort of disassociation from her mother and her sister. For a year they'd been all each other had. They'd comforted each other, spurred each other on, cheered their victories and softened their defeats.

But now her mother and her sister each had someone, and Prue was the odd woman out. Their unity would never be challenged, but their lives now had a different emphasis than hers.

They had families.

She'd almost had a family, but instead she now had an act, a fantasy.

A lie.

The impromptu party began to disperse when her

mother and Jeffrey left. Prue and Gideon thanked everyone again, and she watched him give Paris a quick hug, then shake Randy's hand.

"I'm so glad you're my brother-in-law again—" she heard Paris say softly "—if only for a while."

"Me, too," Gideon replied.

Paris hooked her arm in Prue's as the four headed out to the parking lot. "Did I tell you I'm selling the cab?" she asked.

Prue stopped in surprise. She'd felt fairly sure Paris would eventually want to find another line of work so that she'd be available on Randy's days off, otherwise they'd never see each other. But she hadn't expected that choice to be made so quickly. She felt an attachment to the cab since she, too, had driven it often.

"No, you didn't," she replied. "To whom? And when?"

"To Beth Childress, Chilly's wife." Paris grinned broadly. "So it's still sort of in the family. He drove for us the night of your show, remember? She spelled him after the show for a while and liked it. The wedding's scheduled for Saturday, and she's taking over Friday."

"*This* Saturday?" Prue gasped.

Paris nodded, unrealistically calm. "You don't have to worry about a thing except being there. And if you don't have time to make up that pumpkin brocade, don't worry about it. Wear whatever you want to wear. I know how busy you're going to be with Gideon's aunt.''

Prue felt major panic.

"But…it's your wedding! I should be organizing a shower, helping you plan, find a house…''

Paris shrugged as though none of that mattered. "I don't really care about all that. Though when I do go house-hunting, I hope you're free to come along. But if you're not—no biggie.''

Prue studied her usually methodical sister in concern. "You're very…relaxed all of a sudden.''

Paris only smiled wider. "I know. Isn't it great?'' She patted her still-flat stomach. "I feel as though I have everything—a man who loves me and a baby coming—and my time is better spent concentrating on them rather than trying to organize a life that suddenly defies organizing and worrying about things I can't control. And when you decide what to do after Georgette leaves, I want to be ready to help you. If you don't mind having a baby in the studio while your PR person makes you known all over the world. Of course, that'll necessitate you staying here rather than going to New York.''

Prue stared at her in disbelief. Paris had done a complete about-face from the sister with whom she'd grown up.

"No, I wouldn't mind,'' she said. "I'd love that. And when I have to be in New York, you can fax in your work or something.''

They hugged again, and Prue and Gideon climbed

into Gideon's truck as Paris and Randy headed for his.

Prue was quiet all the way home, then disappeared into the kitchen to make a pot of coffee while Gideon built a fire. Then she began fussing with the basket and the silk flowers for the library table.

Looking around for some way to help, he found a box of towels and picked it up. "Downstairs bathroom," he asked, "or upstairs?"

"Half and half," she said. "I'll need some downstairs tonight, and you'll need some."

"You sleeping down here tonight?" he asked.

She looked up in surprise. "Of course."

"Okay. I just wondered how we're going to prove to Aunt George that we're sexually insatiable," he teased, "if we don't get in some practice."

She made a face at him, understanding the reference to the conversation-stopper in the restaurant.

"Haley's the one who came up with that term," she explained, concentrating hard on the flowers to avoid his eyes. "I promised to take them out for Chinese food when this is over if they play along with our charade. And she wanted to know if we'd take them to the tea shop if they convinced Aunt George that we were…sexually insatiable."

"Mmm," he said, heading off toward the bathroom, then adding over his shoulder, "The tea shop does have a lot of great stuff."

They looked through photographs while drinking coffee and selected family photos to leave downstairs, then photos of the two of them to place on the dresser in the bedroom.

"I'm surprised you saved those," he said, standing back and watching, coffee in hand, as she placed them one way, then gathered them all up again and started over. "And didn't even cut me out of them."

"They were in the bottom of my closet," she said, stepping back to admire her arrangement of a cluster of photographs in the middle of the dresser and one on the end. "It wasn't as though I had to look at them." She touched a round frame with a photo of his parents. "And I'll always love your mom and dad."

"Mom's responsible for this game we're playing," he reminded her. Actually, it was his fault and not his mother's, but her insistence that he and Prue would work it out had given him the idea.

"If it means Prudent Designs will become a competitor in the rag trade," she said, speaking to the tray of small plants she'd brought upstairs, "then I should be grateful."

She placed one of the plants in an old blue and yellow water pitcher she'd bought at the Bargain Basement.

"There," she said, apparently satisfied. She looked at the bare space above the bed. "Do you think there should be something up there?"

"Like what?"

"A picture or a tapestry?"

"A picture of what?"

"I don't know. Just something to add warmth."
She tilted her head to the side as she studied the blank
spot. "A quilt hanging, maybe."

"We can look for something when we go back to
town for groceries," he suggested.

She nodded. "Good idea. Mariah Trent has signs
and things on consignment at the Mountain Gallery.
We could check there."

"Okay. Where are the rest of these plants going?"

She picked up a Boston fern. "This one's for the
bathroom. It'll love the steam." She carried the plant
into the bathroom and placed it on a shelf above the
towel rack. She came back to pick up the tray. "The
rest of these can go downstairs." She smiled at him
stiffly. "If it's all right with you, I'll just tidy up a
bit down there and go to bed."

"Sure." This was going to be harder than he
thought. He was very much aware that he still had
strong feelings for her, but they hadn't controlled him
in the old days as much as they seemed to now. He'd
had so much to do then, so much responsibility that,
though he'd adored her, the weight of his office had
demanded much of his focus.

It was curious, he thought as he followed her downstairs to lock up, that now that he was a few years
older, he was more a slave to his libido than he'd
been as a younger man.

Less distracting influences, he guessed. And the
proximity. They'd spent so much time apart in the old
days, he at the office, seldom home before midnight,

she at home or at luncheons or fund-raisers. She'd often been asleep when he'd come home.

He didn't remember the sinuous curve of her body as she tipped her head from side to side and stretched her arms in an attempt to relieve weariness. The light and movement in her hair as she ran her fingers through it to catch it up in a clasp she had in her pocket. He guessed she was about to shower.

He did remember the rose and lavender scent of the stuff she splashed on after she'd dried herself. It surrounded him now as he watched her cross the hall from the downstairs bedroom into the bathroom, a bath towel in hand.

"Good night," he called. Then he hurried upstairs, unwilling to let the image form of her wrapped in a towel, slender limbs exposed, the bloom of her breasts peeking out the top.

"Good night," she replied.

The image formed anyway, and for several hours he tossed and turned. He awoke after a scant three or four hours' sleep to the aroma of coffee brewing and the sounds of activity downstairs. Tired and grumpy, he showered and pulled on jeans and a red sweater, hoping the color would bring him to life. He reached for his watch and keys and was surprised to find only his watch on the dresser. He braced himself to spend another day of frustration with Prue and ran downstairs.

Prue stood at the stove in beige cords and a pink sweater, her hair French-braided in a coil that stopped just between her shoulder blades. A curved silver barrette held the curly end of it. He gave himself a moment to admire her tight little backside, the edges and strings of a white apron tied around her middle providing a frame for it.

He went to the coffeepot pretending that he hadn't been staring at her as she became aware of him. "Good morning," he said, pouring himself a cup. "What's cooking?"

"Stuffed French toast," she replied, her manner suspiciously sparkling this morning. And that had always been his favorite breakfast. Was she up to something? he wondered. And why shouldn't she be? He was.

"Are we celebrating something?" he asked. He topped up the coffee cup on the counter near her elbow.

"I'm rehearsing my role," she said with a smile that had no wry innuendo in it, no suggestion of a snide zinger to follow. "I remember how much you used to like these, so I thought I'd do my best to put you in a mellow mood, too."

He looked in surprise at the cream cheese and strawberries on the counter. "You've been shopping already?"

"I ran to my mother's to get socks this morning," she said. "Somehow I remembered everything else but that. It was easy to stop by the market on my way back. But we'll still have to do major grocery shopping this afternoon. I'm sure there are things you'll want that I don't know about.''

"You drove my truck?"

She pointed to the middle of the table where his car keys rested. "Didn't get a scratch on it.''

"Did I leave these down here last night?" he asked, retrieving them.

She reached into the oven for a plate she'd apparently placed there for warming, put the tantalizingly beautiful French toast on it and carried it to the table for him. "No," she replied casually. "I went upstairs and got them off your dresser.''

He was fascinated by the fact that she seemed embarrassed that she'd done it. Frankly, he liked the thought of her tiptoeing into his room while he slept. He'd have liked it better if the sight of him had lured her into climbing in beside him, but there was still time for that. He could afford to be patient.

"Really." He took advantage of her mild discomfort and said nothing more. He knew her. That would make her crazy. She liked to deal with things, put them center stage and have it out.

That is, she used to before the Maine Incident. Maybe that had changed her.

"I didn't take any side trips," she said, going back to the oven to retrieve her plate. "I parked it far away from other cars in the parking lot and didn't leave even a gum wrapper inside.''

He pretended surprise at her defensiveness. ''I

didn't say a word. You're welcome to borrow my truck.''

She sat at a right angle to him and studied him. "You used to hate it when I borrowed the Porsche."

"That's because you used to pull the seat way up, put the country-western station on the radio and re-adjust the mirrors. And let's not forget your tendency to drive on the sidewalk. It's also not good form when a senator takes a supporter to lunch, reaches into the glove compartment for a pen and pulls out a tampon.''

"I'm sorry about the tampon," she said with a roll of her eyes. "And the other things were hardly ma-licious. I just forgot to change them back for you when I parked."

He shrugged. "At this point, I don't care about it. And I told you to keep the Porsche after you left in it."

She looked momentarily nonplussed. "Then what are we arguing about?"

"Nothing," he said. "I think that was a lot of our problem most of the time. We argued over every-thing—and most of it was nothing."

She opened her mouth to respond to that, then closed it again.

He second-guessed her. "You were going to add— except what happened in Maine."

She tossed her hair—or would have if there'd been anything free to toss. The braid made her look prim and schoolgirlish and lent a sort of stubborn denial to the action. "I was, then I thought better of it. The animosity has to stop here if we're going to get through this. It was…generous of you to do this for me." That seemed to be hard for her to say. "And I appreciate it. I can see that you're more…thoughtful than you used to be." That had been hard, too. "So, I'm going to try harder to be less judgmental and more cooperative."

That was good news. But all he said was, "Thank you."

"I mean…there was a time when we had fun together. I'm sure we can't recapture that, but certainly we can manage to be polite."

"Of course we can." And he was going to keep working toward the fun. "Incidentally," he added, "did I tell you that I've arranged to rent a van while my aunt's here? We can't get everybody in my truck, and we'll need room for camera equipment."

She looked surprised. "Good thought, Gideon," she said finally. "See? The spirit of cooperation is working already."

CHAPTER EIGHT

PRUE AND GIDEON loaded groceries into the back of the truck, fitting them around the table and lamp they bought in a return trip to the Bargain Basement. Prue snatched a bag of cheese and jalapeño potato chips out of the last bag Gideon placed in the bed of the truck. It was past lunchtime and she was starving.

They climbed into the cab of the truck, and she pulled open the bag while he started the engine.

"Where's this gallery that Mariah shows her work?" he asked, delving into the bag when she held it out to him.

She pointed beyond the common. "About two blocks the other side of the square on the right." She held a potato chip between her teeth as she snapped her seat belt into place.

They were there in two minutes. The proprietor, a small, older man in a three-piece suit, approached them as they walked in the door. He had wavy gray hair, a bushy gray mustache and a silky terrier at his heels. It ran to Prue, plumey little tail wagging.

"Hi, Toulouse!" she said, picking up the dog and holding him close. A tiny tongue licked her face.

"Honestly, Lautrec." Pierre Pelletier took the dog

from her. Prue and Pierre had served together at St. Anthony's Christmas tea. She'd enjoyed his company so much that she dropped into the gallery whenever she had time just to chat. "The dog's supposed to be a welcoming committee, but sometimes he's over-zealous."

Prue patted the small head. "I love him and he knows it."

Pierre walked across the gallery hung tightly with oils and watercolors, and placed the dog in the chair behind a cluttered desk. On the back wall was fabric art and a case filled with jewelry. Several pieces of sculpture stood on pedestals around the room.

"Now." The man returned with a smile. He looked from Prue to Gideon then back to Prue again. "I heard you and your husband had reconciled," he said, offering his hand to Gideon. "You must be the husband. I'm Pierre Pelletier."

Gideon took his hand. "Gideon Hale."

"Welcome to Maple Hill," Pierre said. "Are you staying, or have you just come to collect Prudence?"

Prue grew tense for a moment, but Gideon replied easily, "We're decorating the bedroom of the A-frame on the lake. I've rented it for a few months."

She relaxed, smiling gratefully at him for the truth that neatly shielded the lie.

"We have a bare spot above the bed," Prue added, "and I heard that Mariah Trent has several pieces here," Prue said. "That she's gone beyond the signs everyone loves so much."

Pierre nodded and beckoned them to follow him through a doorway to the right. The room was smaller than the other and hung with obviously special pieces. He pointed to the wall behind Prue and she turned, shocked by the four paintings done in brilliant colors. All featured children.

Prue couldn't help the breathy gasp that escaped at her surprise over the skillful, touchingly heartfelt work.

"I had no idea," she said softly. "I loved her signs, but these…"

He nodded, apparently understanding what she couldn't put into words. "I know. She made those nicely crafted, sweet, witty commentaries on life with cartoony flowers and birds, and I suspect even she had no idea what talent lay hidden inside her. She says she started to try her hand at painting about a year ago…"

"When she married Cam," Prue said, unable to take her eyes from the wall of Mariah's work. It was so easy to see what love had done to her gift.

One of the paintings was of children laughing on the playground—not sweet, cutesy children, but real skinned-knees, devil-in-the-eye children. Another depicted several of those same faces looking out school-bus windows, and one was of two children, a boy and a girl in a rowboat on the lake. Prue could see Ashley and Brian in their features.

But it was the fourth painting that caught and captured her attention. It was entitled *Quiet Moment*. It depicted four children sitting in the middle of a carpeted living room—two boys and two girls ranging in ages from about two to eight years old. The two oldest were towheaded boys sitting on their knees, toy trucks arranged around them. The baby laughed at the artist, fine golden hair in disarray, the strap untied on the shoulder of a pink romper. The older girl was a redhead with mischievous green eyes and a tabby cat sprawled out in the lap of her frilly, rose-sprigged dress. It was clear that in a family of little ruffians, she was…the princess.

It felt as though she spoke to Prue.

You're the one, Prue said in her heart, *that I lost. The life that never had a chance to be.*

Prue didn't realize she was crying until she turned to Gideon to see if the painting had affected him as it had her, and saw that his forehead was creased in concern. He put a hand to her cheek and wiped a tear away with his thumb.

She pointed to the picture, wanting to explain, but her throat was too tight to allow it.

He put an arm around her shoulder and drew her closer.

''The children we'd planned,'' he said, studying the painting. ''Aaron, Christopher, Lisa and Annabeth.''

She looked up at him in astonishment, unable to believe he remembered the names they'd chosen one romantic Sunday morning in Maine right after they'd bought the weekend house. They'd been so happy together then—a breakup, a life reclaimed by heaven, had seemed impossible. They were going to have four children, he was going to run for governor, and they were going to change the world for the better, then retire to his parents' vineyard and spoil their grandchildren.

He pointed to the older girl in the painting. "We were wrong about that name, though," he said. "She's not a Lisa. She's a Princess Prue II."

He laughed as he said it, then kissed her temple. The gesture was completely honest and unguarded, and something solid and protective inside her shattered. She tightened her jacket around her, feeling exposed and vulnerable.

"We'll take that one, Pierre," Gideon said.

Pierre took it tenderly off the wall and disappeared into the other room with it.

Prue stood arm in arm with Gideon for a few moments while she composed herself. She couldn't explain her tears to him, because she'd never told him. She'd never told anyone that the day she'd hurried back to Albany from Maine, she'd lost the baby she hadn't even had a chance to tell Gideon about. "I'm sorry," she said finally, pulling herself together. "I...don't know what happened."

"You probably just never expected to have to look that dream in the face again," he said gently. "And it was such a good one. But...you can still have it someday. Probably with some Broadway producer or business mogul you'll be introduced to when you move Prudent Designs to New York.''

She shook her head and sighed. "I don't think so," she said, then moved away from him to follow Pierre.

GIDEON HATED the grief he saw in her eyes, but knew there was no way he could help relieve her of it. Yet the depth of what she felt gave him a curious hope. If the dream had meant that much—if she hadn't simply scrapped it when she'd left him—then there was something inside her for him to reach.

With the painting hanging in the room they'd be sharing for the next few days, there was hope.

Back at the house, Prue washed the linens in the downstairs bedroom and bath and prepared a seafood salad while he vacuumed and scrubbed bathrooms.

He finished the upstairs bathroom and stood to find her smiling at him from the doorway. "You've really become quite handy," she observed.

He shrugged off the compliment. "I got you into this. I have to help you make it work."

She held up the painting. "Let's hang this."

"Okay. I'll get my tools." He left the cleaning stuff in the garage and returned with a hammer and nails to find Prue standing in her socks in the middle of the bed, holding the painting up against the wall. "Is that high enough?" she asked, holding it just above the headboard, as high as she could safely reach on the unsteady mattress.

"I don't think so." He climbed up beside her and

held it up several inches higher. "How's that?" he asked.

She stepped back gingerly to look, and almost lost her balance, grasping his arm for support. Steady again, she nodded. "I think that's perfect."

He put a hand behind the painting to mark the spot on the wall where the wire hung, then handed her the painting and hammered in the hanger. He reached back to reclaim the painting and slipped the wire onto the hook. After an adjustment or two to center it, he took a step to the side so that she could see the canvas unobstructed. "What do you think?"

"It's beautiful," she said in a whisper.

It was. He wondered if Mariah had used children she knew to model for the painting, or if she'd conjured those children out of her imagination. Because he felt possessive about them—as though his DNA was somehow imprinted on them. And the older of the little girls could have been cloned from Prue.

Prue moved in for a closer look, her eyes on the painting rather than where she was going, then stepped on the hammer, lost her balance and started to go down. Forgetting she couldn't possibly hurt herself on the mattress and reacting solely on instinct, he caught her in his arms and they went down together.

He'd fallen onto his back to protect her from his weight and she sprawled over him in torturous intimacy. For the space of several seconds enclosed in a bubble of timelessness, it was all so warmly familiar—the squash of her breasts against his chest, the curve of her shoulder in the palm of his hand, the point of her knee riding up his thigh.

Trapped in the flare of emotion in her dilated eyes, he forgot he was no longer entitled to this intimacy. He cupped her head in his hand and brought her mouth to his. She opened for him eagerly, generously, contributing to his amnesia. He kissed her deeply and she kissed him back. She framed his face in her hands and his hands wandered over her, searching for familiar curves and hollows. He put his hand over her hip and pressed her closer.

She sat up suddenly, gasping for air, her eyes accusing.

It was like falling through the February ice on Lake Michigan. And reality was his life preserver. For a moment, he seriously considered a watery grave.

But there'd been too much emotion in her kiss for him to give up now.

"Yes, I started it," he admitted, still flat on his back in the middle of the bed, trying to regain his equilibrium. She knelt beside him, bristling. "But you were doing your part, so you have to share the blame."

"I wasn't planting blame," she said, pushing herself off the bed. She stood near the edge, looking down on him, her fingers clenching and unclenching. "We've always had a certain…combustibility. That's all it means. We were physically compatible and still are—or we would be if you weren't so physically compatible with other women, as well."

He put a hand over his eyes and counted to ten. As anatomically improbable as that seemed, it prevented bad words from coming out of his mouth.

"I'll get the bedding out of the laundry," she said and he heard her storm away.

He sat up with a groan, hoping he was going to survive this adventure with his brain and his libido intact. It didn't look promising at the moment.

PRUE HEARD the shower running upstairs while she pulled sheets out of the dryer. Her hands were trembling and her heart was still beating quickly. She couldn't deny the conflagration that had taken place inside her when Gideon kissed her. She'd been like a dry pine in a forest fire.

She balled the difficult-to-fold fitted sheet in her arms and carried it into the bedroom. She fitted two corners of the mattress at the headboard, then tugged the foot corners into place. Her actions were testy. It was humbling to realize that even though a man had betrayed you in a most humiliating way, you still reacted to his mouth, to his touch.

The bottom sheet in place, she put the top sheet on, made neat hospital corners at the foot, then put on a thermal blanket.

She was going to have to watch herself. She'd gotten a little cocky because they'd been dealing with each other fairly well and seemed to have found a common ground in preparing for Aunt Georgette's visit. It had been easy to forget how dangerous a friendly relationship could be when a man and woman had knowledge of each other's bodies—and when they'd once revered and enjoyed them so much.

She couldn't keep her distance, or his aunt would notice. She'd have to find a way to appear loving and warm without letting him touch her.

Right, she thought crossly, snatching a bare pillow off the chair. *Like that could be done.*

She held the pillow under her chin and began to pull on its cover. There was no easy way out of this situation. She was going to have to just keep going and remember that whatever it cost her in emotion, frustration and exasperation, the benefits to Prudent Designs definitely outweighed them.

She tossed the covered pillow at the head of the bed and reached to the other one to pull on the case. It was just surprising to discover how vulnerable she'd been in his arms. And how much she'd liked it. She felt a familiar shudder now as she thought about it.

She tossed the second covered pillow beside its mate and yanked up the coverlet. God, she was pathetic.

She looked at the newly made bed, ready for Aunt Georgette's occupancy tomorrow, and wondered where she was going to sleep tonight. Upstairs was definitely out.

He was emerging from the shower wrapped in a towel when she went up to ask him about extra blankets for the living-room sofa. His hair was wet and in sexy disarray.

Life seemed determined to torture her. Now that she'd felt his clothed body against hers, she could look at his near nakedness and see everything she'd felt—the long, corded muscles of his strong limbs, the sturdy, nicely muscled shoulders, the broad chest. She remembered clearly what was *under* the towel, but thinking about it would severely tax her already strained control.

She drew a breath and tried to appear unaffected. "I was wondering if you had an extra blanket. I just made up your aunt's bed, and I don't want to disturb it."

He seemed a little edgy as he reached to the pillows and yanked away the bedspread. "Take this," he said.

She noticed there was only one thin blanket under the spread. "You'll freeze," she predicted.

He gathered it up and thrust it at her. "I'll sleep in my sweats. I'll be fine."

"No, I can't…" she began, trying to give the bedspread back to him.

"Where are you sleeping?" he interrupted without the faultless courtesy he'd displayed since she'd moved in.

"Downstairs on the sofa," she replied.

"Then, unless you're willing to climb into bed with me to keep us both warm, you'd better take this downstairs *now*." The emphasis on the last word was clear. He'd displayed considerable patience over the past few days, but it was apparently at an end.

She turned around, part of the bedspread trailing behind her, and made her departure.

She showered downstairs, pulled on a pair of flannel pajamas decorated in croissants and coffee cups that Paris had given her last Christmas, and folding the spread like an envelope, she climbed into it. She'd forgotten a pillow, but she'd manage without one. She grumbled at herself for not even thinking about decorative throw pillows when she'd been shopping at the Bargain Basement. One of them would have come in handy now.

She listened to the quiet house for an hour. She heard the gentle lapping of the lake against the broken-down pier at the back of the house. Distant howls in the woods came eerily out of the darkness, adding a primitive element to her cozy surroundings.

There was nothing to worry about, she told herself bracingly. Even though the dog-door slide was apparently lost, a coyote or whatever that was would never approach a house, probably wouldn't know what to do with a dog door if it saw one.

In an attempt to distract herself from thoughts of coyotes, she went back to thoughts of her surroundings. *Cozy* was not a good choice of words, considering Gideon was in a temper upstairs and she was freezing on a leather sofa that seemed to hold the cold despite her flannel jammies and the bedspread wrapped around her.

Which just went to prove that you could plot carefully and set the scene and pretend everything was fine, but the truth would force itself to the surface. She just hoped she could prevent it from completely erupting until Aunt Georgette left.

Then she began worrying about filling all the orders taken at the fashion show. This charade was scheduled to take just a week out of her life, and it was intended to do wonders for her career. But what would be the point of gaining a reputation as a designer if the customers who wore her clothes complained about the amount of time it took to actually receive them?

No. She couldn't worry about that. Rosie DeMarco would be available to help. They'd fill orders in record time.

Once her supplies arrived.

Once they'd scheduled fittings. Over fifty of them.

The impulse to scream was almost overwhelming. Only Gideon's ill temper prevented it.

She closed her eyes and thought about relaxing every muscle, one by one. She'd heard somewhere that it helped induce sleep.

You were supposed to start with every toe and imagine it relaxing. She did that, then imagined the muscles in her foot and the dozens of trips they'd made up and down the stairs in the past few days.

Her calf muscles, her thigh muscles.

It was working, she thought drowsily as she began

to experience a definite reduction of tension in her lower body.

She was working on the muscles of her backside, her eyes closed, her focus narrowed on her relaxing body when she felt the sudden leap of something onto her stomach. Startled, she opened her eyes and looked into a pair of gray ones reflecting the dying firelight.

The coyote had found her after all.

She felt the scream build somewhere in the bottom of her chest. It formed in her throat as she struck out at the intruder and encountered whisker and fur. She shrieked at full volume.

GIDEON WOKE out of a deep sleep to the sound of Prue's scream.

He shot out of bed and raced for the stairs, flipping the light on as he passed. He skidded to a stop halfway across the living room where he found her sitting in the middle of the floor. She'd apparently fallen, her legs entangled in the bedspread. Her breath was coming quickly, her eyes wide with fear.

"What?" he demanded, his body braced for combat as he looked around for a predator.

"Something…" She pointed toward a shadowy corner, shuddering. "There!"

"A mouse?" he asked, relieved it wasn't something bigger than he, carrying a weapon.

She took offense. "Not a mouse!" she said, clearly impatient with him. "I'm not the kind of woman who gets hysterical over a mouse. It was big!" She spread her arms about four feet apart. "And hairy! And it had whiskers!"

He tried to imagine what was that large with long hair and whiskers. There was a certain lobbyist he knew who fit that description, but he didn't think Prue would appreciate an injection of humor at that moment.

He was confident that whatever the beast was, it couldn't be *that* terrible, because the shadow she'd pointed to wasn't more than two feet square.

"Okay," he said calmly, hauling her off the floor and easing her onto the sofa. He picked up the bedspread and put it beside her. "Just sit tight and I'll see what it is."

"Be careful, Gideon," she urged in a frightened whisper, drawing her feet up.

He went slowly toward the shadow, scanning it for shape and form, for some sign of life. When he was within several feet of it, a low gray form darted away from him toward the kitchen doorway where it stopped to arch its back and hiss at him.

It was a cat.

Granted, it was a large one, a very fluffy tabby with a big head and ridiculously wide whiskers. Its eyes were gray-green and enormous.

Gideon's muscles relaxed and he expelled a small laugh, getting down on his haunches and stretching a hand out to try to lure the cat back.

"Oh, my gosh!" Prue said in a high, quiet voice,

coming up behind him. "Poor thing! Don't scare him."

He glanced drily up at her over his shoulder. "You're the one who shrieked like a banshee. Does he really look four feet wide to you?"

She got down beside him, crooning to the cat to come back. "Well, it jumped on my stomach in the dark. It was heavy and it felt really big."

"M-m-hmm." He humored her while he beckoned the cat.

It came halfway toward them and stopped, looking from one to the other, then came the rest of the way. But it rubbed against Gideon's extended hand rather than Prue's.

"Must have come in through the dog door," Gideon said, stroking the rough, wiry fur. He supposed, in the dark, it might have felt like something big and wild. In the light, however, it was leaning into him with a vengeance and beginning to purr. "Hank said there was a cat that came with the property. It was a wanderer. This must be him."

She reached a hand out to stroke the wide head. The cat recoiled.

She withdrew her hand, her expression grim. "Now he'll never forgive me."

"Unfair, isn't it?" Gideon said with a significant look at her. He scooped up the cat and carried him into the kitchen. The cat tensed, front paws pushing against Gideon's chest.

He put him down in a corner, then retrieved a bowl

and a can of tuna. The cat reacted to the sound of the can opener, his tail going straight up as he rubbed on Gideon's legs.

Gideon put the bowl on the floor and the cat ate hungrily.

Prue stood in the kitchen doorway, looking worriedly in the cat's direction. "Did Hank tell you what his name was?"

"No."

"Are you going to keep him?"

"As the story goes, he doesn't want to be kept. He moves on and comes back when he feels like it."

She folded her arms and leaned against the doorframe, looking from the cat to Gideon with something new in her eyes, something he didn't understand. It seemed composed of old uncertainties and new interest.

"You and I never had a pet," she observed, taking a few steps into the room. He noticed her silly pajamas for the first time, the way they clung lovingly to the tips of her breasts and the curve of her bottom, the flannels baggy yet somehow revealing. The wild and rumpled cloud of her hair brought back to him the fragrance of it—roses and spice. He had to look away before it made him feel weak. "Paris and I had dogs when we were growing up. I missed that."

"We were in a condo in Albany," he said unnecessarily because she knew that. She seemed to be trying to work out something. "Then we couldn't have one in Maine because we weren't there often enough. It wouldn't have been fair.''

She nodded—then without warning, tears sprang to her eyes. He got the same feeling he'd gotten when she was falling on the mattress—the need to reach out and catch her.

But she put him off with a glance—not a rejection as much as a warning. Never one to mind warnings if he wanted to do something, he went to put an arm around her.

She resisted him for a minute, then she leaned into him and wrapped her arms around his waist. He guessed it was residual fear from the cat's arrival in the dark that stayed with her and made her emotional. Otherwise he couldn't explain the tears.

''I'm sorry I woke you,'' she said against him, then pushed away. He took comfort in the fact that she seemed reluctant to do it. ''You should be getting your sleep, with Aunt Georgette arriving tomorrow.''

''Why don't you sleep in the bed,'' he suggested. ''And I'll sleep on the couch.''

''Because it's your house,'' she said, flattening her tumbled hair with one hand.

''Then I get to say who sleeps where.'' He pointed upstairs. ''Go. The bed's very comfortable. I'll fix a bed for the cat with a towel and one of the boxes you brought over. Go. Take the bedspread with you.''

''What'll you cover up with?''

''I'm going to build a fire, maybe stay up for a while.'' There was no way he was going back to sleep. She'd startled him into full wakefulness, with her scream and the fit of her pajamas.

She opened her mouth as though to argue further, but he threatened her with a look, at the outside edge of his tolerance.

She grabbed the bedspread and went upstairs with it.

He went to the cupboard for a brandy.

Prue couldn't stop crying. She curled up in the middle of his bed, tightly wrapped in the blanket and bedspread, and sobbed into the pillow that carried his scent.

She was so confused. She remembered vividly the love and excitement with which she'd planned that weekend in Maine a year ago. The man downstairs was a lot like the man she'd wanted to spend that time with—the old Gideon who'd been gentle and protective and remarkably tolerant.

Then she'd walked in on him and Claudia Hackett, and lost her future. She remembered the miscarriage, the grim hospital stay and the long year of darkness that had followed.

Well, it hadn't been all dark. She'd loved spending time with her mother and her sister. Forging ahead together had given depth to their affection for one another and changed each of them.

But Prue's love for Gideon had been such a critical part of her. Without it her days had lost their interesting texture, their sparkle. Life had been good, but not the adventure it had once been.

She closed her eyes tightly and, for the first time, really tried to remember that moment when she'd opened the door to their place in Maine. She could see the hallway rug they'd bought together at a flea market, the long expanse of plank floor and creamy walls covered with the work of local artists—seascapes, bright primitives, an expressionist work she hadn't understood but responded to anyway.

She saw a woman's bare back and her bottom in a pair of black lace panties sitting astride Gideon's lap on…on…a brown leather sofa. Just like the one downstairs.

No. She tried not to think of here but of *there*. To focus on what she'd seen. To try to remember some detail that might prove he was telling the truth when he said Claudia had thrown herself at him and he was pushing her away.

He'd been half reclined on the sofa, as she remembered, one hand holding on to the top of the cushion, the other on the woman's breast.

Feelings of anger and betrayal burst in her all over again, but she suppressed them. She needed to remember things clearly.

The woman's arm had been straight, as though she was pushing on Gideon's chest. Pushing him down? Pushing him away? But what had he been doing?

Holding her breast? Holding her away? Had he just tried to push her away as she attempted to seduce him and his hand happened to connect with her breast?

She punched the pillow. She couldn't believe that.

She was obviously desperate to make it seem as though he had a defense.

So, why was she doing it?

Because, she thought wearily, she'd been so certain of what she'd seen, but his kindness now made her second-guess herself. And he'd always been an honest man. He'd been elected and served on that principle.

She pulled the bedspread over her head and tried not to think about it anymore. She had to get some sleep. Aunt Georgette was arriving tomorrow…today, now…and Prue had a role to play.

Curiously, that role had seemed easier to undertake when Gideon had been her enemy. Now that she wasn't so sure she hated him, acting as though she loved him would be difficult and dangerous.

Just what she needed in her life. Another complication.

CHAPTER NINE

GEORGETTE FINCH-MORGAN was something to behold. She wore Chanel—Prue recognized it right away—a Dolce Gabbana hat, Prada shoes and carried a Louis Vuitton handbag. She had a straight, silver-gray bob cut just below her ears and diamond stud earrings that had to be two karats. She was tall and elegant; her sculpted face had a few wrinkles but they were flattering in an I've-lived-and-learned-and-know-everything sort of way. She was followed across the very small airport terminal by a handsome, intense-looking young man in a photographer's vest, who was hand in hand with a pretty young woman with short, bright red hair.

"Gideon!" Georgette came toward him, arms outstretched.

Gideon stepped forward to embrace his aunt. Her affection, like her smile, was lively and genuine. "It's so good to see you, Aunt George," Gideon said. "And a real pleasure to have you in Maple Hill."

"Thank you, Giddy," Georgette said, stepping back to look at him. "You look more like your father every day. He was quite the devil in his youth, you know. Your mother had to fight to keep other girls away from him when we were in college.''

Gideon laughed. ''Mom's still in fighting form. Prue, come say hello.''

Prue, who'd been standing back, trying to brace herself for the meeting and hoping her wifely attitude was in place, allowed Gideon to take her arm and draw her toward his aunt. She was immediately engulfed in an Elizabeth Arden-scented embrace.

''Prudence, you brilliant little designer, you!'' Georgette grabbed her shoulders and drew her away, giving her a small shake. ''I never *suspected* when Gideon's mother introduced us and told me your dream was to design clothes that you had such a sense of style! I mean, I appreciate artistic expression as much as the next woman, but the day I go out in an off-the-shoulder jersey knit over striped silk harem pants is the day they walk by my coffin and say, 'She looks just like she's sleeping!''''

Prue laughed at the description of a design on the last cover of *W*.

''But your work is sophisticated and absolutely stunning. You're going to be the next Donna Karan, there's no doubt in my mind.''

''Thank you, Aunt Georgette.'' Prue had to clear her throat to give her voice some volume. ''I'm flattered that you think so. And it's so nice of you to want to do all this for me.''

Georgette put her free arm around Gideon. ''I'm just so sorry that I was preoccupied at the time of your wedding. I want you to know it isn't that I'd forgotten you.''

''You were getting married yourself at the time,'' Gideon said wryly. ''It's understandable that you were distracted.''

Georgette sighed wistfully. ''That Winston was such an interesting man. It's a shame we had so little time together. We had matching Harleys, you know. Just like Liz and Malcolm.''

Prue blinked. ''Liz and Malcolm?''

''Taylor and Forbes,'' Georgette explained. ''The actress and the entrepreneur. They were an item before he passed away.''

Prue nodded, trying to imagine Georgette on a motorcycle. Surprisingly, the picture did come into focus. She looked and behaved as though nothing was beyond her capability or daring.

Georgette freed Gideon and reached behind her to draw the young couple forward. ''Prue and Gideon, I'd like you to meet Bruno Biazzi, a freelance fashion photographer, and his assistant, Justine Young.''

Prue shook hands with them, aware as Bruno took her hand that he looked her over with a vaguely dissatisfied air. Justine, though, seemed cheerful and friendly.

''You're sure,'' Bruno asked Georgette in elegantly accented English that made Prue think of prep schools and soccer fields, ''that it wouldn't be a better idea to use professional models?''

Georgette rolled her eyes as though this wasn't the

first time they'd discussed this. "No," she said, her tone measured. "As I've already explained, I'm *trying* to do something different. I think promoting the clothes with their very beautiful designer modeling them will be attention-getting."

He nodded, clearly unconvinced. "She's lovely," he said after a cursory glance at Prue, "and her hair's great, but she's short for—"

"Bruno," Georgette said in that same tone. "I'm going for something different."

"I'm just saying, if you want to really *sell* the clothes…"

"Bruno." Justine tugged on his arm, trying to stop him, but he shrugged her off.

"I'm just thinking of the best outcome of this shoot."

"I think," Georgette interrupted, "that her romance with her handsome husband—" she indicated Gideon, who was beginning to frown at the photographer "—is going to be just the thing to sell her romantic designs."

"He's got everything," Bruno agreed with that same cursory look at Gideon, "but she needs to be five-eleven, not five-three."

"I'm five-five," Prue put in defensively, then added to Georgette, "but if you do want to use someone…"

Georgette was shaking her head before Prue had even finished. "This is going to work. Bruno's just too conventional in his approach to see that." She

An Important Message from the Editors

Dear Reader,

Because you've chosen to read one of our fine romance novels, we'd like to say "thank you!" And, as a special way to thank you, we've selected two more of the books you love so well, plus an exciting Mystery Gift, to send you absolutely FREE!

Please enjoy them with our compliments...

Pam Powers

Peel off Seal and Place Inside...

How to validate your Editor's
FREE GIFT
"Thank You"

1. Peel off gift seal from front cover. Place it in space provided at right. This automatically entitles you to receive 2 FREE BOOKS and a fabulous mystery gift.

2. Send back this card and you'll get 2 brand-new Harlequin Superromance® novels. These books have a cover price of $5.25 each in the U.S. and $6.25 each in Canada, but they are yours to keep absolutely free.

3. There's no catch. You're under no obligation to buy anything. We charge nothing—ZERO—for your first shipment. And you don't have to make any minimum number of purchases—not even one!

4. The fact is, thousands of readers enjoy receiving their books by mail from the Harlequin Reader Service®. They enjoy the convenience of home delivery...they like getting the best new novels at discount prices BEFORE they're available in stores...and they love their *Heart to Heart* subscriber newsletter featuring author news, horoscopes, recipes, book reviews and much more!

5. We hope that after receiving your free books you'll want to remain a subscriber. But the choice is yours—to continue or cancel, any time at all! So why not take us up on our invitation, with no risk of any kind. You'll be glad you did!

6. Remember...just for validating your Editor's Free Gift Offer, we'll send you THREE gifts, *ABSOLUTELY FREE!*

GET A *Free* MYSTERY GIFT...

*SURPRISE MYSTERY GIFT COULD BE YOURS **FREE** AS A SPECIAL "THANK YOU" FROM THE EDITORS OF HARLEQUIN*

Visit us online at
www.eHarlequin.com

The Editor's "Thank You" Free Gifts Include:

- Two BRAND-NEW romance novels!
- An exciting mystery gift!

PLACE FREE GIFT SEAL HERE

Yes I have placed my Editor's "Thank You" seal in the space provided above. Please send me 2 free books and a fabulous Mystery Gift. I understand I am under no obligation to purchase any books, as explained on the back and on the opposite page.

336 HDL DZ6U   135 HDL DZ7A

FIRST NAME	LAST NAME

ADDRESS

APT.#	CITY

STATE/PROV.	ZIP/POSTAL CODE

(H-SR-06/04)

Thank You!

The Harlequin Reader Service® — Here's how it works:

Accepting your 2 free books and gift places you under no obligation to buy anything. You may keep the books and gift and return the shipping statement marked "cancel." If you do not cancel, about a month later we'll send you 6 additional books and bill you just $4.47 each in the U.S., or $4.99 each in Canada, plus 25¢ shipping & handling per book and applicable taxes if any.* That's the complete price and — compared to cover prices of $5.25 each in the U.S. and $6.25 each in Canada — it's quite a bargain! You may cancel at any time, but if you choose to continue, every month we'll send you 6 more books, which you may either purchase at the discount price or return to us and cancel your subscription.

*Terms and prices subject to change without notice. Sales tax applicable in N.Y. Canadian residents will be charged applicable provincial taxes and GST.

BUSINESS REPLY MAIL
FIRST-CLASS MAIL   PERMIT NO. 717-003   BUFFALO, NY

POSTAGE WILL BE PAID BY ADDRESSEE

HARLEQUIN READER SERVICE
3010 WALDEN AVE
PO BOX 1867
BUFFALO NY 14240-9952

NO POSTAGE
NECESSARY
IF MAILED
IN THE
UNITED STATES

patted Bruno's cheek in a gesture Prue felt sure only she could have gotten away with. "I'm paying you, darling," she said. "You have to do what I say."

He looked troubled and annoyed for one moment, then he smiled. "Okay. I'll get our luggage."

Gideon went with him while Prue took Georgette and Justine to the van they'd rented that morning.

Gideon drove to the Yankee Inn where Bruno and Justine would stay. Georgette occupied the front passenger seat, Prue in the two-seater in the second row. Bruno and Justine sat in the back. Prue turned, concerned about their comfort, and found them in the middle of a serious kiss. She turned back quickly, keeping her face forward for the rest of the drive as the kiss went on and on.

Everyone went into the inn, Prue introducing Bruno and Justine to Jackie Whitcomb, who was working the desk. She was prepared for their arrival.

She handed them room keys and rang for a bellman to carry up their bags.

"We'll be by to pick you up at eight in the morning," Georgette declared. "We'll all have breakfast, then we'll scout out locations." She looked to Prue and Gideon. "All right?"

"Yes," Prue replied. "But don't they want to have dinner with us tonight?"

Bruno and Justine leaned closer to each other. "No, thanks," Bruno replied. "We'll just rest up and see you in the morning. We can get something to eat here if we want to."

Prue nodded, thinking she was grateful there wasn't room at the house for them to stay. She'd go crazy if she had to watch them fall all over each other twenty-four hours a day.

The bellman led Bruno and Justine to the elevators, the couple gazing into each other's eyes, their plans for the afternoon clearly written in their smoldering looks.

"I hope we can drag those two out of bed in the morning," Gideon laughed when the elevator doors closed.

"I'll see that they're left a wake-up call." Jackie jotted a note down in a book near the phone. She smiled at Prue. "We'll get you started on time."

Prue waved at her as they headed back to the van.

Georgette seemed pleased with her bedroom. Prue imagined her room in her London town house probably had marble columns, Palladian windows and a bed draped with curtains streaming down from a gold crest.

"I'm going to take a nap," Georgette announced, "and when I wake up, I'm going to take the two of you for a five-course meal."

Gideon put her bags on the bed. "Could you be happy with the best meat loaf and mashed potatoes this side of my mother's? Not many five-course meals in the vicinity."

She smiled. "I'm really a peasant at heart when it comes to food. I just like to dress like royalty. A little nap and I'll be good as new."

Gideon nodded. "I could use one myself. Sleep as long as you need to, Aunt George."

Gideon was about to follow Prue out the door, when the closet squeaked open and the cat came sauntering out, pausing to stretch before moving into the hallway.

"Your mother didn't tell me you had a cat," Georgette said. "What's his name?"

"Ah…Drifter," Gideon replied with a quick glance at Prue. "He's a fairly new addition. Just moved in yesterday."

"Really?"

"It was cold and windy, and he found the dog door."

"You have a dog, too?"

"No, the door just came with the house."

"Ah…well. See you in a bit."

Gideon closed her door behind them just in time to see Prue try to pick up the cat. It scampered away from her, heading for the kitchen.

"Why don't you feed him," Gideon suggested, finding her another can of tuna. "He'll come around."

"I hope I have enough time," she said, opening the can and turning it into the cat's bowl.

Gideon preferred not to think about the brief amount of time he had to make this plan work. Every once in a while he was surprised by a promising turn of events, then Prue would look at him with that suspicion that made it seem hopeless.

Right now she was studying the cat with the same sense of helplessness he felt. "Drifter is a good name," she said and yawned, putting a graceful hand up to cover her mouth.

"Come on," he said softly. "A nap is a good idea. Neither one of us got much sleep last night."

She closed her eyes and expelled an exasperated breath, as though she'd forgotten something.

"What?" he asked.

"I forgot to get bedding for the sofa bed."

"Then I guess you'll have to sleep with me," he said, turning his back on her and heading for the stairs.

She caught up to him, apparently prepared to argue about it.

"But you have to stay on your side," he stipulated as they began to climb.

She shushed him with a finger to her lips and a glance in the direction of Aunt Georgette's room.

He cleared the top of the stairs and sat on the foot of the bed to pull off his shoes. "I remember how insatiable you can be," he went on, tossing his shoes aside and standing to pull the coverlet back, "but that'll have to wait. A coyote came through the dog door last night and I—"

A pillow whacked him on the back of the head. "Just shut up!" she snapped, climbing under the covers on the other side and curling up, facing away from him.

He smiled at the ceiling as he closed his eyes. He

heard a very small sound, then felt a not-so-small weight land on his stomach. Drifter had joined them.

RITA ROBIDOUX at the Breakfast Barn looked Georgette up and down as she brought menus. Prue guessed Georgette could seem snooty and superior if you didn't know her. Prue explained she was Gideon's aunt, and she'd come to help Prue advertise her designs. "Rita ordered a cloak for her daughter," Prue told Georgette.

"Smart woman," Georgette praised, her glance bouncing off Rita's burgundy-colored hair, then returning to her eyes with a smile. "Do you have wine?"

Rita poured water into their glasses. "We do—Chablis and Mountain Rhine," she replied a bit defensively, as though expecting a complaint over the limited selection.

Georgette looked at her companions. "What's your preference?"

Prue didn't want to influence her decision, but Gideon said, "Prue's into whites."

Georgette smiled at Rita. "A bottle of Mountain Rhine, please."

Rita nodded and disappeared. Prue was surprised at the lack of questions, then realized there were few people around who could match Rita for simple audacity and directness. But Georgette could.

"So the two of you are planning to stay here?"

Georgette asked, taking a sip of water. "You don't miss New York or politics?"

Gideon shook his head. "No. Politics is too much of a cooperative venture—and not always in a good way. It was frustrating trying to get things done when there's someone opposed to everything you try to do, and many of those wanting to help you have ulterior motives."

"Corporate life's a lot like that," Georgette sympathized. "It makes me insane. But I have an assistant who's very geared to the battle and I often travel and leave him in charge. Now, I know Prue's designing clothes, but what are *you* doing?"

"I work for a company that provides all kinds of services to homes and businesses. I'm developing a security model for them. You met my boss's wife at the Yankee Inn when we dropped Bruno and Justine off. Her family's owned it for generations."

Georgette blinked. "Security? You mean…putting in alarms and things like that?"

He shook his head. "That, too. But mostly person-to-person security," he said. "Security guards, bodyguards, some personal training."

"That's right. You have all that training from your days in the service. But is that really what you want to do with the rest of your life? I mean…it's dangerous!"

"No, it's not," he assured her. "I'm not doing the guarding, I'm just developing the plan on how it should be done. I did a lot of that in the Gulf War."

"You were a kid then."

He pretended offense. "I'm hardly a geezer now."

She laughed and patted his hand. "Of course you're not, but this is the time of your life when you should be having babies and making yourself indispensable to your wife so that when you do become an old geezer, she'll still want you."

Gideon put an arm around Prue's shoulders and leaned back with her as Rita arrived with a bottle, a corkscrew and three glasses. "No danger there," he said with a theatrically weary sigh. "Prudie wants me all the time. It can be embarrassing. I'm sure if you weren't here, we'd still be home and she'd be all over me right now."

Prue accepted that he was playing the role and thought deflating his ego would be considered an appropriate response. "He's a little full of himself," she told Georgette with a wink. "I think because Bruno said I was short but Gideon was perfect."

"You're both perfect," Georgette insisted, thanking Rita with a gracious smile as she poured the wine. "And I wish someone wanted *me* all the time. I miss Winston and his randy, old prep-school ways. Sometimes death seems to have an affinity for those particularly full of life."

She grew sad suddenly, and Prue noted Rita's quick glance at her as she put the bottle in the middle of the table. Even the most sophisticated and wealthy could feel lonely.

"Have you thought about coming home for a

while?'' Gideon asked with a gentle solicitousness Prue found touching. ''I'm sure Mom and Dad would let you have the guest house on the vineyard. If you needed something to do, the holidays there are always very lively.''

Georgette turned her wineglass by the stem and sighed. ''I'm all right in London for the most part. I just get melancholy sometimes.'' She patted his hand again and smiled. ''Like when I see my brother's children as adults and realize how much time has passed. I was the one always looking for something, you know. The middle child who was never satisfied with what everyone else wanted, but longed for bigger and better things.''

''But you got them,'' Prue pointed out. ''You lived your dreams.''

''I did,'' she agreed. ''But every time I realized a dream, it was taken away. So I live in London, but my life's not really there anymore. And I've been so busy living and working, that I seldom saw my siblings, so my life isn't with them, either.''

''I think you're wrong about that,'' Gideon insisted. ''I'll bet the folks would be happy to have you spend some time with them. Then you'll know if you want to come home or not.''

It occurred to Prue that Georgette might be undertaking this ad campaign as much for herself as for Prudent Designs. She'd wanted to come home and test the waters, and this had been an excellent excuse to do it.

Georgette raised her glass. "Maybe. But that's enough of that. Let's toast Prudent Designs and your brilliant future. If Prue makes the fortune I think she'll make when word gets out about her, she's going to need a top-of-the-line bodyguard. How lucky that she has one built in."

Prue smiled lovingly at Gideon as she knew she was expected to and, his arm still around her, he squeezed her closer. She was a little disappointed he didn't kiss her as well, but instantly dismissed that notion as insane and self-destructive.

Though that had been some kiss last night.

Tonight she was sleeping on the sofa bed whether or not she had linens.

They ordered meat loaf, then dessert, though Prue declined. "I have a deadly red dress," she explained to Georgette, "that shows every indulgence." Then she teased Gideon with a grin as he ate hazelnut cheesecake. "If you have a gut hanging over your belt when we start shooting, you won't be perfect anymore."

"I can hold my stomach in," he responded, "but you'll still be short."

She elbowed his arm and he cried out dramatically.

"Children!" Georgette chided them. "You have locations lined up for us to visit tomorrow?"

Gideon nodded. "I'll just drive you around and we'll make a list of where you'd like to shoot. If we need city permission for anything, we're on good terms with the mayor."

"Good. And I was thinking that cloak would be dynamite on a trail in the woods where the leaves are turning."

Gideon nodded. "We can go up into the Berkshires if you have time."

"I'll make time. There's some board business I should be back for soon, but I don't imagine we'll need too much."

"The weatherman says the weather will hold out for us," Prue said. "There's a cold front keeping rain at bay all week."

"Perfect." Taking a last sip of coffee, Georgette collected her purse and gloves. "Shall we head home and get our beauty sleep?"

Gideon helped her on with her coat, then Prue with her jacket. He ushered them out to the car and was helping Georgette in when they heard a scream at the far edge of the lot nearest the stream. It was pitch-black, and though Prue turned toward the sound of the scream, her heart beating faster, she couldn't see a thing.

"Stay here," Gideon said, taking off in that direction.

"Gideon!" she called after him, trying to grab his jacket sleeve, but he was loping across the parking lot, already out of her reach.

She took her cell phone out of her purse, shoved her purse at Georgette and followed him.

The screams were now steady, and she could see a man and a woman apparently struggling over a purse.

The man was determined to have it but the woman seemed to have no intention of parting with it.

"Hey!" Gideon shouted, stopping within several feet of them.

The man turned in Gideon's direction, and Prue felt a cold shiver of fear run along her spine. His features were indistinct in the darkness, but his shadow was large. Prue blindly punched out 9-1-1 in the darkness.

"Drop it, buddy," Gideon advised calmly.

"Mind your own business!" the shadow snarled at Gideon. Then there was an ominous click and the gleam of a blade in the dark.

There was a quick slash, the straps of the handbag were cut, and the shadow took off at a run.

Gideon followed and tackled him before he was halfway across the lot. The man fell with a thud and a lot of profanity. He turned, prepared to resist with everything he had.

Prue felt panic, wondering how the police would possibly get here in time to prevent Gideon from being hurt. She ran toward them, picking up a two-by-two from the back of a pickup in her path.

When she arrived, the man had his arms on Gideon's, but Gideon freed himself with an upward swing of both arms, blocked a blow with one arm and struck the man a ringing right cross with the other. The attacker landed like a felled tree.

Prue stared at him in stupefaction, the two-by-two still riding her shoulder, ready to be swung.

Gideon, hardly a hair out of place, grinned at her

as he readjusted his jacket. "Where you going with that?" he asked, indicating the lumber with a jut of his chin.

"To your defense," she replied, sounding distracted. In the four years they'd been married, nothing like this had ever come up. He'd occasionally shown her some moves, wrestled playfully with her, but those incidents usually broke down into something else entirely. She'd never really seen him in a serious situation.

She was a little stunned.

"You want to call 9-1-1?" he asked.

"I already did," she replied.

A young woman in her early twenties materialized out of the dark. She grabbed her purse off the pavement and clutched it to her chest, the cut straps dangling. Her eyes were wide with fear and disbelief.

"You all right?" Gideon asked her.

She nodded. "Yeah. Thanks."

"You know, you shouldn't fight an attacker like that," he said gently. "If that ever happens again, let the purse go and call the police. Your money isn't worth your life."

She tightened her grip on the purse. "It has my son's inhaler in it." She pointed to an old gray import. The back door was still open, the interior light picking out the frightened face of a child about four sitting in the back in a car seat. "I don't have insurance."

Gideon was taken aback for a moment. "That was

very brave of you," he said finally, "but he had a knife. There'd be some way to get another inhaler. You wouldn't be that easy to replace."

The police arrived, took control of the purse snatcher, then an officer followed the young woman home.

The other officer gave Gideon a lecture similar to the one he'd given the young woman. "You should never interfere with a crime in progress. Call 9-1-1 and let us handle it."

Prue expected Gideon to tell the officer his qualifications, but he simply thanked him for coming so quickly, answered all his questions about what had happened, then when he was told they were free to go took Prue's arm and turned her toward their car.

"Where did you get that?" he asked, taking the two-by-two from her.

She pointed to the pickup whose bed was filled with lumber. He replaced the wood, then caught her hand and headed back to the car.

"That was amazing," she said.

He bobbed his head from side to side. "Well, when you've got it, you've got it."

"I didn't know you were that good."

"There's a lot about me you don't know."

She didn't want to touch that subject, curiously invigorated by the frightening events. "Were you scared?"

"No."

"*I* was scared."

"With that big stick over your shoulder?"

Georgette came toward them, meeting them in the middle of the parking lot. She wrapped her arms around Gideon. "My goodness!" she exclaimed. "Are you okay?"

"I am. He didn't touch me."

Georgette freed him and turned to Prue. "And you, young lady. Taking off after him like Sundance after Butch Cassidy!"

"I thought he was going to need backup," she explained. "I didn't realize he was Stallone in disguise."

They reached the van, and Georgette climbed into the front while Gideon pushed the sliding door open for Prue.

"Thank you," he said, stopping her as she prepared to climb into the middle seat. "But I told you to stay."

She looked up into his suddenly grave expression, remembering the strong response that had risen in her when she'd watched him take off after the purse snatcher. He was her man and he'd been in danger.

It shook her to the core as she realized what that response meant.

She was still in love with him.

CHAPTER TEN

"I HEARD YOU," she said, covering that heavy discovery with a casual smile, "but I'm not a poodle you can point into a corner. I thought you were in trouble and I wanted to help."

"Well, that's interesting," he said as he drove out of the parking lot. "But I believe it's customary in times of physical danger for the person with the least acuity in self-defense to accede to the instructions of the one with the most."

She knew he was taking advantage of the fact that Georgette heard everything and thought all was well with their marriage. She might think him within his rights to challenge her failure to listen.

"It's a marriage, sweetheart," she said, taking advantage herself, "not a government operation. If I want to run to your aid with a two-by-two, I'll do it. Live with it."

"So there," Georgette added. But Prue caught his eye in the rearview mirror and suspected she hadn't heard the end of it.

Georgette excused herself and went right to her room. Prue went upstairs while Gideon locked up.

She opened out the love seat and took the bedspread as she had last night and folded it. Then she went into the bathroom to put on her pajamas.

Gideon was standing near the bed in sweat bottoms when she came out, the top halfway over his head. She watched with breathless admiration as his abdominal muscles rippled with the action of pushing his arms through the sleeves. He yanked the hem down and his face emerged, his eyes tumultuous and dangerous.

GIDEON WATCHED PRUE cross the room to the sofa bed with its folded bedspread held in place by Drifter. It amazed him that just an hour ago she'd been prepared to come to his aid with a piece of lumber from the back of a pickup.

She gave him the same defensive look now she'd given him then. It was proof that she still cared.

He'd have preferred to learn this by being pinned to the bed while she kissed him passionately, but this would do for now.

"Have you forgotten everything I taught you about self-defense when we were married?" he asked, turning off the overhead light. All that remained was the small pool of light cast by the lamp near the love seat.

She looked puzzled by the question and stood uncertainly by the sofa bed. "Not entirely. Why?"

He shrugged, folding his arms, intrigued by the careful way she kept her distance. "Well, I just assume since you got a two-by-two to help you out, you're no longer feeling confident about your abilities in hand-to-hand.''

''Ah.'' She nodded understanding. ''I thought the danger was immediate, and I was never that good anyway.''

''I kept telling you that you just have to put more aggression into your approach. If we could just get your body to react with the same conviction your mouth does, you'd do very well. Want to try a few moves?''

She took a step backward. ''No.''

Drifter, considering her too close, ran off.

He looked into her eyes and understood her reticence. She didn't want him to touch her, but it wasn't fear of him, it was fear of herself. He closed the distance in two steps. ''Why not?''

She swallowed. ''Because…we'll wake your aunt.''

''I can attack in absolute silence.''

She nodded, laughing nervously. ''But you know me. I'll scream bloody murder. I'll just forget in the exertion of the moment that it isn't…real…combat.''

Oh, but it was.

He waggled his fingers at her invitingly, circling her. ''Come on. Surely, if you get to attack me, you'll be able to be quiet about it.''

''I don't want to attack you,'' she insisted, backing away.

''Why not?'' he taunted. ''Can't do it without a stick?''

"Can't do it without provocation," she replied.

That stopped him an arm's length away from her. She was now halfway between the bed and the love seat, with her back to the bed.

"I thought you considered that you have a lot of provocation. I cheated on you, embarrassed you..." He drove her backward with the words. "Caused you to have that breakdown."

She put her hand to his chest and held it firmly there. "I'm...I..." Her eyes brimmed with tears, filled with confusion and sadness. "I'm trying to remember that night," she said finally, her voice hoarse.

The playful mood of their encounter was changing. He'd been enjoying trying to deal with the obvious desire emanating from her over their adventurous evening. He didn't want this to turn into a serious discussion of the wall between them.

But a tear fell down her cheek and the mood change was complete. He drew a breath to switch emotional gears.

"Really. Why?"

"Because," she said breathlessly. He could feel the warmth in the hand with which she held him away. "The man you are now seems incompatible with the man who'd have done that. I'm trying to remember if I...if I misinterpreted something, or..."

The old anger tried to move in on him.

"You can spare yourself the trouble," he said. "You saw what you saw. Claudia Hackett was in her underwear and sitting on top of me. The picture's not going to change.'' Instead of letting the anger take him over, he held it at bay. If he was going to get her back, he had to stay cool. ''What has to change,'' he continued, ''is your analysis of what you saw. Do you really believe I'd have done that to you?''

''I *saw* it,'' she insisted, then on a ragged breath, shook her head and dropped her hand from him. ''But...was I wrong?''

That was halfway home, he thought wearily. ''When you can answer that for yourself,'' he said, ''we can talk about it. Take the bed, I'll take the love seat.''

''No, it's a foot shorter than you are.'' She climbed into the bedspread envelope then leaned over to turn off the light. ''I'll be fine. Good night.''

Too tired to argue, he went to bed.

Gideon awoke to the sound of someone rapping on the door to the loft. He flipped on the bedside lamp and sat up to find Prue also sitting up on the love seat, looking confused.

Drifter, sleeping on the other side of the bed, opened one eye.

The clock read just after 5:00 a.m.

''Yes?'' Gideon called.

''Gideon, it's Georgette. Does your master bath have a tub?'' she asked.

''Ah...yes,'' he replied. Prue was already on her feet, balling up the bedspread and tossing it at the bed.

''Darling, I hate to be a beast at this hour of the

morning, but my legs are all crampy, probably from the flight, and the only thing that helps me is a soak in the tub. And all I've got downstairs is a shower.''

Prue fought with the love seat, which seemed to refuse to close. He scrambled up to help her, found the latch she'd neglected to loosen and put away the love seat's alter ego.

He and Prue ran for the big bed together as Drifter scrambled off and ran under it. Prue reached down to pull the bedspread up as Gideon shouted, trying to hide his breathlessness, ''Sure, Aunt George. Come on in.''

As the doorknob turned, he hauled Prue into his arms and pulled the coverlet up high so that it looked as though they'd made a burrow out of the blankets. He could feel Prue's heartbeat as she snuggled into him.

''Thank you, darlings,'' Georgette said, hurrying past their bed. ''Much as I try not to notice, I think I'm just an aging old broad with all the usual ailments. I hate it!''

''Relax, Aunt George,'' Gideon said. ''It's okay.''

''Go back to sleep,'' Georgette encouraged, tapping his blanketed feet as she went past. ''I'll just have a little soak and I'll be good as new.''

''Take your time,'' he said lazily.

The moment the bathroom door closed behind her, Prue moved out of his arms, her hand to her heart. ''Geez!'' she whispered.

The bathroom door opened again and Prue fell back against his shoulder.

"Any bath salts?" Georgette asked.

Gideon opened his mouth to say no, but Prue put her hand over it and lifted her head to reply. "In the drawers under the sink, Aunt George. Bottom right."

Gideon blinked his surprise at her.

"Thank you, sweetie."

When the door closed, Prue dropped her head to his shoulder again. "I put my aromatherapy in there when I moved in," she whispered.

He was grateful. A bathroom shared by a woman would probably not seem normal without bath salts in it.

Gideon pulled the blankets up over her shoulder. "You'd better relax. No telling how many times she'll be in and out."

She huddled closer. "It is nice and warm in here."

"Nothing like body heat. Feels better to me, too."

Then an ice floe somehow crossed their path and collided with his shins.

"Holy…" he began to exclaim.

Again, Prue covered his mouth with her hand. "My feet are frozen!" she complained, withdrawing them from him. "I'm sorry. I guess I'm no longer entitled to…"

His feet went out in search of hers and found them. He caught them in his and drew them back to the middle of the bed. "The coldness just startled me. God, do you have any circulation below the knees?"

"It's just simple cold feet."

"I remember."

He felt the slight inclination of her weight against him and guessed her feet were warming up. For him, it was like having ice-cube trays strapped to his legs. But he was happy to put up with it as her nose nuzzled into his throat and she heaved a sigh that probably meant she wasn't too unhappy to be there.

For an hour, while Prue slept against him, he heard Georgette add more hot water to the tub. Drifter jumped onto the foot of the bed to give them one more chance to enjoy his company.

Gideon was unable to move or think. He simply lay there, Prue next to him, and absorbed the bonus granted him by his aunt's postflight distress.

At one point, Prue shifted her weight, flung an arm around his neck and hitched a leg over him. His control strained to the absolute limit of his endurance, he made himself lie quietly while his body tried to riot, tried to prepare him for what would normally be the outcome of such an exercise.

The moment Georgette tiptoed out of the bathroom in a thick yellow terry cloth robe, Gideon slipped out from under Prue. Drifter watched him leave, but curled up again near Prue's feet.

Gideon jumped into a cold shower.

PRUE FELT CHEERFUL, even effervescent. She wasn't sure what accounted for it unless it was that hour of deep sleep she'd enjoyed in Gideon's arms while

Georgette was in their bathroom, and the fact that Drifter had let her pet him without shrinking away.

Gideon, however, seemed curiously subdued this morning. He was quiet while they picked up Bruno and Justine, and said little during breakfast. Georgette had done most of the talking, and Bruno and Justine had eaten with their arms linked. Justine, fortunately, was left-handed.

Gideon didn't seem angry or out of sorts, just quiet. As the five of them wandered over the Maple Hill common, he and Georgette talked. And Bruno, whose skill as a photographer seemed to be overcoming his desire to be a lover, left Justine behind him as he examined the square from various angles.

"Is this your first trip to the States?" Prue asked as they wandered along behind the trio.

"No," Justine replied. "My father lives in Seattle. I'm here once, sometimes twice a year. He's a photographer, too. He has a portrait studio."

"So you come by your interest in photography naturally."

She rolled her eyes in self-deprecation. "My mother was a model, and it became pretty clear early on with these curves and lack of height that I wasn't going to go in that direction, but my father is so in love with looking for the light in his clients that I started to think in those terms. I helped him in his studio when I stayed with him over the summer. So when I started taking photography classes after college, I wanted a job in that field and found Bruno's help-wanted ad.''

"He seems to really…appreciate you," Prue said.

Justine smiled beatifically. "We hit it off immediately. He's even helping me pay for my photo classes.''

"What's your favorite subject?"

"Oh, I love back roads and country lanes, and England has so many, you know. I entered a contest sponsored by the London Tourism Board using a series of photos I'd taken in Yorkshire.''

"Well, good luck. Or have you already won?" Prue asked eagerly, then remembering that could have had another outcome, asked with a wince, "Or lost?"

Justine laughed. "It's being judged this week. I don't have high hopes because the competition's really stiff. I don't think anyone loves the work more than I do, but I'm certain many photographers are better at taking pictures.''

Everyone climbed into the van again, and Prue and Justine resumed their conversation when they all got out to walk around the lake to consider it as a backdrop.

"I understand from Georgette that Bruno's very well respected here and in Britain," Prue said.

Justine nodded, her eyes going to his tall form pointing something out to Gideon and Georgette. "He is. I've always admired his confidence. I suppose that comes from experience.''

"He looks as though he's only a few years older than you are."

"Yes, but he worked for a studio right out of high school. And he's been on his own for seven or eight years."

Prue did appreciate the respect Georgette and Justine had for him, but he seemed more arrogant than confident to her. Or maybe that was because he thought *she* was too short.

"When you finish your classes in photography," Prue asked, "you're probably going to want to work as a photographer rather than as an assistant."

Justine spread her arms as though anticipating that eventuality. "Bruno will make room for me at his studio when that happens."

"So you've talked about it?"

She shook her head. "Not much. He's always so busy with his work. But I'm sure when the time comes, he'll be happy to have a partner rather than an assistant."

Prue couldn't help but wonder if that was true.

They stopped for coffee at the Perk Avenue Tea Shop, where Georgette thought a sumptuous background of decadent desserts might be a possibility, went back to the Yankee Inn and looked it over because Bruno liked the lobby, checked out the white church with its classic steeple, explored the very old shops on the square.

They went to Prue's studio to look over the clothes Georgette had seen only in a faxed image. Prue uncovered the rack on which she kept them, and Georgette studied them one by one. She selected several garments—a red dress, a green casual outfit with a crop top, a little black dress and a cloak—which she hung face out to study them more closely.

"The fabrics are wonderful," Georgette said reverently, running a thumb over the rich wool of the cloak. "And the cut…" Her fingertips followed the side gather at the waist of the red dress. "I'll bet that looks like a dream on a shapely body."

Prue nodded. "Paris looked wonderful in it."

Georgette turned to study Prue's curves. "I'm sure you do, too." She turned up the hem on the red dress. "Have you shortened this for yourself since Paris wore it?"

"I've hemmed a few things since you called to say you were coming. I'll take the others home with me and do them as we go. Except for the wedding dress." She smiled widely. "Paris is getting married Saturday and asked if she could wear it."

"Well, how lovely! Will she let us photograph her, do you think? It'd make a nice element in our scenario."

"I don't think she'll mind."

"Good. Well—these four pieces *definitely*," Georgette said, touching the garments she'd selected. "And the green wool dress and the beige pants with the white shirt and the vest. Oh! And look at this!"

She found a white cat suit at the back of the rack.

It had sophisticated beading at the neckline and sleeves. "This is wonderful! Let's do this, too!"

Prue shook her head. "I made that some time ago, but its just *too* revealing. That would require Kate Moss's body."

"But it's stunning," Georgette wheedled.

Prue held firm. "I can't wear it, Aunt George. Makes me look pudgy."

"Okay." Georgette put it back, finally accepting her refusal.

"First of all—" she walked around her nephew, standing to the side "—we have to pick up a few things for our handsome prop here."

"Prop?" Gideon complained mildly with a raised eyebrow.

Prue patted his shoulder. "I like to think of him as my security force, my furniture mover..." She grinned at him. "My foot warmer."

"Are we going to be able to find the clothes we need in this town?" Bruno asked doubtfully. "It is charming, but will it have a tuxedo? There won't be time to wait for one to come in."

Georgette smiled at her nephew. "He used to be a senator. I'm sure there's a tux in his wardrobe."

Prue felt her smile waver. She wasn't sure what was in his wardrobe at the moment, but she knew he'd come to Maple Hill with only an overnight bag.

"I have one in storage in Albany," Gideon said easily. "I didn't think I'd need it in Maple Hill."

"We have a friend who owns one," Prue put in,

relieved at his logical explanation. "We used it for the fashion show. Gideon's a bit bigger than he is, but I think we can make it work."

Georgette nodded. "We can always pin it in place or leave the back of the shirt open, or something. If we're shooting from the front, it doesn't matter how it looks in back."

"Pin it in place?" Gideon questioned. "I don't like the sound of that."

"Not *to* you, sweetheart," Prue assured him, the endearment slipping out in her relief and excitement. "To itself or to the jacket."

"And he'll need a business suit." Bruno said. "Something gray to balance the black dress. And the red one."

"I left those, too," Gideon replied.

That wasn't quite as convincing, Prue thought, but no one seemed to notice. "There's a wonderful men's shop on the square," she said, "where we can get a suit."

They had lunch at the tea shop, then went shopping for Gideon's wardrobe.

Gideon headed for the round-neck sweaters, but Georgette redirected him to the turtlenecks.

"They make me feel like I'm going to suffocate," he complained.

"It won't if you get one that fits you," she argued. "And there's a lot of drama in a black turtleneck."

"Isn't that a little casual to go with all her dressy stuff?"

"No. We don't have to give you the same image we give her." She was obviously thinking through the idea as she spoke, walking up and down a rack of sports coats and frowning. She stopped suddenly and turned to Bruno.

"Prue said she thinks of him as her security force."

Everyone nodded, remembering that.

"That's the drama I want to go for in the shoot," she said, her eyes sparkling, her excitement mounting. "While it's true that the third-millennium woman is competent and confident and completely capable of taking care of herself, these are tough and scary times. I think having a strong man in her corner speaks to something elemental in her, something that harkens back to the days when women allied themselves with a man who could hunt, hold his own in the tribe and protect her and her children from harm."

"Today's woman might be offended," Bruno said.

Justine frowned at him. "No, she wouldn't. Protection in today's world is a practical consideration. And it'd be subtly presented, anyway."

"I'm afraid it'll detract from Prue as the focal point."

"No, it won't," Georgette insisted. "He's always beside her or behind her. Partially hidden, but very much there. She's strong because she's got backup." She swept a casual hand in the air. "And in today's world, having muscle at a woman's side just frees her up to do what she has to do. What do you think?"

Bruno shrugged. ''I'm outnumbered, I guess, but I think we should go for the romance.''

''Isn't that romance?'' Gideon asked. ''A man standing by to defend his woman—not because he considers her inferior, but because she's the most important thing in his life?''

Prue watched her female companions melt. And she felt a little hot puddle in the center of her being as well.

Where had *this* man been, she wondered grimly, when she'd been married to him?

CHAPTER ELEVEN

GIDEON EXPECTED the shopping experience to be torture. Generally he preferred a casual style, and since he'd left the New York State senate, he'd enjoyed not having to wear a suit or a tux every other night for some charitable or political function or other.

But there was a certain fascination in watching women pick out his clothes. The black turtleneck was pulled over his head, paired with black slacks, topped with a gray jacket, which was pulled off him and exchanged for a beige one. A young male clerk had tried to approach them to help, but the three women were so clearly on a mission and in control that he'd backed off and watched from two aisles over.

Gideon tried on several suits, and even Bruno agreed on a gray Perry Ellis. They paired it with a silver-white shirt and, unable to decide on a tie, chose several.

''But what'll he wear when she wears that top with the pants?'' Georgette asked, talking to herself.

''Slacks and a more casual sweater,'' Bruno suggested.

''No,'' Prue countered with a smile. ''It's a dinner-club, dancing kind of outfit. He'd be wearing a suit.

Only maybe stripped down to the shirt and tie. Or maybe, no tie.''

"That's it!'' Justine agreed. "There's nothing sexier than a man without his suit coat.''

Bruno, tired of being countermanded, lost interest and walked away.

"What'll he wear when she wears the cloak?'' Georgette asked.

"He has a cashmere coat that'd be perfect,'' Prue replied.

"Good. Let's see.'' Georgette's eyes scanned the racks and counters. "We need suspenders for a shot without the suit coat, an interesting scarf for the winter coat.''

Bruno wandered back to them. "We done here yet?''

Prue dusted off her hands. "I think we are.''

They took everything back to the house—Prue's designs, Gideon's clothes and Bruno's cameras and equipment—and set up a sort of headquarters in the living room. Drifter watched from the safety of the blue wing chair. Gideon smiled privately at the memory of Prue's careful placement of everything to create the best impression. A lot of the furniture was now shoved aside in the interest of lights, tripods and other things.

Prue made baked chicken for dinner, with Gideon and Justine helping while Georgette and Bruno planned strategy.

Justine told them about her favorite places to eat in London and Seattle.

"It must be nice to be able to go to Langan's Brasserie all the time," Prue said, slicing zucchini and onions. "I've only seen pictures of its fine art collection and wild lampshades, but it sounds wonderful."

"I don't get to go very often," Justine admitted. "There's this pub Bruno really likes on Coventry Street, so we usually end up there."

Gideon, washing and tearing greens, raised an eyebrow at Prue.

"Your lives are a lot about what he likes, aren't they?" Prue said.

Justine considered that and shrugged. "A lot of the time they are, but only because I don't insist on my way. I'm sure if I did, he'd take me to Langan's."

"You shouldn't have to insist," Prue said, scooping the greens off the cutting board and dropping them in a bowl. "He should take you there because he wants to make you happy."

"I'm happy," Justine said. "Mostly."

"If you are," Prue added, "it's because you are naturally, not because of him. Because from what I've observed, he doesn't value your opinion."

"He's a pro," she said defensively, "and I'm just...an assistant."

"Maybe. But he should also value your brain. You seem to have a lot of good ideas."

Justine appeared surprised by the praise, even unused to it. Then she took her coat off the back of a chair. "If you'll excuse me, I'll just step out the back and get some fresh air."

"She seems like such a nice kid," Gideon said, after Justine had left. "But it sounds as though he treats her like a work slave one minute and a love slave the next."

Prue nodded. "She was telling me she's taken lots of photography classes and she thinks when the day comes that she wants to strike out as a photographer, Bruno's going to make room for her in his studio."

"I can't see that happening. I think he likes having her around because she's adoring and works hard. But he doesn't like competition. The moment she tries to be his equal, I think the relationship will be over."

"I think you're right," Prue agreed, "but don't tell her that. I think she's beginning to see that for herself already." She opened the oven, pulled out the rack with the chicken and basted it. It was just beginning to brown.

"I miss having dinner at home together," Gideon said, inhaling the aromas of garlic and butter. "We didn't have that many quiet evenings at home, I guess, but the ones we had sure stick in my memory. I remember your baked chicken, microwaved popcorn and rented videos, and going to bed early."

"I do, too." She pushed the pan back in and closed the door, telling herself the heat in her cheeks was from the oven. "I have a lot of good memories of our life together."

He was suddenly tired of tiptoeing around the issue. He'd intended to be patient, to do everything in his power to convince her that she'd been wrong about that night in Maine and lure her back to him.

But he'd never been one to dance around an issue. He thought if you were honest, the best course of action was to be direct. What he'd hated most about politics was that his philosophy simply didn't apply there.

And—partially because of the way he'd set up this scenario with Georgette—honesty didn't apply here, either. He was beginning to chafe under the strain, and the adventure had barely begun.

He reached into the refrigerator again, this time for the bottle of white zinfandel, and poured two glasses, handing one to Prue. "So, are you convinced it's over?"

She blinked. Apparently he'd paused too long to think.

"Is what over?" she asked, leaning against the counter to face him. "Thank you." She toasted him and took a sip.

"Our life together," he replied, toasting her in return. "Have you given up on it?"

She looked stricken, as though she wasn't prepared to talk about it. But he considered it hopeful that she didn't refuse. "I had thought *you'd* given up on it," she finally said.

"Because you thought I was fooling around with Claudia. But you said last night you weren't sure about that anymore."

"I'm not," she admitted, looking into his eyes. Then she lowered hers and seemed to be having difficulty saying what was on her mind.

"We used to talk so easily," he reminded her. "Tell me what you're thinking."

"I'm thinking," she said, pausing to take a sip of wine, "that so much was wrong that last year. That...maybe I jumped to a wrong conclusion because it all seemed to be going to hell. You were never home before midnight, and when you did come home you seldom spoke to me. I pleaded with you to come to Maine with me that weekend, but you couldn't find the time."

"I explained that," he said. "And I'll be the first to admit that everything took me more time than it should have because I had so much to learn about political life and about getting things done. And I wanted so much to do the right thing for everyone, to validate their trust in me."

"You sacrificed me for that," she accused gently.

He nodded his guilt. "I did. I thought you'd see as I did that the working of government was bigger than what happened between us. The trouble is that doing what was right for my job was hard on our family. I was between a rock and a hard place."

Her eyes grew sad, heavy with the burden of an old pain. "Why didn't you come after me, Gideon?"

He had to tell her the truth. If they were to clear a foundation to build again, it had to be free of all the old debris. "I followed you back to New York, and when I found out you were in the hospital, I tried to see you, but your friend said you didn't want to see me. I thought it was a chicken way for you to hide from me.

"Then I began to realize," he said quietly, "that maybe I'd been right worrying about my constituents first because they voted for me, they trusted me, and it was clear when you ran away and believed the worst that you didn't." He sighed. That had been hard to say and probably hard for her to hear. Pain was visible in her eyes, but she drew a breath and held his gaze. "So I finished my term," he continued, "and figured I had to rebuild my life on my own. I expected every day to be served with divorce papers. Why didn't you file?"

"I…was broke," she said, looking away. "Why didn't you?"

He sighed. "I don't know. I suppose deep down I didn't want to give up on us. I sent you the money from the sale of the condo."

"I know. But that was just a couple of weeks ago. And I've had a lot going on since."

"So you intend to file?"

"I don't know!" she shrieked at him with sudden violence. "I think yes one day, no the next! I don't know! I love you and I hate you and I'm so confused I could scream!"

Prue did hear screaming and was shocked to discover it was her. Drifter ran off into the shadows at the back of the house.

Gideon arched an eyebrow and glanced over her head in the direction of his aunt and the photographer, and she could only guess they were staring at them, wondering what on earth was going on, why the blissful couple was fighting.

Oh, God. Had she blown everything?

Gideon cleared his throat. "Well, Prudie. If you have that kind of relationship with the tea shop's cheesecake, maybe you should try going cold turkey. I don't think it's worth all that angst, do you?"

Prue heard conversation begin again between her aunt and Bruno and knew Gideon had saved the moment, using her love-hate relationship with cheesecake as the excuse for her outburst.

She had to smile as she straightened away from the counter and pushed him out of her way so she could get a pan for the green beans. "Thank you," she said under her breath. "Always the problem solver."

"I live to serve the princess," he returned just as quietly.

PRUE AND GIDEON slept in the same bed, dutifully keeping to their own sides. Georgette's propensity for knocking on the door made it too risky for Prue to sleep on the sofa bed. Besides, Drifter had laid claim to it.

They lay on their backs in the darkness, a body's width between them, and pretended to sleep. But tension had her wound so tightly, she was sure one false move would shatter her.

"What's it going to take," he whispered, "to get you to stop making those little whining sounds?"

She jumped at the sound of his voice. "I'm not whining," she denied.

"Yes, you are," he insisted. "Are you hungry? Thirsty? What?"

It irritated her beyond reason that he apparently felt none of the tension she felt. For someone torturing her with questions about whether or not their relationship was over, he seemed completely unaware of her frustration.

She propped up on an elbow and glowered down at him. He probably couldn't see her in the dark, but she was sure the threat carried in her voice, as well.

"I'm going crazy!" she whispered harshly. "And you're not helping!" She tried to shove him but he didn't budge. "I don't think this is going to work after all, and I can't just lie here beside you as though…as though…"

Unwilling to say, "As though I'm not still attracted to you, as though I'm not remembering being wrapped in your arms, as though I'm not dying with the need to touch you right now," she simply jerked to a sitting position and prepared to move to the sofa bed.

But he caught her upper arm and pulled her back to him. She felt the heat of his bare chest through her pajama top and heard herself make that disturbing noise again. "As though you don't wish we were naked right now," he asked, his voice velvety and quiet as he spoke right into her ear, "and making love the way we used to."

She tried to clear her mind to calculate an answer when his hand reached beneath her flannel top and she lost whatever thread of good sense she'd been able to hold on to. His fingers splayed against her in a dearly familiar way, pressing her to him and surrounding her with all those delicious memories.

Her control shattered just as she'd been afraid it would when his hand moved over her, tracing her spinal column, dipping into the elastic band of her pajama bottoms.

"Gideon!" she whispered.

He turned them so that she lay on his supporting arm and he leaned over her, his free hand catching hers and carrying it to his lips. "I've heard you say my name in my dreams for a year," he said. With a tender stroke of her cheek, he added gently, "I've missed you, Prue."

She looped her arms around his neck and drew him down to her. "I've missed you, too!" Tears clogged her throat, a new tension threatening. There was so much unresolved. If they made love now, it would only confuse this already complicated game they played. She pushed against him, and to her surprise, he leaned back with a ragged breath.

"We haven't fixed anything," she said, expecting him to be angry.

He surprised her again by agreeing. "No, we haven't."

"Isn't that important?"

"To a reconciliation, I'm sure it is," he replied. "But that's not what's going on here, is it? This is just communication. I remember times when we didn't understand each other on other levels but managed to come together this way."

She felt a grinding disappointment. "Then this isn't about love?"

"Damn straight it's about love," he corrected, moving closer again, leaning over her as she rested in the crook of his arm. "I've loved you since the day I met you, and will until the day I die. But in between, we've hurt and disappointed each other, and before we ever get together again, we have to fix that. I just don't know how to reach that place when the words don't work. Maybe this will do it. Because I do love you."

The words washed over her like a warm balm. "I love you, too," she replied, wrapping her arms around him again and holding him close, kissing his shoulder. "I do. I love you!"

THERE'D BEEN TIMES during the past year when he'd been sure he'd never hear those words from her again. He'd managed to suppress the need for them, managed to convince himself that he could go far away and start over without her, but now as she melted in his arms, he knew that wouldn't happen.

She was home to him, and he had to find the way back into her life.

Even as they undressed each other, he was aware of how this endeavor had changed in purpose from its conception five days ago when his aunt called. His intention had been to get her back, but he hadn't understood until they'd spent time together how much he'd hurt her even *before* the Maine Incident she'd so misunderstood.

Now he needed desperately to make it clear how sorry he was that he'd sacrificed her to the job, that he hadn't made more of an effort to assure her of his feelings and his devotion.

And how much he wanted to bring that portrait of the children above the headboard to life.

Coherent thought left him as they lay side by side, flesh to flesh, for the first time in more than a year. She was cool and silky in his arms and he pulled the blanket up over her to cover her bare shoulder. She huddled closer, rubbing a frigid foot along his calf.

He caught that leg and hitched it up over him, tracing the line of her thigh up and down.

She kissed him hungrily, hotly. He felt her hands roam his back, his spine, then move between them to explore his chest. With a single fingernail she began to blaze a trail downward.

He followed the line of her thigh and dipped a finger right inside her. She tightened on him at the same moment that her hand closed over him and made him forget all romantic metaphors and remember only that he needed desperately to be inside her.

She lay back against the pillows and drew him to

her, apparently needing him inside her as much as he needed to be there.

He entered her with mild trepidation, afraid his eagerness to be there would overpower her own eagerness to have him. It had been a long time.

But she welcomed him, clasped her legs around him, and all the old power came back to fuse them together.

The little whimpers she'd been expelling all night changed into one long, sighing sound of satisfaction.

PRUE FELT like a collection of sequins and rhinestones being twirled and catching the light. Life spun and sparkled and made rainbows all around her. The ultimate solution to all her problems with Gideon didn't matter if she had this back. Because it had never been just sex between them. It had been deep and significant, hearts and souls meeting, lives being altered every time they touched.

She and Gideon climaxed together, clinging to each other, holding on as long as possible to the memories and the magic they'd recaptured.

Then he lay beside her and tucked her into his shoulder. He pushed the damp hair out of her eyes and pulled the blankets over her again. ''You okay? Warm enough?''

''Fine,'' she replied, exhausted physically and emotionally. She wrapped an arm around his broad middle and kissed his chest, marveling that after that long, dark year, they'd come back together again as though nothing at all was missing. "Are you okay?"

"Okay hardly says it," he replied, "but I'm too spent to search for a superlative. Just know that it's in my heart."

She put a hand over it, feeling its strong and steady beat.

"Got it," she said, and let the rhythm of it lull her to sleep.

CHAPTER TWELVE

THE SHOOT WENT remarkably well thanks to the rapport Prue and Gideon had reestablished. It was strange, he thought, that they were relaxed about it considering the way the last year had been. Prue didn't seem to want to talk about where this might take them—which was good because he didn't think she was ready to hear that he had no intention of letting her go again.

So they stood around hand in hand, waiting for Bruno to set up on the common. As Justine ran to and fro, doing his bidding—another tripod, a different lens, a cup of coffee—Georgette smiled at Gideon and Prue, and they smiled back. And when Prue turned away to return a greeting from a passerby, Georgette winked at Gideon in appreciation of the obvious success of their venture.

It was probably clear to a blind person that they'd made love last night. Prue glowed with the look of a woman in love, and Gideon had seen in the mirror while he shaved that his expression reflected the closely held pride of the man who'd made her love him.

He didn't feel guilty about the little charade because it was working so well. Prue seemed eminently happier than she'd been when he'd first arrived in Maple Hill, and God knew *he* was.

He was wearing the sports jacket over the black pants and turtleneck, and she was wearing the green wool dress, her hair caught up into a neat bun, just a few wispy lengths of hair trailing past her ears. Bruno, cameras finally ready, posed them in front of the statue of a man and woman clearly prepared to defend themselves from…judging by their period dress, Gideon guessed the British.

"Who are these two, anyway?" Gideon asked as Bruno made a few readjustments. His movements were swift but tense this morning, as though he was in a temper.

"Elizabeth and Caleb Drake," Prue replied. "They helped drive away the British."

Gideon laughed lightly. "At about that same time, there was a young woman living in the room I occupied at the inn who saved a wounded British soldier." He told her the story Jackie had told him. "She said they lived to raise eight children in that house."

"Love accomplishes big things," Prue whispered with a significant look.

She was trying to tell him something. "Do you want big things accomplished?" *Like our reconciliation?*

She admitted with a shy smile, "I'm confused about what I want. Are you okay with that?"

"There's a lot going on right now," he said, wrapping his arms around her as a cool wind whipped across the square. Flags and awnings fluttered and the tall trees whispered. "It's hard to be sure about anything."

Bruno came to position them with Gideon behind Prue. "You'll be just visible in the frame," he told him as he tipped Prue's chin up and told her to widen her stance. "As though giving her a clear field, but ready if she needs you. You, Prue, are invincible in your little green dress."

As Bruno walked back to his camera, Prue turned to grin at Gideon. "You okay back there?"

He grinned back. "I'm used to being four paces behind the princess."

Bruno shot the photo from several angles, then came back to reposition them. He drew Gideon forward and directed him to wrap his arms around Prue from behind. "Lean in so that I get your chin against her hair. Georgette wants to show off the unusual collar on the dress."

That was doable. Difficult, but doable. With his arms wrapped around Prue, he had her backside right against him where only sheer self-control kept his body in check. Prue, apparently comfortable, leaned back into him and wrapped her hands on his wrists.

"Perfect!" Georgette shouted. "Get that, Bruno."

He did.

Bruno moved them around the site, took more photos, then they finally packed everything back into the van and moved on to the Yankee Inn. It became even more clear in the van that something was wrong between Bruno and Justine. The couple who couldn't keep their hands off each other were now careful to avoid even eye contact.

At the inn, Georgette directed Gideon to remove the jacket and Prue to change into the caramel knit pants and vest over a white shirt.

The plan for the shot was a cozy night at home for two lovers. Bruno directed Prue to lie on her back on the sofa with Gideon sitting on the edge and leaning into her. But it was soon obvious that while it was romantic, the outfit, the object of the shot, was rendered invisible.

"Put Prue on top of Gideon," Justine suggested, rearranging a light behind the settee.

Bruno dismissed the idea until Georgette seconded it.

"You're probably the only man alive," Justine said under her breath to Bruno, "who can't appreciate a woman-on-top scenario."

Bruno gave her an injured and angry look. "I just think if we want to project this protective image," he said to Georgette, "he wouldn't let her block his movement by being on top of him."

"She weighs a hundred and ten pounds," Gideon put in reasonably. "I could have her out of my way in an instant. And with her on top of me, I haven't turned my back on what could be behind me."

"Let's try it," Georgette insisted.

Gideon exchanged places with Prue. He lay on his

back on the settee, his head resting on an opulent gold and burgundy pillow, one leg bent at the knee on the arm of the settee, the other propped on the floor.

Georgette came to pull the pins out of Prue's hair and let it fall to her shoulders. Gideon lay quietly, enjoying the unobstructed view of Prue's slender but nicely rounded hips, her shapely legs in the pants. Then her hair caught the glow of the fire, lit just for their shoot, and he was reminded vividly of several occasions when she'd come to him just this way, a small smile on her lips that said she wanted him and something in her eyes telling him she had no idea what was happening to their relationship.

He should have taken the time then, he knew now, to make her understand how important she was to him, how much he loved her. But he'd been enduring his own insecurities about his job and how difficult it was to affect the changes he'd hoped to accomplish. Instead of uncertainty in her eyes, he'd wanted to see confidence, belief in him. Each had been looking to the other for the strength and sense of security they lacked, but finding only more of the same.

He reached up to help her down to him as she put a knee on the settee and lowered her weight. The moment was delicious, the silk of her hair falling on his face, the softness of her body in the elegant fabric lying atop him. He lifted her by the waist to settle her comfortably.

As Bruno and Georgette argued over whether or

not they should be able to see Gideon's face, Prue smiled sweetly and kissed his lips.

"What was that for?" he asked.

She giggled. "I weigh a hundred and fourteen."

He laughed, unable to resist the impulse to kiss her again.

"Try a couple with his face hidden by her hair," Georgette directed. "We can see his hand on her, and in this scenario, that's even better."

It took an hour for everyone to be satisfied with the work. By then Gideon was nearly paralyzed with frustration while Prue seemed to sparkle. Bruno took several shots of her alone while she and Georgette carried on a running conversation about the knit, the body-hugging fit of it, the versatile color.

They were still talking when it was time to pack up. Bruno was throwing lenses into a camera bag with alarmingly little care for their vulnerability to damage. He pointed Justine to the lights behind the sofa.

"Get those," he ordered.

The lights were tall and hot, but she handled them with the skill of someone who set them up and took them down a dozen times in a day. As she fought a stand set particularly high and adjusted tightly, Gideon went to help her.

He'd watched Bruno make that adjustment when he'd been angry over Justine's woman-on-top remark.

"Let me get that," he said, taking it from her and loosening it. The pole slid into itself and she removed the light.

She smiled. "Thank you. The shot's going to be great."

He had to agree. "Prue looks good in everything."

She glanced at him as she packed the lights into a padded case. "I envy the way you two are together," she said with a sigh. "I suppose you've always been that way. Some relationships just fit better than others."

He ignored the irony of that statement. "Bruno seems to have a disposition that'd be hard for anyone to fit into."

She nodded. "Yes. The intense artist."

"The selfish egotist," he corrected. "Don't fool yourself into thinking that's a creative quality."

"Today was my fault," she said, taking the poles from him and tucking them into their fitted corner. "I entered a photo contest at home and got a call this morning telling me that I was a winner. I'll have to have a week off and he's upset about it."

It seemed criminal to Gideon that she should be made to feel guilty because she'd succeeded at something that made Bruno resentful. "If he's not happy for you that you've accomplished something wonderful," he said, taking the case from her as she would have lifted it, "then you should think twice about him."

She followed him with an electrical cord looped over her shoulder. "I'm beginning to come to that conclusion myself."

"I would *kill* for Chinese take-out," Georgette said

as they headed home. "Does that sound good to anybody? But I'm too pooped to decide between mu shu pork and kung pao chicken."

"I'll take you home," Gideon said, "and I'll come back for the food."

Bruno shook his head. "I think Justine and I'll go back to the room. I didn't sleep very well…"

"Chinese take-out sounds good to me," Justine interrupted with a casual smile in his direction. "Would it be a problem to take me back to the hotel later?" she asked Gideon.

"It'd be my pleasure," he assured her.

He dropped Bruno at the inn. Bruno gave one quick look over his shoulder at Justine and went inside.

"I want to know what happened between the two of you," Georgette said. "He's been like an angry wasp all day long."

Justine explained as Gideon headed back in the direction of the lake.

"You *won* that contest?" Prue asked. She and Justine sat in the second seat together. "We should have been celebrating today! That's wonderful!"

Georgette turned in her seat to add her congratulations. "Justine, that's marvelous. And I know that contest. It's very prestigious."

"I know, I was thrilled about it until Bruno got upset because it means I'll have to take a week off."

"Bruno got upset," Prue corrected, "because it means you have the potential to be as good as he is.

That's what he doesn't like. Well, I think that calls for mandarin duck.''

Gideon dropped everyone off at home, then returned to town with a long list of takeout to which they'd all contributed. He thought he'd add a bottle of champagne in honor of Justine's victory—over the contest and the stirrings of her liberation from Bruno.

He sat in the Chinese restaurant perusing a magazine while waiting for his order, when the door flew open and Paris rushed in.

''Hi!'' she said, throwing her arms around him. She was breathless and pink-cheeked. ''I saw your rental van in the lot and I wondered if you could save me the trip to your house with this stuff.'' She handed him a magazine and several envelopes.

''Sure,'' he replied. ''What is it?''

''It's Prue's mail. I thought it could just wait until…'' She hitched a shoulder, obviously unsure how to put it. ''Until your aunt goes home and the act is over. Until you two can decide what you're doing with your lives. Until you move on to Alaska and she goes home to Mom.''

''Okay,'' he said, taking the mail from her.

''I was going to deliver it,'' she said, ''but I got a call on the way. Somebody's late for the airport. I wouldn't have worried about it, but there's something there from a hospital. I had to sign for it.'' She frowned at him, seeming to slow down for a moment to focus on the question that presented itself. ''I didn't even know Prue had been in the hospital.''

He nodded, looking at the envelope with the hospital's return address. "She spent a few days there after that whole fiasco in Maine," he explained.

Paris gasped. "What happened?"

"The doctor wouldn't let me in," he said. "Her friend said Prue had suffered a nervous collapse."

"She never told me that! Or Mom."

"Yeah." He hated to think back to that time. "It was a rough period for her. She probably just didn't want to have to think about it again."

"Have you guys been able to talk about what happened in Maine?" Paris asked gently.

He nodded. "Actually, we have. And though we haven't really resolved anything, it's looking more hopeful than it has been."

She hugged him again. "That's what I wanted to hear. Gotta go, Gideon."

"Okay. I'll see that she gets the mail."

PRUE COULD NOT remember when she'd had a better time. Gideon had come back from town with a bottle of champagne as well as a veritable Chinese feast.

Justine told them about the photos she'd entered in the contest, about her dreams for the future, even shared a little about her disappointment over Bruno's attitude.

Georgette had stories about her various husbands, about life in Europe, and as they read their fortune cookies, she laughed over the prophetic nature of hers. "Keep your eyes open," it read. "The best part of life is still unfolding."

She smiled at Gideon and Prue. "That's true," she said. "I think I'll take your advice, Gideon, and see if your parents would mind if I spend some time at the vineyard. I've so enjoyed being involved in your lives. When the children start coming, I don't want to be too far away to watch them grow."

Children. Prue felt a fist of pain and tension develop in the pit of her stomach.

Gideon, topping up everyone's champagne, noticed the sudden change in her expression.

"What's wrong?" he asked, refilling her glass, then sitting beside her on the sofa. Justine and Georgette talked about working together on another project.

She shook off the mood and smiled. "Nothing. It was a long day and all the food and champagne has made me sleepy."

"You look sad," he argued quietly, "not sleepy."

She took a deep sip and leaned back, resting her elbow on his shoulder. "Well, it is sad, isn't it? The way two people start out loving each other, then somehow get lost to one another along the way? Like us. Like Bruno and Justine."

"Their only problem is his ego," he said. "You and I were a bit more complex than that. And that's kind of taken a favorable turn, don't you think?"

She nodded. "Yes. It's just that some things were lost that can't be reclaimed."

That startled him. It was something she'd never said before. He tried to imagine what she meant. Last night had felt to him as though all the love and passion they'd ever had flared to life between them.

But he had to remember that his responsibility in their breakup was that he hadn't listened to her, had been too engrossed in his own problems to notice hers.

"What have we lost that's unredeemable?" he asked.

"Oh, you know," she said, suddenly offhand, as though she'd become afraid of his attention. "Youth, I guess."

"You're not even thirty," he disputed. "And I'm thirty-four. Hardly time to be picking out assisted-living accommodations."

She nodded and sipped more champagne. "I know. I guess I'm talking about that first blush of your life together when everything's perfect."

He had a feeling she wasn't telling him the truth about what was bothering her, but he didn't want to press her. They weren't alone for one thing; and for another, what he felt for her was too complicated for him to explain to himself, much less to her. He could only hope she felt the same.

The party finally broke up with a toast to Justine's success, and her promise that whatever she decided about Bruno, she wouldn't let him get in the way of having her own career as a photographer.

Gideon prepared to drive Justine back to the inn,

then remembered the mail. He delved into his pocket and handed it to her. "Here's some reading material," he joked, "to keep you occupied while I take Justine home."

She looked surprised as she accepted the letters.

"Paris had to sign for the thing from the hospital," he explained, then told her how Paris had found him and asked him to take the mail home to her.

"Oh." He heard the slightest intake of her breath, then she smiled at him. "Thanks. I'm going to go up. I'm tired."

"Okay. I'll be right back."

She hugged Justine, then him, then disappeared upstairs.

Justine, newly excited about her win after being surrounded by loyal support all evening, seemed full of ideas about what to do with her future. Gideon walked her into the inn on the chance there was a problem with Bruno, but he'd already left for home and Jackie had saved the room.

Gideon returned home to find the downstairs darkened and quiet, except that the porch light had been left on for him. And a wall lamp at the top of the stairs left a small puddle of light to guide his way up.

He was happy to see Prue curled into herself on her side of the bed, though she appeared to be asleep, Drifter on his spot on the sofa bed. She'd seemed unlike herself tonight, and it had worried him. That was what came of lying, he told himself judiciously. He now found himself wondering if she'd find out that he'd orchestrated this cohabiting thing, and if it would make a difference to their reignited relationship.

He changed quickly out of his clothes, leaving on his briefs and T-shirt, and climbed into bed, careful not to wake her.

He was completely surprised when she turned toward him and settled into his shoulder. "Hi," she said sleepily, throwing the corner of the blanket over him.

"Hi," he replied, kissing the top of her hair. "I thought you were asleep."

"I want to be," she said, "but I heard you come in."

"Everything okay?" he asked.

"Yeah," she replied.

"What about the mail?"

"That was nothing," she answered, expelling a deep sigh. "Just my insurance company and the hospital haggling. G'night."

"Over your hospitalization last year? Or did something else happen?"

"Last year," she replied.

"You might want to explain that to Paris and your mom when you have a chance. Paris was worried that you'd been in the hospital."

"Okay. Good night, Gideon."

"Good night." It was clear she didn't want to talk about it, and that was fine. Neither did he. That nervous collapse, as her friend had called it, had taken an issue that should have been discussed immediately and put enough time and distance between them that misunderstanding festered and suspicion grew.

He pushed the thought away, happy that they might survive that difficult episode after all. There was no point in dwelling on how it should have been handled.

He was awake with the first shaft of light. Prue was still snuggled to his side, though she now had an arm hooked around his neck and a leg thrown over him. He loved the way that felt.

He slipped out from under her to go to the bathroom, then tried to decide whether to go back to bed for another half hour or put the coffee on and enjoy a few minutes of quiet solitude. Women were wonderful, but the constant discussion of clothes and accessories was beginning to get to him. And it was going to last another few days. Small price to pay, he decided, to have Prue within his reach.

He had decided on climbing back into bed with her, when she rolled over in her sleep, wrapped an arm around her pillow and snuggled her head deeper into it with a groan. He smiled at the action, thinking she was having trouble getting comfortable because he wasn't there, when he noticed the corner of a piece of paper sticking out from under her pillow, the white sharply visible against the gray flannel sheet.

Afraid she might hurt herself on the sharp edge, he pulled the paper easily out from under the pillow. It was a standard-size sheet of paper folded in three. Though the room was shadowy, he thought he saw the hospital logo that had been on the envelope Paris had brought over. What, he wondered, was it doing under her pillow?

Unable—and unwilling—to curb his curiosity, he went into the bathroom with it and turned on the light.

Under the hospital's logo was the simple word Statement. Just as she'd said, it was a bill from the hospital.

The charge was for a…he had to study the words twice.

PRUE AWOKE to bright sunlight on her face. The first sensory impression to reach her was the herbal fragrance of Gideon's cologne under her nose. She inhaled, all the images the smell evoked dancing in her mind. She stretched a hand out for him, smiling even before she opened her eyes.

His side of the bed was empty.

She listened for the sound of the shower, but the house was silent.

Maybe he was preparing breakfast. No. There was no smell of coffee and no sound of puttering in the kitchen.

Maybe he'd gone out for something—doughnuts, the paper.

Or maybe he'd just…gone.

She sat up suddenly, violently, her hair blinding her, her heart beating fast. Maybe his partner had called from Alaska. Maybe things were going together faster than he'd thought. Maybe now that he'd spent five days living with her, he remembered why he'd let her leave him in the first place.

Maybe she'd dreamed this whole scenario—him coming back, his aunt visiting, the photo shoot.

No. She saw the rustic walls of the A-frame she'd lived in for most of the past week. She hadn't dreamed it. She felt a great sense of relief.

Then she spotted him sprawled on the love seat on the other side of the room. He was dressed in cords and a black sweater, and the look in his eyes shattered her relief and frightened her anew. In his right hand was a piece of paper.

She drew a breath and clutched the blanket to her bosom, feeling the need for a shield. She knew he held the hospital statement. She remembered studying it more closely last night, then hiding it under her pillow when she heard him come in.

"Good morning," she whispered.

He didn't reply, apparently in no mood for civilized niceties.

He held up the paper. "I found this sticking out from under your pillow," he said. "I was afraid you'd open your eye on it and hurt yourself, so I removed it."

He waited for her to speak.

Refusing to feel guilty, she waited for him to go on.

"You told me it was your insurance company and the hospital warring over charges." He got up and came toward the bed, sitting on the edge of it and looking her in the eye. "You didn't tell me it was for a D & C."

Her throat closed and her eyes filled. It still astonished her how much that could hurt even a year after the fact. She didn't trust herself to speak.

"Granted, I don't know that much about procedures in the area of women's health," he went on quietly, "but isn't that often done when a woman's had a miscarriage?"

She sat up straighter. "Sometimes," she replied. She tossed her head, and the need to sob abated. "Sometimes it just helps in the case of other female complications."

He asked directly, "Was it for a miscarriage in this case?"

She looked away from him as the sob rose in her throat again, guilt surfacing in her despite her efforts to hold it off.

"Yes," she replied.

CHAPTER THIRTEEN

THIS WAS A GIDEON she hardly remembered from their four-year marriage. In the beginning, he'd been kind and funny, gentle and loving. Then, as time and pressure wore on both of them, he'd become impatient, occasionally distant, sometimes angry.

But the fury she saw in him now was something he saved for dishonest colleagues and self-serving lobbyists. He controlled it with a careful tone of voice, but it was very much alive in him.

"I suppose you have a good reason for not telling me you were carrying our baby?"

She tried to remember that this was understandably shocking to him, but she was also overwhelmed with all the feelings from that horrid time in her life, and she was in no mood to deal with his righteous indignation.

"That was why I wanted us to have that weekend in Maine."

She spoke in a very controlled tone, a fact that surprised her, considering she didn't seem to be able to draw in any air. "I had bought booties to hide in your slippers, but things didn't work out as I'd planned."

Volley successful. Guilt in his court. He closed his eyes in acceptance of how that scene had played out, then opened his eyes again and pinned her with a dark glance.

"So, the nervous collapse was a miscarriage?"

The old hurt stabbed right through her. Lost him, lost the baby, lost everything.

"Yes."

"And you were comfortable punishing me that way?"

Her control snapped like a strained cable on a bridge. "Punishing *you?*" she screamed at him. "I was the one who thought I might be able to get through the rest of your term with a baby to keep me company. You were the one who didn't even have enough time to give me to find out you were going to be a father!"

He withstood her shrieks, then dismissed them all with a shake of his head. "How could you not have told me that you lost our baby?"

Guilt back to her. She'd lived with this one a while, but she'd managed to explain it to herself. "Because I thought you had someone else."

"If you'd let me explain it to you," he said grimly, "you'd have learned that I didn't."

"I only knew what I saw."

"And I only knew what you told me. Nothing. No clue that I was going to be a father, that we were going to be a family."

She shook her head, tears falling, guilt winning.

"After the miscarriage, telling you about it would have only looked like a ploy to get you back."

He exploded to his feet at that, jamming his hands in his pockets as though afraid they might reach for her of their own accord. "And my knowing the truth wasn't more important than whether or not you looked needy?"

"I shouldn't have had to lose a baby to get your attention!" she yelled. Then she raised the blanket to her mouth as sobs came in painful gulps.

He stood there for a moment, then grabbed his jacket off the chair and stormed out of the room.

Prue fell back to her pillow and turned into it, crying out all the pain of that horrible time and all the regret of the intervening year. She felt Georgette's cool hand on her forehead, nodded at her suggestion of a bracing cup of tea, then collapsed again the moment she was gone, hating what had happened.

She had hoped never to feel that pain again. And she'd hoped never to have to inflict it on Gideon.

GIDEON HAD NO IDEA where he was going, he just got into his truck and drove. It crossed his mind that Georgette and Bruno intended to take pictures today, that Georgette was paying for the photographer's time and it was precious, even if the man wasn't.

He had to pull himself together, remember how horrible and confused that time had been, and try to understand how Prue could not have told him.

But her not telling him the truth had been mean

and small and deliberately hurtful. Anger coursed through his veins and darkened his perception.

He found himself in the parking lot of the Breakfast Barn, but he sat behind the wheel, unable to get out of the truck. His stomach was growling, but food had little appeal. He wanted to punch and kick. He'd have given anything to have the purse snatcher come back.

He finally got out of the truck, but went in the direction of the stream that ran alongside the lot rather than toward the restaurant. The trees on the other side of it were bright red and gold in fall dress, though the water trickled musically as though it was still summer.

He took a breath of the sweet air and drew it as deeply into his lungs as possible, as if he was preparing for a confrontation. But the moment he got the anger under control, the sadness took over. He'd had a child and lost it.

He imagined Prue pregnant with his baby. In the old days, that thought had been on his mind often, but they'd never conceived and the pressures of the job became such that he'd thought that was probably a good thing until there were better days.

Right beside the sadness surfaced a terrible guilt. Prue had been pregnant and he hadn't even noticed? Of course, if she'd just been about to announce it to him, she couldn't have been very far along, but still... Had she been sick? Had she craved strange foods? Had she been emotional and he'd completely missed it?

Well, she'd always been emotional, so that would be a hard indicator to go by. But there must have been some signs that had gone right by him.

"Hey."

He turned in surprise at the sound of a familiar voice. It was Randy in jeans and a gray sweatshirt. He apparently was off duty today.

"What are you doing out here?" Randy asked. He was looking him over, Gideon noticed, like a mother—or a doctor. He hooked a thumb over his shoulder. "Food's in there."

Gideon tried to smile but it didn't quite work. "I'm not really hungry."

"You're in the parking lot of a *restaurant*," Randy pointed out.

Gideon nodded in self-deprecation. "Sorry. It's not a day for making sense."

Randy seemed to suddenly understand. "Woman trouble," he guessed. He slapped Gideon's shoulder and pushed him toward the Barn. "Come on. I'll buy you a high-cholesterol omelette and you can tell me all about it."

"I don't understand what's going on well enough to talk about it," Gideon grumbled. "But coffee sounds good."

"Keeping us confused is a woman's stock-in-trade," Randy said as they stood just inside the double doors. He pointed to an empty booth by the window and led the way there. Rita was on them in an instant with menus, two coffee cups and the pot.

She frowned at Gideon as he sat opposite Randy. "You look a little green. Want some dry toast and a soft-boiled egg?"

"A waffle?" Randy suggested. "Not too hard on the stomach but gives you something to go on."

Gideon nodded. "A waffle, please, Rita."

"All right." She scribbled on her pad, then turned to Randy. "And you, I suppose, are having sausage and eggs?"

He smiled at her and handed back the menu. "You understand me, Rita. I'm getting married in three days. If you're going to make a move on me, the time is now."

She sighed regretfully. "Inviting as that sounds, I respect the strength of the O'Hara sisters. I wouldn't want to answer to either of them. You'll just have to go through with the wedding and pine for me afterward."

Randy sighed theatrically. "You ask a lot of me, Rita."

She whopped him on the shoulder with the menus. "That's what a woman does, Band-Aid Boy. Keeps a man on his toes."

As she walked away, Randy laughed. "So, there you have it directly from one of the women who knows everything. Don't get between the O'Hara sisters and what they want." His laughter turned suddenly to a worried frown. "Tell me you didn't try to do that."

"Well, not on purpose," Gideon replied, sipping

the hot coffee. It was strong and delicious but too hot to guzzle as he needed to. He added a little cream. ''I found out something she'd kept from me,'' he said, watching the cream swirl into the coffee with a new fascination for things that didn't matter. Things that *did* seem to pose problems that had no solutions.

''Well, that sounds familiar. Go on.''

Gideon didn't know how much to share. Randy was a nice guy, though he didn't know him well, but Prue hadn't even told her sister about the miscarriage and Randy was about to marry Paris. Still, he seemed levelheaded and compassionate and completely trustworthy.

''Prue hasn't told Paris or Camille about this,'' he said on a warning note. ''So it has to stay between us.''

Randy nodded. ''No problem with that.''

''Okay.'' He started with the background of what had happened in Maine.

Randy nodded. ''Right. Heard all that.''

''Okay. Well, what Prue doesn't seem to have told anyone is that she'd wanted to spend that weekend in Maine with me to tell me she was pregnant. When I couldn't go because of the investigation I couldn't tell *her* about, she went anyway and that's when she saw me with Claudia Hackett.''

''Geez,'' Randy said.

''Yeah. When she ran back to Albany and I followed...'' Gideon told him the rest.

''Dear God.'' Gideon leaned against the back of

the booth and closed his eyes. "I don't know if I'm more angry at myself for being completely unaware of her pregnancy, or at her for not telling me she'd lost the baby."

"Did she explain why she didn't tell you?"

"Yes," Gideon replied grimly. "Because it would have looked like a ploy to get me back."

"Oh, boy."

Gideon put both hands to his eyes, grief and anger connecting to form a biting pain in the middle of his chest. "You know what the worst thing is?"

"What?"

"I wonder if she lost the baby because of the shock of what she saw. Even though it was innocent on my part and she misinterpreted what she saw, she thought I'd destroyed our lives together—and lost the baby almost immediately after that." The pain ground into him like an auger digging a hole in his stomach.

Randy pushed his coffee toward him. "Drink some of that."

The coffee had cooled to a drinkable temperature and Gideon took a deep sip, feeling the hot caffeine burn a line down through the pain to reach his stomach and gain his bloodstream.

Their food arrived and they leaned back to give Rita space as she placed their plates, dropped extra butter, several kinds of syrup, hot sauce and ketchup on the table.

"I'll be right back with more coffee," she said.

Gideon looked at his waffle with complete loss of appetite.

"Okay, listen," Randy said, leaning toward him over his steaming plate. "I wouldn't go blaming yourself for the miscarriage without more facts. I'm an EMT and I can tell you that ten to fifteen percent of pregnancies are lost in the first eight weeks, and three percent in the twenty weeks after that. It's often hard to explain why, it just happens. While it's true that the whole Maine thing was a shock to Prue, women have carried babies successfully through the most incredible conditions and against odds that seemed insurmountable. I think a baby's destined to live to birth, or it's not."

Gideon studied Randy's face, trying to decide if he was being honest or telling him whatever he thought would make him feel better.

"It's true," Randy said, reading his mind. "And to prove that I wouldn't sugarcoat anything for you, I'll tell you that Prue seems just like Paris when it comes to matters of pride and determination. She thought you'd cheated on her, so she endured the loss of your baby alone rather than let you think she'd use it to gain sympathy. Look what Paris did to me when she thought I didn't want a family."

Gideon nodded. "I'm just wondering how you live a lifetime with a woman like that. First, she wouldn't believe me, then she wouldn't tell me the truth. I can't get on the winning end of the situation."

Randy smiled grimly. "That's because you're deal-

ing with an O'Hara sister. Their mother was a star—
still is. Paris thought she didn't have that center-stage
quality and tried to live it down, but she found herself
on a runway in Prue's fashion show and the town
went wild. Prue, on the other hand, has star quality.
You only have to meet her once to know it. She's
probably convinced that she has the power, and the
right even, to manipulate the lives of the people she
loves, to work things out the way she thinks they
should be.''

"Okay," Gideon agreed, "but this wasn't what
kind of furniture to buy or where to go on a vacation.
This was the loss of our child!''

"I know. But my guess is she was too grief-
stricken herself to think straight. I'd give her the benefit of the doubt."

Gideon closed his eyes, letting that possibility sink
in. It sounded plausible. He was surprised that it
hadn't occurred to him. Possibly he was too grief-
stricken himself at the moment to have thought that
through. But he couldn't get over the notion that she
lost the baby because of him. Maybe he could forgive
her, but could he forgive himself?

"Eat up," Randy advised. "Sounds like you're going to need your strength."

Giving Prue a generous motive for her behavior
eased his mind a little and relaxed him sufficiently to
allow him to eat the waffle.

"WELL, YOU'D THINK he'd have sufficient consideration for the rest of us," Bruno said, pacing the liv-

ing-room floor, "to either be punctual or let us know whether or not to cancel the shoot."

Prue, sitting in a wing chair in the living room, her knees folded up against her chest to ease her misery, heard Bruno's complaint for the fourth time with growing impatience.

"I've explained over and over that we had a quarrel, and it really isn't his fault. He needed to walk it off, or drive it off, or whatever he's doing. He'll be back. He wouldn't leave us in the lurch." She'd listened to Bruno's complaints through the breakfast of fruit and French toast that Justine and Georgette had prepared.

Bruno rolled his eyes. "Personal issues shouldn't affect business."

"This isn't *business,*" Justine said, coming out of the kitchen with a cup of tea for Prue, who hadn't been able to eat anything. "This is photography. It's an art. It's better served by emotion and drama."

He expelled an impatient breath. "Oh, little miss contest winner now knows all about photography."

"That's it!" Georgette sprang to her feet and said to Justine, "Can you finish this job?"

Justine straightened, the steaming teacup still in her hand, her eyes wide with surprise. "Finish it? You mean…"

"I mean take the photographs," Georgette demanded.

Justine blinked once, handed Prue the tea, then nodded. "Yes," she said. "I can."

"Good." Georgette turned to Bruno. "You're fired, Bruno."

Bruno went white, then red. "We have a contract," he reminded her flatly.

"I'll pay you for the whole shoot," Georgette said. "And if you'll leave the film you've already shot, and your cameras so we can finish the job, I'll give you thirty percent more. Someone will bring your cameras back to you. This will only take us a couple of days."

Bruno squared his shoulders. "You're making a mistake. She has no experience…"

"She has heart," Georgette said, "and she's not continually treating everyone like underlings. Can we keep the work you've done and borrow your cameras?"

"No one uses my cameras." Bruno began to pack up his things, but tossed Georgette several rolls of film.

"It's all right, Georgette," Justine said with a smile. "There's a photo studio in town. I'll go talk to them. If I can get one good camera and a tripod, we're in business."

Georgette raised an eyebrow. "You're sure?"

"I'm sure. Fancy equipment is nice, but I can make do without it. I won the contest with a 35mm Minolta."

"This isn't a contest," Bruno argued, stacking his things by the door, "with a bunch of sympathetic judges wanting to give some wide-eyed newbie her big chance. This is business. If your photos aren't superior, this ad campaign is going nowhere.''

''Bruno, darling, you forget that I own the company,'' Georgette said. ''And I'm sure Justine's going to do a brilliant job.'' Georgette handed Prue her cell phone. ''Call your sister's cab and see if she can take Bruno and his cameras to the airport.''

''I'll drive him,'' Justine said, ''if I can use the van.''

''I'd rather take the cab,'' Bruno huffed.

He was gone in ten minutes.

Prue gave Justine the van keys Gideon had left on the dresser. ''Go talk to the photo studio about a camera,'' she asked. ''If that doesn't work, I know the woman who owns the *Maple Hill Mirror*. She might be able to help.''

Justine nodded. ''All right. Is it okay if I throw your name around?''

Prue laughed. ''The photographer's wife did order my little black dress. Tell him she can have it for nothing if he'll rent us his cameras.''

''I'll come along,'' Georgette volunteered. ''When subtle courtesy doesn't work, I've learned to browbeat.''

Prue was putting a load of laundry in the washer, Drifter sitting in front of the bathroom's heating vent, when Gideon came home. He looked tired and hurt, as though all the wit and energy with which he usually bristled had been sucked out of him.

They stood at opposite ends of the long living room, she with her arms full of towels. She opened her mouth to try to explain why she hadn't told him about losing the baby, and simply couldn't organize the thought. It had made sense once, but it didn't seem to any longer.

He raised both arms halfway in a gesture of help-lessness.

"I'm sorry," he said, shocking her out of her speechlessness.

"For what?" she asked, hugging the towels.

He seemed surprised that she'd asked the question. "Because you lost the baby. Because it was probably the shock of opening the door and seeing Claudia with me that did it."

She was horrified that he seemed absolutely sin-cere. She tried to remember their conversation earlier, wondering what she'd said that had prompted him to believe the miscarriage was his fault. Then she re-called that she'd put forth the story that her stay in the hospital had been because of a nervous collapse, and she'd been happy to let him think he'd been re-sponsible for that. But the miscarriage was another story.

She tossed the towels into a corner and walked halfway toward him, stopping when he made no move toward her. "The miscarriage wasn't your fault," she insisted. "The doctor said that sometimes it just hap-pens. That there was probably something wrong that would have been a problem later, and it's best just to believe that nature knows what it's doing.'' Her throat tightened when she remembered how she'd felt hearing that. ''It's no comfort, of course. Nothing is. But I never considered you responsible.''

He drew a breath that caught in his chest. He coughed and folded his arms. ''I still feel responsible. We had a baby when you went to Maine, but when you left, we lost it.''

''I never considered it your fault,'' she said again, and took a few steps closer to him. He still made no move toward her. ''In fact…I think a lot of the reason I didn't tell you is that the miscarriage made me feel like a failure. As though I'd done something wrong that made me lose the baby. Maybe I shouldn't have driven all that way. I didn't feel well and I was tired.''

''That's ridiculous.'' He dropped his arms and took a step toward her. ''How can you blame yourself?''

She shrugged, all that old guilt coming back, filling her eyes with tears and clogging her throat. ''I guess when you can't explain something bad, you try to blame somebody for it. And I was the one carrying her…''

He took another step closer, his eyes darkening. ''It was a girl?''

''No.'' She wrung her hands. ''I don't know. It was too soon to tell. I just felt it was a girl. She was Lisa. Princess Prue II.''

He closed the gap between them and took her into his arms. She clung to him, crying out all the grief she'd borne alone at the time. The event was frighteningly fresh now as she explained it all to him, but his arms around her, the pain in his voice, somehow helped ease hers.

"I'm so sorry," he whispered again.

"I know. I am, too."

IT DIDN'T SEEM to matter that Prue had absolved him of guilt in the loss of their baby, or that Randy had tried to explain that it was often impossible to tell why a fetus was lost without warning. Gideon knew only that he'd had a child he hadn't known about, and Prue had lost it after the shock of finding him with Claudia.

He had to make up to Prue in some small way for all the heartache she'd endured alone. And at the moment, the only way he could do that was to help her with this ad campaign. If it was successful, she would have everything she'd ever wanted. She'd lived all of their married life devoted to his job as a New York State senator. The least he could do now was dedicate the next few days to her.

He couldn't see beyond that time. He couldn't imagine them living in harmony the rest of their lives with the death of their child between them. So he pushed the future out of his mind and focused on the present.

"Did you have something to eat?" he asked, leading her into the kitchen.

"I wasn't hungry," she said, "but Georgette and

Justine made French toast for themselves and Bruno. What about you? Want me to fix you something?''

''I ate with Randy at the Barn,'' he said, reaching into the refrigerator for the strawberries they'd bought the other day. ''How about a bowl of berries? You always used to like that. With some yogurt?''

''Okay.'' She went to the cupboard for two bowls. ''Did you call him?'' she asked.

He explained about running into him there as he poured the berries into a colander and washed them. ''We commiserated about being married to the O'Hara sisters.''

''Mmm.'' She smiled, making a disgruntled sound. ''He's not even married yet and he's complaining about Paris?''

''Not at all,'' he corrected, finding a knife, hulling the berries and cutting them up into the bowls. ''He adores her. Where is everybody, incidentally? Where's the van?''

''Bruno's on his way back to London,'' she said with a wide grin. ''Georgette fired him when he kept grumbling about you being gone. And she and Justine went to the photo studio to see if they could borrow some cameras so we can still shoot today.''

''Aunt George fired Bruno because I was gone?''

''Because he kept complaining that you were gone, even after I explained that we'd quarreled over something important and you needed time. Then Justine came to your defense, he climbed all over her, so Georgette fired him.'' She spooned berry-flavored yogurt onto the strawberries. "It was glorious. You should have been here."

"So…Justine's going to do the shoot?" He carried the bowls to the table and Prue followed with spoons.

"Yes. And I bet she'll do a great job. Georgette seems convinced she will."

"Well, good. Eat up so the color in those berries gets into your cheeks. You look a little pale at the moment."

She picked up her spoon, but looked at him with blue eyes dark with concern. "So you've forgiven me for not telling you about the miscarriage?"

"It's hard to blame you," he said, "for anything that happened."

"Then we're agreed that, though you worked too hard and I behaved like a princess, neither one of us is responsible for the loss of the baby?"

He *wasn't* agreed, but he didn't want to do anything that would thwart the photo sessions.

"Right," he replied simply. Then he grinned at her to get rid of that frown on her forehead. "So eat, then do something about your hair. It's scary."

She swatted his arm, but the frown line dissolved as she smiled. "Thank you. That'll make me smile for the camera."

Drifter leaped up onto the table. Prue put him down on the floor, going to the cupboard to get his tuna.

"How long does Drifter stay when he comes home?" she asked. "Did Hank say?"

Gideon shook his head. "As long as he feels welcome, I guess. Isn't that what keeps us all in place?"

CHAPTER FOURTEEN

GIDEON WASN'T FOOLING her for a minute. He was harboring bad feelings about this morning, and she couldn't tell if he was angry at her, though he continually denied it, or if he was blaming himself despite her insistence that he shouldn't. Something was wrong.

All she could think to do was pretend as he was doing, probably for the sake of the shoot, that everything was all right. When she understood the problem, she could take more appropriate action.

Justine and Georgette returned home with a camera, film and a tripod, and several other pieces of equipment the helpful Douglas Helm of Helm Portraits had refused to rent but allowed them to borrow. Georgette grinned broadly. "We're on our way, and I'll wager we won't miss Bruno one bit."

They shot a Prudent Designs burgundy pantsuit in the Perk Avenue Tea Shop, Gideon also in a suit, studying a sheaf of papers between them on the table. The decadent stuffed croissants on their plates provided an interesting counterpoint to the "business meeting" set.

Prue sat sideways at the table so that the suit was visible.

"Put a little cream from the filling on her chin, Gideon," Georgette advised, "then flick it off with your finger for the photo."

Gideon did as she suggested, teasing Prue in a whisper as he leaned closer to remove the cream with his index finger. "She obviously doesn't know what a tidy eater you are. You're the only one I know who can crack crab without a paper bib."

She'd forgotten about that. He was referring to a cookout at his family's home when they'd been short one bib, and his father had tried to give her his because she'd been wearing a new white sundress. She'd refused, insisting that he had to protect the shirt she and Gideon had brought him back from their honeymoon in Hawaii. His mother had wanted to wrap a simple tea towel around her, but it had turned into a wager to see if she could get through the meal without spotting her dress.

Gideon, she remembered, had put his money on her. "The princess," he told his family, "never gets a spot on anything."

She'd won the bet, she recalled, and he'd rewarded her with a long night of lovemaking.

She could see in his eyes that he was remembering the same thing.

Georgette's face suddenly appeared between them. "Shot's over," she said emphatically, as though this wasn't the first time she'd said it. "It would save time if you two didn't zone out to that place you go to every time you look into each other's eyes. Up, up. We're going into the kitchen.''

"Did you clear that with the ladies?'' Prue asked worriedly.

"Got their approval while you were making googly eyes. Come on.''

The four of them spent half an hour in the kitchen with Cecilia Proctor and Bridget Malone, the two sisters-in-law who owned the tea shop. They were middle-aged and lively, and ended up in several of the shots. They sent a box of pastries with them when they left.

"How's the camera working?'' Georgette asked Justine as Gideon drove them into the Berkshires.

"Beautifully,'' Justine replied. "I think this whole thing is going to work.''

Gideon drove an hour into the wooded hills until Georgette spotted an aesthetically perfect grouping of flame-leaved trees.

"There!'' she said, pointing to a grove of maples that were so beautifully shaped and colored they might have been placed there specifically for the purposes of Prudent Designs ad campaign.

Gideon pulled off the road.

Justine pointed to a low branch heavy with giant red and gold leaves. "We'll put you right under that branch, Prue, so that it frames the top of the photograph.''

Prue pulled the cloak on over the suit she still wore,

while Georgette fussed with her hair. "Hair up or down?" she asked Justine.

"We'll do some of each. And hood up and hood down, so we can see what looks most dramatic."

"All right."

Gideon pulled on his alpaca overcoat and they went to stand together under the tree while Justine set up.

"I'm thinking it's a clandestine rendezvous," Georgette said. "Gideon's come to rescue you from a cruel husband." She pulled the hood up over the updo she still wore from the "business meeting" in the tea shop.

Something flickered in Gideon's eyes at the cruel-husband remark. Prue wasn't sure what the look meant—a flare of guilt, maybe. Curiously, his insistence on being responsible for her miscarriage made her hurt for him as much as she hurt herself.

"Paris said the cloak made her feel like a smuggler," she told Georgette to distract him.

Georgette flicked lint off her shoulder. "We've got a protective scenario going here, and it's working. You can be a smuggler with a cruel husband, if you want." She turned her attention to Gideon and pulled up the collar of his coat. "If you could re-create the look you had in your eye at the tea shop, that'd be good." She stepped back and went to sight through the lens with Justine.

"It's going well even without Bruno, don't you think?" Prue asked.

Gideon nodded. "I do. And this is a breathtaking

setting.'' He looked around at the beauty of the trees against the bright blue sky, an afternoon wind blowing leaves all around them as though they were charmed. It reminded him of their place in Maine.

''It makes me think of walking out the kitchen door of the summerhouse.'' She looked wistful. ''Remember when I dried all those leaves and made a mobile for the stairway that we left up all year?''

He remembered that very well. They'd made love under it once on the landing. They'd been teasing about the first to use the shower and she'd taken off at a run for the upstairs bathroom, and he'd tackled her on the landing.

A frown appeared between her eyes. ''When *was* that?'' she asked.

''What do you mean?''

''What year of our marriage?''

He had to think about that. ''Ah…the last year, I think. It seems to me we were getting ready for a dinner party with the Watsons. And he worked with me on the budget crisis, which was in my last year.''

Her gaze remained unfocused as she thought back.

''Why?'' he asked. ''What does it matter?''

''I was just…remembering…how warm and wonderful that time was,'' she said quietly, refocusing on his face. ''I have this picture of the last three years of our marriage being difficult and filled with contention, but…we had some very good times.''

Her lip trembled dangerously.

''We did,'' he agreed, looking worriedly toward

Justine and Georgette, but they were still sighting through the camera lens. "But I was working too hard, and you were feeling insecure. I think worry is stronger in memory than happiness."

She said nothing, but looked up at the spray of leaves over her head, her mouth still unsteady. She reached up for a particularly large, brightly colored leaf, but a gust of wind lifted the branch out of her reach.

Gideon raised a hand and snapped the leaf off the branch. "Here," he said, eager to do anything to chase away whatever thought was about to make her cry. "You going to start another mobile?"

She twirled the leaf in her fingers and drew a breath, the dangerous moment passed. "Unfortunately, we don't have a landing."

"We have a vaulted ceiling."

She smiled into his eyes, and he thought he saw the old affection for him in them. "Yes, we do."

"You guys ready?" Justine called from across the small clearing.

Prue sighed and squared her shoulders, turning toward him for the sake of the camera. "In my next life," she said with a wry smile, "remind me not to model my designs in an ad campaign while trying to restore my marriage at the same time."

He'd wanted to restore their marriage, but now that he knew about the miscarriage, it was planted firmly in the forefront of his mind, casting a shadow over his plans. He'd lost a baby he hadn't even known he

was having. What kind of husband and father had he
been, could he ever be?

But Prue looked stressed and vaguely upset and
he'd promised himself he'd get her through this shoot.

"You have to lighten up," he said, tucking his
hand inside her hood to cup her cheek. "For today,
pretend we are this couple meeting on the sly in the
woods because we're willing to risk anything to be
together."

Her hands went to the chest of his coat. She smiled
and tossed her head, seemingly willing to play the
game.

"Where are you taking me?" she asked.

"To my plantation in South Carolina."

"Really. And how did a Yankee like me meet up
with a Southern gentleman like yourself?"

"I came North to sell my cotton to your husband.
He runs a mill, you know."

"Ah." She giggled. "I'd forgotten that."

"We met at a party."

She smiled at the fantasy. He heard Justine clicking
away. He had to continue the story.

"Did you fall in love with me the moment you saw
me?" Prue asked.

"Yes. But you were married and I had to go home.
We were separated for a year."

She stared at him wide-eyed, ensnared by the tale.

"Then I came back," he added.

"Why?"

"Because a mutual friend wrote me that your husband mistreated you. I'm taking you home with me to show you what love and marriage can be like when it's right.''

"But…the law?"

He sighed, the character he'd assumed bored by the suggestion that the law could confine him. ''It doesn't exist for me. I'm a law unto myself.''

She smiled indulgently. "Surely you know that loving me will change that for you. I'm used to the pleasures of Boston. I'll want fine clothes and pretty things.'' She frowned. ''I could be trouble on a plantation.''

He shook his head. ''You'll be so grateful to be loved and treated well that you'll be happy and adoring and do everything I ask.''

She leaned into him, laughing, and he swore that for those few moments she'd forgotten entirely that there was a camera on them.

''Prue, drop the hood and take your hair down!'' Georgette called.

Prue rolled her eyes and handed him the leaf. ''They will insist on bursting our bubble.'' She lowered the hood and undid her hair, then Georgette handed her a brush. She pointed to a trail.

''We're going up there to shoot the two of you walking toward us. Okay? You're doing great. We got some spectacular shots this time. And keep the leaf. That's a nice touch.''

Georgette and Justine headed up the trail, and Prue brushed out her hair, then turned to him, the silky cloud of it gleaming in the sunlight, rippling with the breeze.

"There better be a big pot of spaghetti at the end of that trail," she said with practical sincerity, unconsciously looping her arm in his, playing with the leaf with the fingers of her other hand. "Do you have spaghetti in South Carolina?"

"Ah…I think we're big on ham, sweet potatoes and collard greens."

"But I want spaghetti."

"You warned me you were going to be demanding."

They walked up the trail talking nonsense, the wind blowing down the corridor of trees and sending leaves flying.

"Do you think we'd still be together," she asked with sudden seriousness, "if I'd stopped in the doorway and listened to your explanation?"

The question surprised him and forced a reality on him he didn't want to deal with at the moment.

"I guess it depends on whether or not you'd have believed me."

"There was a naked woman in your lap."

"That's what I mean. It would have taken a lot of faith in me and our marriage."

She sighed. He felt her grip on his arm tighten. "I think I believed in you," she said after a moment. "But we'd spent so little time together those last few months that I sort of forgot everything that went before."

She stopped abruptly in the middle of the trail. He had to retrace a step. "I don't think it was a deliberate thing on my part, but being adored was so much a part of my identity. When I no longer had that, I...maybe...lost faith in myself." She thought that through, as though coming to a new clarity about the situation. "Maybe it wasn't you I doubted, but me."

In the last ten hours or so, her miscarriage had absolved her in his mind of any responsibility for anything.

"Any woman would have probably reacted in the same way," he said. "And we've beaten that subject to death, anyway. Let's just let it go."

"But...it's the root of the problem," she insisted, her expression urgent. "The wall between us."

"I'm not aware of a wall," he said, surprised to find that he meant that.

She gasped. "You aren't?"

"No." He put an arm around her shoulders and indicated Justine ahead of them encouraging them to come toward her as she looked through the viewfinder.

Nothing separated them but his own inability to reconcile his responsibility in the loss of their baby.

PRUE SAUTÉED onions and celery in olive oil for spaghetti sauce. Georgette rested and Justine went to the portrait studio's lab to make a contact sheet for the day's work.

When they'd finally finished for the day, Gideon

closed himself upstairs to work on the security plan for Hank Whitcomb while Prue tried to relax in the kitchen. She and Gideon had reached a mature connection they'd never quite accomplished when they were married, yet she felt him drifting away from her despite the love in his eyes, the tenderness of his touch, the insistence that there was no wall between them.

He was right, though, she thought. It wasn't a wall but a chasm—a long trench that extended from the moment she'd opened the door in Maine and across the past year to the present. They understood each other better than they ever had, seemed able to accept their share of the guilt for their breakup, yet the coming together that would be the natural result of such an epiphany wasn't happening. There was no animosity, no disagreement, just a giant hole where reconciliation should have been.

She added a bottle of spaghetti sauce to the onions and celery and turned down the heat, then tried to remember where she'd stored the angel-hair pasta. She tried several cupboards, the drawer under the silverware, a corner of the counter where she'd grouped several tins. She checked them all, forgetting what she'd stored in them. No angel-hair.

Drifter watched her primly from behind his bowl, his eyes widening when her search grew more desperate.

She slammed cupboard doors as she started over, the need to find the pasta making her feel frantic.

She stood on a kitchen chair, searching behind canned goods and boxes, then stepped onto the counter to see in the back of the top shelf, when she heard a loud crash behind her. She turned carefully in her stocking feet to see Drifter sitting near the overturned chair. He'd probably leaped onto it and knocked it over.

She was marooned.

It was the last straw in a weirdly emotional day. Nothing was going the way she wanted—except the shoot. That seemed to be progressing well. But if she didn't resolve her relationship with Gideon and did decide to move her operation to New York, she'd probably never see him again. He'd go to Alaska, file for divorce, and they'd communicate through their attorneys and live the rest of their lives apart.

She began to cry.

LIFE WITH PRUE had always had a curious skew to it. Gideon had gotten used to her unpredictable reactions and curious behavior. But when he ran downstairs to investigate a lethal-sounding crash and found her standing on the kitchen counter in her stocking feet, her face contorted in tears, he considered it a new high in eccentricity.

Then he saw the cat, the overturned chair, and figured out what had happened. Except for the tears.

"You're looking for high tea?" he teased, approaching her with care. She looked both upset and volatile.

"Ha, ha!" she snapped at him, folding her arms when he would have reached up for her to help her down. She turned away from him with her chin in the air as though she was on a street corner waiting for a bus.

"I was looking for the pasta," she wept. "Only I can't find it because I don't remember where I put it." Then she added in a loud, angry whisper, leaning down toward him for emphasis, "Because I don't *really live here!*"

He raised his hands to catch her, certain she'd overbalance. But she didn't. She turned away from him on her narrow perch. "I should never have agreed to this."

"But it's working," he pointed out, wondering what was going on in her mind. "You're going to become a household name among best-dressed women."

"Is that all my life's ever going to be about? Clothes?"

He frowned up at her. "I thought that was what you wanted."

"So did I." She sniffed and leaned back against the upper cupboard, looking up at the ceiling in dismay. "I love designing, but it doesn't make up for everything else like I thought it would. It doesn't make up for my mistakes—or yours. It doesn't make up for the fact that you couldn't trust my discretion enough to tell me what you were doing about Senator Crawford, and the fact that I didn't have enough faith in our marriage to believe you when you tried to explain. It doesn't make up for the loneliness or the disappointment or the sense of failure I feel because I lost a baby and a husband in the same week.''

''Now you're just willfully torturing yourself.'' He caught her around the thighs and let her fall over his shoulder, then deposited her on her feet. ''What's the matter with you? You can't blame yourself. That's what you keep telling me, and I have more reason to feel responsible than you do.''

''You're withdrawing from me,'' she snapped at him, ''because you feel responsible. Or it's a handy reason if you just don't want to be with me. I think we both behaved badly. We both want to assume guilt for our baby's loss because we think that'll somehow make us feel better or make the situation better. But it doesn't! I don't want to think we've just screwed it up so badly it *can't* be made better. Can't we just forgive each other and start over?''

He liked that thought, he just wasn't sure how practical it was.

''I mean,'' she cajoled, putting a hand to his chest, her eyes dark with emotion, ''you did all this for me.'' She spread her arms to indicate their surroundings. ''You let your aunt believe we were still married so she'd do the shoot for me. You brought me back into your life just to help me out. That was openhearted and generous.'' He held her gaze while wondering if she could see in his eyes the plotting that had gone into this. She apparently caught sight of something and squared her shoulders. He waited breathlessly for her to question his motives. "Unless you've regretted having me here?" she asked.

He wrapped his arms around her and pulled her close to reassure her that he did not regret it—as well as to prevent her from seeing the relief in his eyes. "The warming drawer under the oven," he said.

She looked up at him in confusion. "Pardon me?"

"The pasta. It's in the warming drawer under the oven. You bought that really long stuff that didn't fit anywhere else."

"That's right!" She pulled out of his arms and went to retrieve it. "I thought I was going insane!"

A loud rap sounded on the door and Gideon went to answer it. Paris and Randy stood there arm in arm. Prue came to the door at the sound of their voices.

"Hi, guys!" She hugged her sister, then Randy, and drew them inside. "What's going on? Is everything okay?"

"Everything's great," Paris said. "But I need something borrowed for the wedding. And I wanted to make sure you found something to wear." She went to the wing chair where Drifter had resettled. "When did you get a cat?"

Prue explained about his habit of coming and going, then apologized abjectly for not having done anything about her maid-of-honor dress.

Paris turned to her with a smile, the cat hanging limply in her arms, purring. Prue looked offended by his preferential behavior.

"I've been thinking about it," Paris said, "knowing how busy you've been. Couldn't you just use that little black dress in your collection? It was the in thing a couple of years ago for attendants to wear black. I don't see why it wouldn't work. Then you wouldn't have to stress out over finding something else when you have the shoot going on."

Prue looked doubtful. "You think black would be all right?"

"I think it would be fine."

"Okay. And I've got just the thing for the something borrowed." She turned to Gideon. "Can you stir the sauce while I find my wedding garter for Paris?"

"Sure," he said as the two women left the room.

"Things must be better," Randy observed, leaning back against the counter while Gideon stirred the contents of the big iron frying pan. "She seems very cheerful."

"Yeah. We're holding our own." Gideon opened the refrigerator door. "Beer? Wine? Cola?"

"Cola, please."

Gideon handed him a can and took one for himself. "We're talking about starting over."

"That's great. Paris will be thrilled. She keeps telling me how much she and her mother loved having you in the family."

Gideon took a pull on the cola and stirred the sauce, wondering how a usually bright man like himself had created this complex predicament.

"Yeah. I love them, too. But what Prue doesn't know is that I set up this whole thing. My aunt knew we were separated, and I suggested she pretend she didn't so I could get Prue here to win her back."

Randy closed his eyes and shook his head. "Man! Don't either of you believe in telling the truth?"

"I was a very honest senator," Gideon said, the whole thing mystifying him, too. "I just seem to be a cagey husband. I think she does that to me. I don't always understand her and that makes dealing with her directly difficult. So, here I am. Hoping she doesn't find out."

"Good luck," Randy said wryly. "Nothing ever gets by Paris. We can only hope Prue's different."

PRUE DUG INTO the bottom of her closet and located the box that held the memorabilia she'd been so sure would lend a convincing quality to her and Gideon's life together. In it, she found the little plastic bag with the ruched white garter, its decorative blue bow centered with a tiny pearl heart. She stepped backward out of the closet, her hair rumpled, and handed the bag to Paris.

"There you are!"

Paris sat on the edge of the bed and pulled the garter out of the bag, smiling over it. "I remember helping you get dressed that morning. I was sure you were going to be so happy and that I'd never find that kind of love."

Prue thought back to that morning, surprised to remember how innocently selfish she'd been, how completely convinced that the world was hers, that Gideon had been sent to make her happy and all she had to do was enjoy it and *be* happy.

"And here's your something blue. Just a loan, though." She gave her the cloisonné earrings Paris had given her. "And here we are, everything different for both of us."

Paris took her hand and squeezed gently. "Thanks for the loan of the earrings. But what's happening between you two? You look deliriously happy one moment and troubled the next."

"That's about the way it is." She leaned sideways on an elbow and plucked at the bedspread. "We've fallen in love all over again, but there's so much old stuff between us."

"You still convinced he was cheating?"

"No," Prue replied, surprised to find that she truly no longer thought so. She felt as though she'd gotten to know him all over again, only better this time than she had before. "But…something happened when we split up that I never told you or Mom." She regretted that now, but then she had so many regrets.

"Something to do with the hospital bill I brought over?" Paris asked.

Prue drew a breath and told her about the miscarriage.

Paris's eyes brimmed with tears and she wrapped her arms around her. "I'm so sorry, Prue. We'd have only wanted to help you."

"I know that." She drew away and tried to find a way to explain. "I was just so…wounded and brokenhearted. I couldn't even say the words. And I never told Gideon."

Paris closed her eyes. "Oh, no. Until I brought over the bill and you had to explain."

"It was my fault. He found it."

"And he was angry," Paris guessed.

Prue met her gaze with a roll of her eyes. "To put it mildly. But he was as mad at himself as he was at me. He thinks that I lost the baby because of what I saw at the Maine house when I opened the door. So he feels responsible."

"Do you blame him?" Paris said sympathetically.

"Not at all. But we're each having trouble forgiving ourselves for the whole thing, so it's making it harder to come together with real enthusiasm."

Paris smiled and hugged her again. "Maybe you just need to come to a wedding for inspiration."

"I'm sure that'll help." Prue made herself think positively. "Can you guys stay for spaghetti?"

"Fine with me. I'm sure Randy will want to, but I don't want to start accepting things for him until *after* the wedding. Let's go ask."

The evening turned into a party. Randy was happy to stay, and Prue called her mother and Jeffrey to join them. Georgette came out of the bedroom in a wild-colored caftan, discovered the collection of guests and walked right toward Camille with her arms open, as though it hadn't been five years since the last time they'd met.

Justine returned from the lab with a contact sheet they all looked over after dinner. Prue thought it was hard to see a difference between the photos Bruno had taken and the ones Justine shot—unless it was to see more excitement in Justine's.

She'd apparently been snapping the shutter while Gideon reached to the overhead branch in the woods and snapped the leaf off for Prue. She had several shots of them talking, smiling, looking into each other's eyes with discovery.

"The two of you were made for the camera," Justine said.

"And for each other, apparently," Camille added.

Prue found a moment during the evening to take her mother aside and tell her about the miscarriage. She explained the reasons behind her silence, and how the whole issue had come up again to haunt her.

Camille hugged her fiercely, then held her away and gave her a little shake, her eyes brilliant with tears and annoyance.

"Sometimes, Prudence, you're your own worst enemy. You cannot exist above the struggle. You have to get in there and get dirty. You have always been a princess, but it's now time for you to be queen. The queen makes the hard choices, does the dirty work of keeping a family going, endures the hardships and rises above. And she never runs away. Understood?"

"Yes."

"All right. I want you to love that man as he deserves. He came here to find you—I'm sure that was hard and humbling for him, and adequate proof to me that he'll love you wholeheartedly in return. And I want you to make me a grandmother. Is *that* understood?"

There was no other reply. "Yes, ma'am," she said smartly.

CHAPTER FIFTEEN

JUSTINE PHOTOGRAPHED the green pants outfit at the Breakfast Barn. Prue had called Mariah Trent, who called the upper echelon of Whitcomb's Wonders, who all came in jeans and work shirts to lend blue-collar authenticity to the shoot. They crowded around a table over which Prue leaned with a map, obviously asking directions. Gideon stood back, looking on protectively, almost out of the photo.

When directed to ogle and stare, Gideon thought the Wonders did remarkably well. Paul Foster, single and rowdy, was a bit over the top. Justine reined him in.

"Mr. Foster," she said in her stylish accented English. "You're crowding my shot, and you might bear in mind that the model is married to that big man off to the side."

The Wonders hooted. "He's a martial arts pro," Hank warned. "He's preparing our security program."

Foster seemed more amused than embarrassed. He grinned up at Gideon. "Sorry, man. Beautiful woman."

Gideon nodded. "It's all right. Just remember that I can kill you with my thumb."

"I'll bear that in mind." Foster waved at the camera. "Consider me chastised, Your Ladyship."

There was more hooting and the suggestion that Justine should be helping to write the security program.

"Or implement it," Foster added.

Kibitzing and laughter made for slow progress but much fun. Prue, Gideon, Georgette and Justine all stayed to have lunch with the Wonders, then moved on to a lounge on the other side of town. The band had been called in early to provide a backdrop while Gideon and Prue danced, she wearing the little black dress.

He liked having her in his arms. He was still feeling horrible about the miscarriage, but everyone's insistence that he wasn't responsible was slowly sinking in. For the first time since they'd begun this drama, he held her without overwhelming guilt or a sense of frustration.

She leaned into him trustingly and flirted very deliberately, telling him she was doing it for the sake of the photo. She was made up for evening and her hair was tied in a glittery clip, a curly ponytail bouncing as she moved.

When Justine had suggested the ponytail for this particular shot, Georgette had looked doubtful. "It's a deeply romantic evening. What's sexy about a ponytail?"

Justine had shrugged. "The innocence of it."

Gideon decided the young woman was going places.

Prue's waist felt small under his hand, her breasts firm and round against his chest. He could feel the whoosh of her skirt between his knees as he moved with her, felt the difference the sparkly dress made in how she perceived herself.

She was the princess now, all the harsh realities she'd had to face the past year gone in the fantasy of the moment.

He wondered how she would take the news that he'd manufactured the reason for their cohabitation.

It didn't take much thought to come to the conclusion that she wouldn't like it. Each of them had learned hard lessons about being honest, and she was the one who'd suggested they start over, straight with each other.

No. He'd keep the whole thing to himself rather than risk upsetting her. His plan had worked well so far. He had no reason to believe it wouldn't continue until Georgette went home.

He put himself into the role of eager lover for the sake of the shot.

"Maybe we should make dance lessons a part of our future," she said as Justine knelt on the piano, clicking away.

"You think we need lessons?" he asked.

"Can you samba?"

"No."

"Rumba?"

"No."

"Tango?"

"No."

"Me, neither. Lessons would lend us a South American influence that couldn't help but loosen us up."

"The rumba is Cuban," he corrected.

She nipped his earlobe. "You're missing the point. I'm thinking in terms of moving with abandon instead of in a box step."

"Ah. Abandon."

Prue screamed when Gideon dipped her backward without warning. Her entire body weight was suspended on the flat of his hand, except for her hand clutching the sleeve of his jacket. She felt like someone dangling from the top of a building or over a shark tank. Until she saw his smile and put her own surprise aside to realize that she felt completely secure. He wouldn't drop her.

"I do know one element of the tango," he said.

She still lay suspended over the hand splayed at her waist. The band was grinning. Georgette scolded with a halfhearted, "Gideon!" Justine cried, "That's great! Hold it!"

"It reminds me of a medieval torture to get the truth out of a prisoner," she joked. "Only it involved crocodiles and a moat."

He brought her up and tightly against him so

quickly that she saw stars. "So," he said, his eyes darkly grave. "The truth, then. Do you love me?"

Her heart thudded. "I do."

"Do you forgive me for all the ways I've hurt you?"

"I do. And...*I'm* sorry for what I've done to you."

Pain shot through his eyes. "How can I make it up to you for the baby?"

"You can give me another one," she whispered.

JUSTINE PHOTOGRAPHED Paris in the wedding dress the following day. Rosie DeMarco arrived early with the headpiece. It fit like a skullcap and was covered with pearls, a modesty veil attached to the front and a long veil at the back. Paris had also come early and Georgette was doing her makeup.

Prue noted Gideon's second look in Rosie's direction. She was tall and elegant with bright blue eyes and thick, long, dark brown hair. She wore pencil-slim jeans and a bulky blue sweater that made her eyes even brighter.

"She is beautiful," she whispered to him as Rosie, Paris, Georgette and Justine chatted together. "But don't get any ideas. She's off men."

He gave her another glance as he put their breakfast dishes in the dishwasher. "Somebody done her wrong?"

"I'm not sure. Something bad happened to her family. I was in Albany with you at the time, and Paris was at school. Mom knows them a bit. I guess their family's been around forever, like Jackie's, and Rosie's father was a powerful man. He committed suicide, Rosie's brother died, Rosie's husband left. It was like a general exodus of all the men in her life. Except for her little nephew. Her mother got custody of him when her son died."

"Sad," he said.

She agreed. "And Rosie's just the nicest, smartest woman you'd ever want to know." She grinned at him. "Well, not *you* particularly, but some nice man. I think Addy's trying to fix her up."

"Matchmaking usually leads to trouble," he said, closing the dishwasher door.

"Actually, Addy's got a fairly good record. Randy and Paris are one of hers, in fact."

"You're kidding."

"No. They fought it hard, but finally got together on their own and realized she was right. If you hadn't come back when you did, I was probably next on her list."

He caught her to him and kissed her soundly. "Lucky me."

Storm clouds gathered and the wind blew, but the sun came out brightly for the shot of Paris on the church steps. It was classic, Paris in the middle of the stairs with a duplicate of the bouquet of orchids she would carry the next day at her wedding. She looked breathtaking, and Camille, who'd come to the church to watch the shoot, put a hankie to her nose.

Prue placed a comforting arm around her.

"I can't believe she's getting married!" Camille said. "And modeling! All my dreams come true."

"Are you going to retire now that Jeffrey's in your life?" Prue asked as everyone moved inside the church.

"He says I don't have to. I'm still thinking about it. And he's trying to decide whether or not to stay in Florida where he has established gigs, or let his boys take over there and establish himself here. We've even thought about doing dinner theater together. We once worked very well as a team."

"Mom, that sounds like so much fun."

Georgette came to stand with Prue and Camille, indicating Paris with a jut of her chin. "Isn't she the perfect bride? You did good work with your girls, Camille."

Camille smiled smugly. "Yes. I like to think so."

RAIN FELL in buckets the following day, but nothing could dim the excitement over Paris and Randy's wedding. Prue pinned up the skirt of the wedding dress to save it from puddles and bundled Paris into a raincoat. Rosie, a self-appointed wedding coordinator, carried the veil and the shoes as Paris ran from the car to the church in tennies.

Gideon and several of the Wonders stood outside the church with umbrellas, escorting people from their cars and up the steps.

In the tiny dressing room off the vestibule of the church, Rosie helped Paris into her shoes while Prue unpinned the hem of the dress and fluffed it out. Then Rosie put the headpiece on Paris and drew the modesty veil over her face.

With a straight face, Rosie gave Paris a hand-lettered sign that read, "Veil and Shoes Courtesy of Happily Ever After. Open 9–5 Mon thru Sat."

"Just carry that instead of your flowers," she said seriously, "and be sure that each side of the aisle sees it."

Prue laughed as Paris hit Rosie with the cardboard sign. "Very funny. It isn't bad enough that Prue wants me to tell everyone it's a Prudent Designs dress instead of saying, 'I do.'"

They all laughed again, then Paris sobered and hugged her sister, then Rosie. "Thanks for helping me. I couldn't have done this so quickly without you two."

Prue shrugged off the praise. "I didn't do anything. I've been so busy with Georgette's ad campaign."

Paris held out the skirt of the dress. "Are you serious? The dress? Do you have any idea how hard it would have been to find one half this beautiful?"

"Well, I for one expended a lot of time and energy," Rosie continued to tease. "And I'm expecting a bonus, or at least a large tip."

Paris pinched her cheek. "How about my undying gratitude?"

"I guess that'll do. Well, I'd better get out there and look after the guest book." Rosie smiled at Prue. "You look lovely, too, by the way. I'd love to have that dress. When we finally get down to filling your orders, I'd like one.''

She was as tall as Paris, and Prue thought she remembered she'd been a little fuller-figured. Now she was so slender, she probably could have stood in for a model on the runway. Prue imagined it had to do with all the sadness in her family.

"We'll do yours first," Prue promised as Rosie hurried out into the vestibule.

Prue turned her attention to Paris, looking her over from head to toe to make sure everything was perfect.

"Is this really happening to us?" Paris asked, catching her hands. "You and Gideon together again and me getting married to the nicest man in the universe?"

"It is," Prue assured her, confidence in her own love for Gideon and his for her giving her faith in everything. "We're going to pile over to Mom's with our children for Sunday dinners and have noisy birthday parties and Thanksgivings and Christmases that last for days. It's happening for us, Paris. The O'Hara sisters came out winners."

Paris hugged her tightly. "We were always winners. We just weren't very good at contests."

THE CHURCH WAS PACKED WITH friends despite the last-minute telephoned invitations. All of Paris's regular fares came, and most of the Maple Hill Fire Department, though half of them had to leave when someone's beeper went off.

The remaining firemen then cohosted the reception

with the women of the Congregational church's Events Committee in the basement of the church. Buffet tables of sandwich makings and salads lined one wall, a three-tiered cake taking up an entire table in the corner.

Children dressed in their Sunday best chased each other through the adults gathered in conversation groups, some dancing to the Old-timer's Band in another corner of the room. Justine was taking wedding pictures, a thank-you, she said, for the kindness Prue and Gideon had shown her.

Prue stood alone near the cake, watching the room, and experiencing the most curious sensation of having turned the corner from girl to woman. She was sure it should have happened years ago, but it was just at this moment that she felt her heart open to truly appreciate all she had, to accept and mourn her losses and look forward to the challenges to come.

She veritably tingled with life.

Rosie appeared and put an arm around her shoulders. "You look very smug," she said. "What are you thinking?"

Prue laughed. "That it's taken me a long time to grow up, but I think I've finally done it. I feel generous and hopeful and forgiving."

Rosie frowned teasingly at her. "Hey. Don't go setting standards the rest of us will find it hard to live up to. Hopeful and forgiving. That's asking a lot. But since you *are* in a mellow mood, Forsythe Fabrics just called me because they couldn't reach you. Your fabric's in. They wanted to know if you want it shipped or, since there's so much and some pretty expensive stuff in it, if you'd rather pick it up.''

"Gideon and I can go pick it up—if I'm not completely messing up Georgette's shooting schedule.''

"I could pick up the fabric for you if I can get my sister to watch the shop.'' As Prue remembered, Rosie's younger sister, Francie, was smart but had taken a wild turn when tragedy struck the Ericksons.

"I thought she was away at school,'' Prue questioned.

"She met someone over the summer and decided not to go back. She's getting married instead.'' Rosie shrugged, an indication, Prue guessed, that she wasn't sure if the decision was good or bad. "So, she's been helping me in the shop. Although you should probably go to make sure the order's complete.''

"Go where?'' Gideon asked, coming up beside them with two glasses of champagne, one for each of them.

"Thank you, Gideon,'' Rosie said, toasting him with her glass.

"To Boston,'' Prue replied, extending her thanks with a kiss on the cheek. "My fabric's in. We should go pick it up tomorrow if it doesn't mess up Georgette's schedule too much.''

"Boston?''

"Yes.''

"I'm sorry,'' he said. "I just promised Hank I'd talk to some guys he's collected for the security program. He got them all together for tomorrow, and Jackie's reserved the conference room for them." He smiled at Rosie. "Could you go with her?"

Rosie smiled. "I was just offering to go *for* her."

"Why don't you go together? I'd feel better if she wasn't alone in Boston traffic." He grinned. "Particularly the way she drives."

Prue backhanded his upper arm. "Hey! You were doing so well as the loving, adoring husband."

He caught her neck in the crook of his arm and brought her in for a kiss. "I still am. I'm just trying to protect you from your weaknesses."

Rosie laughed. "I'll go call Francie right now."

His arm still around her, Gideon drew Prue toward the small dance area and took her into his arms. The truth was, she thought as she melted against him, he was her biggest weakness.

THE GROUP OF MEN Hank had assembled to talk to about the security program seemed to Gideon to be tailor-made for the project. Two were former state policemen out of jobs because of budget cuts, one was a former cop friend of Evan Braga's and one had been a private investigator in Los Angeles. All the men had experience in self-defense and weaponry.

"If trained together," Gideon told Hank after he'd interviewed them, "they'd be good enough to be used as an elite force. I can't imagine where the need for it would come up in Maple Hill, but if it did, you'd be ready. Berger's a sharpshooter, Ransom's got com-

mendations out the wazoo, Phillips has hostage negotiator experience, and Martin, the P.I., has more
official and underground connections than seems safe
for anyone to have.''

Hank nodded, looking pleased. They sat at a table
in the back of the Barn. ''That's what I thought. I'm
thinking about putting them on salary so they don't
get away from me until you have the project ready,
and I wanted to be sure I was right about them.''

''I think you are. But what are you going to do
with them? It seems like overkill for little old Maple
Hill.''

''We'll provide local security,'' he replied, ''but
then we can contract out for special jobs that need
muscle or simple investigation.''

''Like what? Surveillance? Intelligence gathering?
That sort of thing?''

Hank nodded. ''Why not? We deal in all kinds of
talents, fill all kinds of needs. Why not branch out
into something for which there's always a need but
seldom anyone to fill it. There's a lot we can do on
a local level—provide practical security personnel, of
course, but we could get the information needed for
abuse cases, insurance fraud—you name it. The kinds
of things an ordinary police force can't devote much
manpower to. And then there could even be—other
stuff.''

Gideon's concern was deepening. ''What other
stuff?''

''National stuff. International stuff.''

"Do you have any idea what you're considering?"

Hank pushed his coffee aside and leaned toward him. "Probably not, but I imagine you do. I'm presuming by the fact that you and Prue are glowing like a couple of halogen lights that the phony-marriage setup on the lake isn't phony anymore?"

Gideon remembered that one of his first conclusions about this town was that there were no secrets. "That's right."

"Then, you're staying?"

"We haven't talked about it. Prue has dreams of going to New York."

Hank nodded, apparently accepting that he had no control over that. "Well, if you move to New York, then I'll have to find another solution to the problem of a security boss, but if you're staying, I'm offering you the job. You can just oversee, if that's your preference, or you can take an active part—that's up to you. I think what we have to offer could ultimately be big." He named an impressive salary. "Anyway." He downed the rest of his coffee and pushed his chair back. "I've got to go pick up the girls at the pool. You think about it, talk it over with Prue and let me know what you decide."

They stood and shook hands over the table. "Nobody could accuse you of thinking small," Gideon said as Hank handed Rita their ticket and a bill as she passed.

Rita caught his arm and said quietly, "If you need an operative no one would suspect," she said, apparently quite serious, "I'm your woman. I have a permit to carry a gun, and I'm the best groin-kicker in the business."

Hank took a self-protective step back. "I'll bear that in mind, Rita. Until then, everything you overheard is not for publication."

She nodded. "Gotcha. Bye."

Hank's eyes widened as they met Gideon's. "I didn't hallucinate that, did I?" he asked. "Rita Robidoux did offer to work for our security team?"

Gideon laughed as they walked toward the doors together. "That'd be enough right there to encourage me to move to New York."

They parted company in the parking lot and Gideon went home, surprised to spot another rental car pulled up near the porch. Justine and Georgette had planned to go over the contact sheet again today to determine whether or not anything had to be reshot. They hadn't mentioned they were expecting guests.

He let himself in and stopped in complete surprise several feet into the room when he spotted Claudia Hackett on the sofa, petting Drifter.

She closed the distance between them at a run and threw herself into his arms.

CHAPTER SIXTEEN

ROSIE DROVE the van back from Boston. It had been several hours of easy driving and fun conversation on the way up, followed by a stressful and traumatic drive across the city to get to Forsythe Fabrics.

Prue forgot the terror of Boston's famous offensive-driving experience as she looked over her fabric order and found it to be even more wonderful than she'd hoped. Everything she'd ordered was there and even more sumptuous in large yardage than it had been in the small amounts she'd purchased to create her line.

She and Rosie packed the wrapped fabric lovingly into plastic boxes in the van, then had lunch to fortify themselves for the trip back across town.

"I'll drive," Rosie said as they paid their bill. "I've grown accustomed to playing chicken without flinching."

Prue had noticed that about her. She had a curious fearlessness usually associated with someone who had nothing to lose—or nothing to live for.

They'd talked about some personal things on the drive over. Rosie had said that she knew everyone in town talked about the misfortunes that had plagued her family, just as they'd talked about Prue and Gideon's Maine Incident.

They picked up the thread of the conversation on the way back, as though a hair-raising drive through Boston hadn't separated the thoughts. "You seem to function beautifully anyway," Rosie said as they headed west, the traffic sparse. "To behave as though you still feel normal. All I want to do some mornings is hide in the closet."

Prue smiled in Rosie's direction as Rosie drove with confidence. "I had a miscarriage," she admitted, finally able to say it without feeling guilt attached to it—the guilt that she'd somehow failed her baby and the guilt that Gideon never knew it had happened. Now that she'd resolved those questions, the pain had abated considerably.

Rosie glanced in her direction, her mouth open in surprise. "Because of the..."

"No. Just because."

"I'm so sorry."

"I brought it up to make the point that the miscarriage was the only loss I suffered—and, of course, a great deal of embarrassment. But you lost a father and a brother, then your husband just..."

"Ran off," Rosie said with a shake of her head. Then after a moment, she added, her voice tight, "I had a miscarriage, too."

It was Prue's turn to stare with her mouth open. "I never knew that! I was away at the time, though, so

I didn't realize you'd been…pregnant. What happened?''

"I fell down the porch steps," Rosie said in a calm tone, though her knuckles were white on the steering wheel. "When I found my father's body on the swing."

"How awful!"

"It was. It was an ugly, horrible time, and it lives with me every day." She expelled a deep sigh, then sat up straighter and added in a steadier voice, "I started a bridal shop so that I could focus on happy times with people and hopefully be busy enough not to think about that time anymore."

"Does it work?"

"Mostly. When I'm at the shop. It's harder at home, though I've moved into the guest house at my mother's. I sold the house my husband and I shared at the top of the hill to the developer who built the condos. I knew he'd tear it down and I wanted that."

"Were you that unhappy together?"

She thought about that. "No, actually. But I thought we understood each other until my whole world crumbled and he walked away without looking back."

"What a rat."

"Yes."

They were quiet for a long time, then they stopped at a drive-through to pick up soft drinks and for Prue to take over the driving. They were about an hour ahead of schedule.

"It's probably good to be near your mom," Prue speculated as she drove on.

Rosie laughed lightly. "It isn't good for anyone to be near my mom. She's snooty and grumpy and leans a little heavily on the Paxil these days."

Prue put a hand out to Rosie's knee. "I'm sorry you're having such a tough time. How does she handle your nephew if she's having these difficulties?"

"She seems to have an endless amount of patience for him," Rosie said without the resentment that might have accompanied such a statement. "My brother Jake was Mom and Dad's favorite, you know—" she went on "—so she's happy to have Chase, but when she feels stressed, he spends time with me since I'm right across the yard. And Francie dotes on him, so he's in good hands."

Prue nodded. "It's good that you're looking out for each other. Paris and I moving home was difficult at first but finally solved a lot of the problems we had with each other when we worked together."

Rosie rolled her eyes at the passing scenery. "Yeah, well, it'll take a miracle for us to all appreciate each other again. And there aren't many of those around anymore."

"You want me to come to the studio with you?" Rosie asked as Prue pulled into the driveway of Bloombury Landing, Rosie's family's home. "To help you bring all that stuff up to your studio?"

Prue shook her head. "No, you've done more than enough. Thanks so much for coming with me today.

It made what's usually a horrible trip very enjoyable."

"It was my pleasure," Rosie replied. "Call me when the shoot's over and you're ready to start filling Prudent Designs' orders."

Prue made a quick stop at home to see if Gideon was there to help her carry up the fabric, but he was gone. Georgette and Justine were also out. Drifter, sprawled out on the wing chair, looked up to see if food was coming, but when he was simply patted instead, he went back to sleep.

Prue jumped back in the van and headed for the studio.

She was surprised when she pulled into the Chandler Mill parking lot to see Gideon's truck there. What was he doing? she wondered. There was also a rental car with Massachusetts plates parked beside his truck.

Anxious to see him again and to show him the wealth of fabrics in her possession, she put a paper-wrapped bolt of black silk chiffon over her shoulder and pressed the button for the elevator.

When the doors opened on the second floor, she readjusted the burden on her shoulder and pushed the studio door open, a smile on her lips for Gideon.

But what she saw instead made her drop her burden to the floor, convinced she'd suffered some weird mental reversal and was going insane. Blood rushed to her face, throbbed in her temples, felt as though it might fall from her eyes in large red tears.

Claudia Hackett stood in the middle of Prue's studio in black thong panties and a matching, barely-there bra from which her breasts seemed to be trying to escape. The moment was so vivid, so clearly what she'd finally convinced herself *hadn't* happened once before that it froze time and seemed to go on and on.

Then someone stepped out from behind a screen in the corner, a look of horrified surprise on his face.

It was Gideon.

"Prue…" he said cautiously, taking a step toward her. "Think a minute. This…"

She ran. Or she tried to. He caught her at the elevator and pulled her back to him. "Listen to me!" he shouted at her.

She hit him in the shoulder with a doubled fist, connecting with real power, anger fueling the blow as every process in her body tried to make up for that frozen moment. And while she experienced a rush of physical power, every emotion she could identify— rage, agony, desperation—seemed to have to fight for survival.

Gideon's head shot back with the blow, but he didn't lose his grip on her.

"Are you going to do this to us a second time?" he demanded quietly, obviously enraged himself. His eyes blazed. No wonder. He probably hadn't expected her home for another couple of hours.

"Why not? You did!" She raised her arms to dislodge his—one of the few moves he'd ever shown her that she'd been able to master. Or maybe he let her do it; she didn't care. The full heart she'd been so proud of only yesterday was suddenly a small, black shriveled thing landing like a weight in the pit of her stomach.

He opened his mouth to speak, but she raised a hand to stop him.

"Save it!" she said, her throat so tight the words were barely a whisper. "You may have explained her away once, but you can't do it a second time."

Something seemed to go dead inside him, too. The blaze went out of his eyes, and all his strength and energy was suddenly gone.

"You know what?" he asked in a flat voice. "I'm not interested in explaining anything to you ever again. Goodbye, Prue." He went to the stairway and she heard his angry tread all the way down.

When she looked up again, she was surprised to see Claudia standing in the hallway in her underwear, flanked on either side by Georgette and Justine. She hadn't noticed them before. She blinked and looked again, so convinced of what she thought she'd seen, it crossed her mind ridiculously to wonder if there'd been some sort of orgy going on in her studio.

Then Georgette came toward her, a grim, almost pitying look in her eyes, and Prue got a terrible sense of foreboding—or was it déjà vu?

"This is Claudia Hackett," Georgette said, extending a hand toward the nearly naked young woman as Justine put the smock Prue sometimes wore when she worked over the girl's shoulders.

Claudia slipped her arms into it and, holding the front closed, took Georgette's hand. She allowed Georgette to lead her toward Prue, though she looked as though she'd prefer to run in the other direction.

"Tell her why you came, Claudia," Georgette said.

It was the first time Prue had ever heard the young woman speak. To contribute to the Hollywood quality of the whole situation, she had a voice like Judy Canova from the old fifties musicals—high and squeaky with the suggestion of the Bronx in it.

"I came with Roger to a pharmaceutical conference in Boston," Claudia explained. "And while he was in meetings, I came to Maple Hill to thank Gideon in person for everything he did for me—talking to me about changing my life, getting me money to go to school." She smiled cautiously. "I'm on the dean's list at Purdue and I've got a great husband, and his family likes me."

Justine appeared again with the long-sleeved white cat suit over her arm. "Georgette wanted a shot of this," she said, "but since you refused to put it on, she was just going to shoot it on the hanger. Until she saw Claudia."

Claudia shrugged apologetically. "I can't gain weight if I try."

It occurred to Prue, in a corner of her mind not occupied with the horrible thing she'd just done, that that was reason enough to kill Claudia, even discounting the mistake she'd caused Prue to make.

No, Prue thought grimly. No one caused her to make it. She did it on her own.

"He was standing behind the screen while I changed my clothes, Mrs. Hale," Claudia said, tears in her voice. "And Justine and Georgette were both in the room."

Making a last-ditch stand for dignity, Prue looked at Justine and said stiffly, "I didn't see you."

"I was in the bathroom," Justine explained gently.

Prue turned to Georgette.

"I was standing near the worktable against the wall when you opened the door. You never even saw me."

Prue drew a pointed breath. "You could have said something."

"I was too...shocked," she admitted, her tone accusatory. "I guess I couldn't believe you'd do that a second time after all he did to get you into his house."

In emotional self-flagellation, Prue was going to accept that as just criticism, until a second thought made the words suggest something suspicious.

"Get me into his house," Prue repeated, raising an eyebrow. "What do you mean, Georgette?"

Georgette shifted her weight impatiently. "Don't get uppity with me, Prudence. And if ever a woman was misnamed, young lady, it's you!"

She was getting that a lot lately, Prue thought.

"I called Gideon because I wanted photos of your brilliant designs. I knew you were separated and I didn't care. I figured if you were silly enough to mistrust a man like him, then you could damn well live your life alone if that was what you wanted. But he saw it as an opportunity to get you close to him, to work on that stubbornness of yours. He asked me to pretend that I thought you were still married so that you'd move in with him for the duration, and then I'd agree to the article and the ad campaign.''

Prue was indignant and embarrassed until she realized that he'd gone to an awful lot of trouble to reestablish communication with her. It probably would have been a lot easier for him to go to Alaska and live in a tent until the lodge was rebuilt.

''Just so we're straight,'' Claudia said, looking pale and worried. ''I did come on to him that time in Maine.'' She spoke quickly and urgently. ''I'd never met a man like him before. My father took nudie pictures for a living—sometimes of my sister and me— and my boyfriend put me on the street to make extra money. I got away from him to start dancing, and when Senator Crawford became interested in me, I thought my life was going to change. But he did all the same things I'd seen before, only with more money.''

''Claudia…'' Prue wanted to stop her, feeling guilty for having thought her own past troubling. She couldn't begin to imagine what Claudia's had been like.

''Please.'' Claudia twisted her fingers. ''I need to explain what happened.''

Prue nodded and made herself listen, feeling a hole

grow at the heart of her where just this morning there'd been so much enthusiasm for the future.

"When your husband and I were stuck alone in your home in Maine," Claudia continued, "we started talking about our lives...you know, like people do. Only no one ever wanted to hear what I had to say before. They just wanted to look at me. But when he said I should go back to school, if he could fix it because of what I was doing for the attorney general's office, I thought..." Her eyes filled and she looked suddenly ashamed. "I was so stupid. I thought I had to say thank-you the way I was...the way I was taught. Only he got mad at me. He pushed me away. He told me I had to have more respect for myself than to think I had to buy my dreams with my body." A tear fell down her cheek.

"But I still didn't get it. I tried one more time to show him how grateful I was and...that's when you walked in. I was sure he was playing some kind of teasing game, but he was trying to push me away."

Prue put both hands to her face as the corridor began to spin, and her stomach began to spin with it.

Georgette put a firm arm around her and Claudia took hold of her other arm. "Come inside," Georgette said as they supported her weight between them.

"I'll get a glass of water." Justine hurried on ahead.

The words screamed in Prue's head. *What have I done?*

GIDEON DROVE HOME by the quiet back streets, afraid his anger had so much of his focus that he wouldn't be safe on the highway. He ground to a halt at the house, slapped the truck into Park, removed the key with a yank, then hit the steering wheel for good measure. Then he jumped out of the truck and slammed the door.

He walked around the porch to the front, looking at the lake and trying to mellow out. He felt something slam against his ankle and looked down to find Drifter rubbing on him. He picked up the cat and scratched the back of his head, the resulting purr sounding like a motorboat on the water.

The lake was turbulent this evening, wind scudding along the surface and causing little eddies to run like whitecaps from shore to shore. And the same thing was happening inside him. Reason was overtaken by emotion as he realized the Maine Incident was happening all over again.

He couldn't believe it. As he remembered the tableau Prue saw when she opened the door, he could understand a momentary confusion. But after their lengthy discussion of how she'd misunderstood what had happened the first time, after all their discoveries about each other and their admissions of mistakes, after all their promises of love and trust—she'd walked away again without even letting him explain.

Drifter protested as Gideon apparently scratched too hard, and jumped out of his arms.

This time Gideon decided he wasn't stopping to

agonize over what he might have done differently, he was just moving on. He took his overnight bag out of the bottom of the closet and packed up the few things he'd brought with him. What the women had bought for him here, he was leaving behind. He didn't want anything to remind him that he'd risked his dignity and his peace of mind to create a situation that would bring Prue close to him so that he could try to win her back.

Well. He'd certainly piled up the mistakes, he thought as he threw the few things in the medicine cabinet that belonged to him into his shaving kit. His plan had been a stupid move. He should have left well enough alone, but no. He'd gotten one good look at Prue, remembered all they'd shared and how good the sex had been and forgotten that she'd also spent a lot of time driving him crazy and making him miserable. He'd been an idiot.

That wasn't going to happen again.

He picked up Drifter, who'd settled in the corner of his bag, and put him on the bed. He dropped in the small alarm clock from his bedside table and made room for his shaving kit.

He wished he could just take off for Alaska tonight, but he had to finish the project for Whitcomb's Wonders' new security arm. He snapped his bag closed and thought about what an exciting project that could be. Hank had big plans and the intelligence and the manpower to back them up.

''I'm going to have to leave you with her,'' he said

to the cat, stroking him as he bumped his head against Gideon's thigh. "I'm sorry about that, but I'm going to the Yankee Inn for a couple of days and cats aren't allowed. But then, Prue likes *you,* so you won't have the same problems with her that I've had."

He took one last look at the painting of the beautiful children that should have been his, remembered the one he'd never even known about and lost, and stood rooted to the floor for one really bad moment.

Then he picked up his bag and started for the door. Prue stood there, however, a hand to the doorframe as though she needed its support. She looked pale and desperate, the neat coil her hair had been in that morning when she left now coming apart. Her eyes held misery and uncertainty when they met his.

They went from his face to his bag. "Where are you going?" she asked softly.

He wasn't sure why that question annoyed him so much, but it did. Had she really thought he could stay after that reprise of the Maine Incident?

"To the inn," he said, moving toward her, certain she'd step out of his way. *He* wouldn't want to be in his way with the mood he was in. "I have to finish the project for Hank and I obviously can't do it here."

She didn't move, but held her ground, looking up at him and speaking quietly as though she was the most reasonable woman in the world. "But *you* live here."

"*We* lived here," he corrected sharply, not ready to feel at all reasonable about it. "And I don't want to be anywhere that's going to remind me that I was stupid enough to want you back. Now, if you'll move out of my way…''

She flinched but she didn't move. ''Gideon,'' she said, putting a hand out to him. He blocked her touch with a raised arm, as though she'd tried to strike him.

She made a little gasping sound of dismay and barred his way with her hands on the doorway molding.

''You're not leaving here until you listen to me!'' she shouted at him, tears brimming in her eyes. ''I'm sorry! I'm *so* sorry! But you keep—''

''I don't want to hear it!'' he shouted over her. Then he lowered his voice and paraphrased her own words back to her. ''You may have thought you had an excuse for your behavior once, but not twice. I'm out of here, Prue, and *I'm* filing for divorce.''

''No!'' she shouted, bracing her position. ''I won't let you leave until you listen to me.''

''You never listen to *me!*''

''Because I was an idiot! But Georgette and Claudia and Justine explained…''

He caught one of her wrists and yanked it away from the doorway. ''I don't care what they explained to you. There was one minute there when you could have proved that you trust me, that you have faith in me, but you blew it!''

She clung to the doorway with her other hand. ''Well, too bad! I'm sure it's not the last mistake I'll ever make! Especially if you keep finding yourself in situations involving naked women! You want blind trust, then maybe you should find a woman who'd let you *be* unfaithful because she doesn't care enough to question you!"

"Bull!" he roared back at her. "I don't think you care whether I'm faithful or not as long as you get to act like the injured, martyred party. That allows you to hold center stage like the princess that you are."

He yanked a little harder and she flew out of the doorway. Since he had the momentum going, he used that hand to fling her onto the bed. "You have the stage, Prudie," he said, his voice curiously flat as his anger morphed into despair. "I'm just not going to be your audience anymore. Goodbye."

PRUE WEPT until her eyes stung and her throat ached and the grief of her own stupidity was too much to bear. Georgette made her tea and Justine used the portrait studio's lab to print the pictures in an attempt to show her how well they'd come out.

But the happiness that was visible between them in the photos only served to deepen her pain. She sat for an entire day in the big chair by the fireplace, going over and over them thinking she could gain some absolution for her idiocy by inflicting more pain upon herself.

But it didn't work. She still felt guilty, and her agony was multiplied by the fact that she couldn't make herself believe that it was over. And just to add more grief to her burden, Drifter hadn't been home all day. She wondered if he also no longer felt welcome.

She called Gideon from the privacy of the upstairs bedroom that evening, hoping that he'd have calmed down in twenty-four hours and be more willing to listen to another abject apology.

Jackie told her he was out.

"Where did he go?" Prue asked. He'd left the rented van parked in the back and she was ready to take off after him.

"He asked me not to say," Jackie replied regretfully.

Prue felt the words like a stab to the heart. He hadn't calmed down at all.

"Is he all right?" Prue asked, her voice tight.

Jackie was quiet for a moment, then she answered Prue's question with another. "What do you think, Prue?"

"He won't listen!" Prue said desperately.

"I know," Jackie replied. "Apparently that's a problem the two of you have in common. I'll tell him you called."

Prue hung up the phone feeling even more hopeless than she had after the last time. Then, she'd been filled with righteous indignation, certain she was the wronged party. This time, she knew better.

She cried for another hour, then finally deciding that was getting her nowhere—and she was determined to get *some*where—she stepped under a hot shower and tried hard to think. There had to be a way to convince him to forgive her. If he wouldn't cooperate in a civilized way...

She uttered a small scream under the rush of water as an idea occurred to her. It wasn't a guaranteed solution, but it *was* an idea.

She stepped out of the shower and without even stopping to wrap a towel around herself, ran to the phone and left Hank a message to call her when he came in.

Then she winked at the painting of the four children.

CHAPTER SEVENTEEN

GIDEON FINISHED the security model two days later. Hank approved it with gratitude and enthusiasm, then pleaded with him to reconsider the move to Alaska.

Gideon shook his head. "Thanks, Hank. I think we'd have enjoyed working together, but I can't stay if Prue's here."

"What if she moves to New York?" Hank asked practically. "Would you consider coming back?"

"No." They sat at a small table in the Breakfast Barn, and he took one last, sad look around. "Too many memories here. I can't look at the lake or the common or even sit in here without remembering how good it was for a while. But it's not ever going to be good again and I have to deal with it. So I'm going to Alaska."

Hank eyed him grimly. "You're sure there's no way to work it out? That you're not just being too proud?"

Gideon groaned. "I told you what happened. I thought we'd restored our relationship after the last time, and she reacted in the very same way. I love her! I wish it could be different, but she's always ready to believe the worst. I'd rather live in misery without her than have to wonder everyday if *she's* wondering if I'm being faithful.''

Hank seemed to understand. ''It's a shame. Personally and professionally, I hate to lose you.''

''Yeah.'' Gideon put money down for the bill, then pushed his chair away. ''I'd better go. My flight to Boston is early in the morning. You'll pick up my truck at the airport and give it to Prue?''

''Right. Any message to go with the truck?''

Gideon considered a minute but couldn't think of anything significant. And it was no time to be smart. ''No,'' he replied. ''I've already said goodbye.''

Hank climbed out of his van in the inn's parking lot and shook hands with Gideon. He gave him his card. ''If you need anything, or something changes and you want to come back, call me.''

''I will,'' Gideon promised. ''Thanks for everything.''

He tried to make his mind a blank as he loped into the lobby where a cheery fire burned in the fireplace. But he remembered playing with Hank's and Cam's kids here, demonstrating a few techniques to the guys in the empty banquet room, Jackie's story about the young girl, the British soldier she'd nursed back to health and the eight children that had resulted from their union.

Apparently, ideological differences had been easier to surmount in those days than the personal differences that stood between him and Prue today.

In his room, he showered, then packed his bag and put it by the door.

Then he went to the window, held the curtain back and looked out on Maple Hill, remembering that he'd done this very thing the day he'd arrived. He saw the lights of town, several smaller house lights scattered between the inn and there. He remembered how comfortable and inviting Maple Hill had seemed to him then.

He dropped the curtain and climbed into bed.

He was staring at the darkness when he heard the subtle sound just before midnight. It sounded like the scrape of a key in the lock. He propped up on an elbow, his eyes well adjusted to the dark, and wondered if Jackie had some kind of problem that required him, or if she'd accidentally double-booked a room.

When the door opened and he saw four men in commando gear and night-vision goggles, he was almost too astonished for his old training to take over. Until a deep male voice said quietly, ''You're coming with us, Mr. Hale. Please get dressed.''

He didn't bother to argue or ask questions. He kicked at the nearest man, doubling him over, then leaped at the man behind him before he went down under the other two. There was a great commotion in the darkness. He kicked and struck out with his hands and heard satisfying grunts and curses. But the confines of the bedroom narrowed his moves and he was finally pinned to the floor between the bed and the dresser. It felt as though all four men held him there.

"Now." The same voice that had spoken originally was breathless with exertion. That gave Gideon some satisfaction. "We're leaving here quietly. This is a respectable establishment and we don't want to cause them any problems."

Everyone scrambled up and Gideon was yanked to his feet.

The clothes he'd discarded and left on a chair by the bed were thrust into his hands.

"Where are we going?" he asked as he pulled on his jeans. Adrenaline was pumping through him, yet his brain was having difficulty taking this seriously.

"Hurry up!" somebody snapped at him.

He pulled on the sweater, then his shoes.

Someone else put his hands together and snapped plastic cuffs on him. Then a hood was yanked over his head.

Gideon was beginning to lose his sense of humor about this. If Hank was behind it, testing him, he was going to pay big-time.

The door squeaked on its hinges, then someone whispered, "Get the jacket on the chair!"

There was something familiar about that voice, but he couldn't quite place it.

Interesting, he thought as he was led away, probably out into the corridor, that his kidnappers were concerned that he was warm. That was good. There was a pocketknife in that jacket.

They walked quickly toward another door, the stairway probably, and he was held firmly by either arm as he negotiated them blindly. There was the whoosh of another door opening, another brief walk, then they were out in the night air.

"Hold on." He was pulled to a stop, then someone called quietly, "All clear."

He heard the unmistakable sound of a van door sliding open.

"Tall step," the man holding his right arm cautioned. That familiar voice again. Someone else pushed his head down.

He half fell and was half dragged inside the vehicle, then hauled into a seat as the van took off.

But now he wasn't worried about the pocketknife any longer because he thought he recognized these guys. That voice belonged to Phillips, Hank's candidate for his security team who'd once been a hostage negotiator. These were the men he'd interviewed the other day.

And judging by the faint smell of chlorine in his nostrils, suggesting a towel left over from the pool, this was Hank's van.

So. It *was* a test.

"Whitcomb," Gideon said. "You're so going to pay for this."

Quiet laughter ran through the van.

"I'm glad you're all enjoying yourselves," he added. "But unless we're on our way to the Barn for pie and coffee, you're all going to pay, too."

They laughed again. But, apparently, they weren't talking.

Okay. He understood the need to work a plan to its conclusion. He relaxed and began to consider methods of revenge.

He'd been giving considerable thought to siccing Rita on them, when they made a turn then pulled to a stop.

The van door opened and he was guided out. Then someone patted his shoulder.

"Come with me." It was Hank's voice. "About five yards forward, then a few steps up."

"*About* five yards," Gideon complained. "A *few* steps up. Are we forgetting I'm wearing a hood? And what is this anyway? If you wanted to test me, you should done it before you hi—"

"Watch it!" Hank interrupted. "Steps. And I think the important thing to note here is that our elite commando group's first time out was a great success."

"Okay. And I'd be excited about that if Maple Hill needed a commando group, and if I still had anything to do with Whitcomb's Wonders!"

They'd reached the top of the steps, went forward several feet, then Hank pulled him to a stop. He turned him around and ripped the hood off him. He smiled at him in a fraternal way that seemed to make little sense under the circumstances.

"I'm hoping the day will come," Hank said, dropping the jacket on Gideon's shoulders, "when you'll be glad we took this job."

"What job? What do you mean?"

"I mean that this isn't a test," Hank replied. "We were hired." Then he reached over Gideon's shoulder, knocked twice on the door behind him, then ran down the porch steps, leaped into the green van and drove away.

It wasn't until the van was gone and Gideon had an unobstructed view of the lake that he realized he was standing on his own front porch.

Or what used to be his front porch.

He heard the sound of a door opening and turned, not entirely surprised to see Prue standing in the doorway. The jacket slipped off his shoulder unnoticed as he observed she wore a bit more makeup than usual, particularly around her eyes. He wondered if the past two days had been as sleepless for her as they'd been for him.

But he didn't care about that. She'd made the choice that determined their fates.

He shifted his weight to one leg and asked wearily, "You hired Hank's new security force?"

"Yes," she replied, opening the door wider. "He wasn't sure how they'd perform, but here you are."

"There were four of them," he said, remaining where he stood. "Hard not to perform well under those circumstances."

"But their quarry was *you*. Certainly that warranted extra force."

"I don't know. I was pretty well defeated in a one-to-one just the other day."

Misery brimmed in her eyes at his reference to that day. The cool elegance of her appearance was suddenly replaced by vulnerability. "Please come inside, Gideon."

He had to fight himself to stay sane. Everything in him responded to her and wanted her as he always did. And it hurt him to see her in pain, but he also hated the pain she could inflict on him.

"Prue, there's no point—"

"Please!" she said urgently. "Just hear me out, then you're free to go if you want to."

"The last time I asked you to hear me out," he reminded her coolly, "you refused."

She nodded her regret. "*Please* be smarter than I was."

While he vacillated, wondering if that was a concession of some sort, she took hold of his still-bound wrists and drew him inside.

PRUE COULDN'T DECIDE whether it helped or hindered her to think about how much was at stake here. Holding the image in her mind of a future with Gideon and the four children they wanted certainly firmed her already strong determination to make him understand why she'd reacted the way she did.

On the other hand, the possibility that he might just walk away as he had every right to do was making it impossible for her to think.

And his expression wasn't helping. He just stood there in jeans and a simple dark blue sweater, his bound hands relaxed, his hair rumpled, his eyes still turbulent with the anger she'd seen in them the day he'd left.

She squared her shoulders and pulled herself together, knowing she had to try. "Would you like a cup of coffee?" she asked. "I know that was a rude way to be awakened."

He shifted his weight again. "No, thank you," he said.

"Would you like to sit by the fire?" She indicated the wing chair. "It's cold out there."

His expression hardened. He stood just inside the door and didn't budge. "I can listen standing up."

"Okay." She expelled a sigh, understanding that he was not going to make this easy for her. And while she certainly could have used a cup of coffee and a chair, she focused on that image of the two of them with their children. She stood several feet away from him and made herself look into his forbidding gaze.

"Just as I misunderstood what I saw—both times," she said, plunging into the explanation she'd thought about for days, "I want to try to make you understand that what you saw me do when I found you with Claudia in my studio wasn't real, either."

An element of confusion entered his dark expression.

"Oh, it happened," she amended quickly, "but that was the princess reaction, and even I can't believe I did that a second time. Unless..." Her throat tried to close, but she swallowed to force the words through. "Unless you consider that I've so enjoyed this time we've had together and the thought of losing you again would be twice as hard now as it was the first time."

He watched her but she couldn't tell what he was thinking. As far as she could determine, his expression didn't change. She plunged on.

"You must have wanted to save our marriage, too," she pointed out a little desperately. "You're the one who plotted with your aunt to trick me into moving in with you."

He didn't look at all guilty or remorseful for the deceit, just completely detached from her pleas.

"I *do* love you and I *do* trust you. It was just that..." She hunched a shoulder and kept talking. "I mean, I know how I am. I'm a lot like Mom and she says that for some men, we're just too much. Too demanding, I suppose, too weird, too...too much trouble."

Still no change in those eyes that she could see, but she forced herself to hold their gaze as she said finally, "So...I wanted to try this last time to explain myself, but I'm sure it's probably an awful prospect for you to have to live that way, so..." Her throat closed again and she could have sworn her heart stopped. Nothing in her wanted to allow the words out, but it was only fair to say them. "So I understand if you want to leave. Just know how much I'll always love you."

Her heart thudded when she thought she saw a

flicker of something in his eyes, then he turned and took the few steps to the door.

Her heart plummeted to her toes when his hand-cuffed hands turned the knob and opened it. He walked out and she put both hands to her mouth to stifle the sob.

Then her breath caught in her lungs when he reappeared, his jacket caught in his bound hands. He held it out to her. "There's a knife in the right side pocket," he said, a small grin quirking his lips. "Get these damn things off me."

Every pulse in her body began to riot as she fumbled through his pockets with trembling fingers. She finally produced a large pocketknife. He opened it for her, then handed it back and held out his hands.

"Remember that if I bleed to death," he warned, the dark expression now gone and replaced with love and longing, "you won't get those four babies."

She slipped the knife unerringly between his wrist and the plastic, and whipped it up with a force that made him snap his head back as the knife split the plastic.

"Well done," he said, reclaiming the knife and dropping it into his pocket.

She threw herself into his arms and cried out all the misery of the past few days, their lost year and their lost baby.

"I'm sorry," she wept over and over. "And I love you. I love you, Gideon."

"I love you, too, Prue. I don't ever want to be

without you again." He held her tightly and kissed her until she had to gasp for air.

They clung together for a long time, nuzzling and whispering promises. Then she felt a familiar weight against her ankle.

She drew out of Gideon's arms to look down at Drifter, who meowed up at her. "You're back!" she exclaimed, picking him up.

"Has he been missing?" Gideon asked.

"I thought he'd left us," she replied, stroking the purring cat. "He hasn't been home for two days."

"Maybe he's finally decided he lives here."

She hugged Drifter, who yowled in protest and leaped down, headed for the bowl she'd kept full, hoping for his return.

"Do *we* live here?" she asked. "Do you want to stay?"

He nodded. "I like it here. I've got a job with Hank if I stay. But didn't you want to go to New York?"

"I could commute," she replied. "This is a great place to raise children." She smiled into his eyes, her own heavy with love. "Incidentally, your mom called."

That surprised him. "What about?"

"Apparently, Georgette told her we were staying together. She wants us to come for Thanksgiving. She wants us to bring Mom and Jeffrey, and Paris and Randy. Georgette will be there. She flew home yesterday for some board thing she had to do, then she's going to spend a month with your folks."

He liked the sound of that. But it posed a question. "How did she know we were staying together if she left yesterday?"

Prue kissed his chin. "I told her what Hank and I were planning. I guess she had faith in my ability to convince you to stay."

He had to accept that Prue was a good strategist. "And where's Justine?"

"Gone to Seattle to visit her father before she flies home."

"So we're alone in the house?"

"Yes."

"You want to make love in front of the fire?" he asked. "Like we used to in Maine?"

She made a contented little sound as she wrapped her arms around his neck. She curled into his chest as he carried her to the hearth rug. "We can *start* in front of the fire," she said, kissing his earlobe. "But I want to make love *every*where."

"I live to serve the princess," he said.

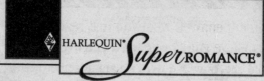

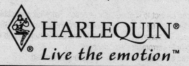

If you enjoyed what you just read,
then we've got an offer you can't resist!

Take 2 bestselling love stories FREE!

Plus get a FREE surprise gift!

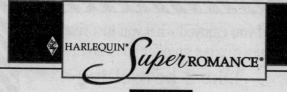

HARLEQUIN® *Super*ROMANCE®

Single
FATHER

He's a man on his own, trying to raise his children.
Sometimes he gets things right. Sometimes he needs a little help....

Unfinished Business
by Inglath Cooper

(Superromance #1214) On-sale July 2004

Culley Rutherford is doing the best he can raising his young
daughter on his own. One night while on a medical conference in
New York City, Culley runs into his old friend Addy Taylor. After a
passionate night together, they go their separate ways, so Culley
is surprised to see Addy back in Harper's Mill. Now that she's
there, though, he's determined to show Addy that the three of
them can be a family.

Daddy's Little Matchmaker
by Roz Denny Fox

(Superromance #1220) On-sale August 2004

Alan Ridge is a widower and the father of nine-year-old Louemma,
who suffers from paralysis caused by the accident that killed her
mother. Laurel Ashline is a weaver who's come to the town of
Ridge City, Kentucky, to explore her family's history—a history
that includes a long-ago feud with the wealthy Ridges. Louemma
brings Alan and Laurel together, despite everything that keeps
them apart....

Available wherever Harlequin books are sold.

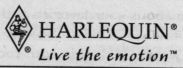

HARLEQUIN®
Live the emotion™

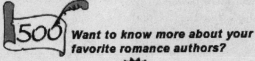

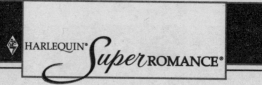

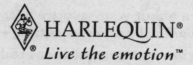